MURDER AT GLENLOCH HILL

Books by Clara McKenna

Stella & Lyndy Mysteries

MURDER AT MORRINGTON HALL
MURDER AT BLACKWATER BEND
MURDER AT KEYHAVEN CASTLE
MURDER AT THE MAJESTIC HOTEL
MURDER ON MISTLETOE LANE
MURDER AT GLENLOCH HILL

Hattie Davish Mysteries

A LACK OF TEMPERANCE
ANYTHING BUT CIVIL
A SENSE OF ENTITLEMENT
A DECEPTIVE HOMECOMING
A MARCH TO REMEMBER

Published by Kensington Publishing Corp.

MURDER AT GLENLOCH HILL

CLARA McKENNA

KENSINGTON
PUBLISHING CORP.

kensingtonbooks.com

KENSINGTON BOOKS are published by

Kensington Publishing Corp.
900 Third Avenue
New York, NY 10022

All Kensington titles, imprints and distributed lines are available at special quantity discounts for bulk purchases for sales promotion, premiums, fund-raising, educational or institutional use. Special book excerpts or customized printings can also be created to fit specific needs. For details, write or phone the office of the Kensington Special Sales Manager: Kensington Publishing Corp., 900 Third Avenue, New York, NY, 10022. Attn. Special Sales Department. Phone: 1-800-221-2647.

The K with book logo Reg. U.S. Pat. & TM Off.

Library of Congress Control Number: 2024940677

ISBN: 978-1-4967-4851-5

First Kensington Hardcover Edition: December 2024

ISBN: 978-1-4967-4852-2 (e-book)

10 9 8 7 6 5 4 3 2 1

Printed in the United States of America

In loving memory of Papa, who introduced me to the world of golf.

CHAPTER 1

Kingdom of Fife, Scotland
June 1906

Aggie Neely lingered in the doorway, the fresh breeze welcome on her flushed cheeks, and watched him go. Dappled light catching the metal cast-off on his suspenders, he disappeared around the bend, swallowed by the thick brush. They'd parted as the commotion up at the manor house grew in volume. Another guest had arrived, with more to come. Reluctantly, she stepped back inside, closed the door, and leaned against it, oblivious to the beaded condensation soaking through the thin cotton of her blue shirtwaist. A smile lingered on her lips as she brushed them with her fingers, tracing where his had been, where her freckled skin burned from the patch of whiskers he'd missed shaving this morning. She could still smell his shaving soap.

"Dinnae worry," he'd reassured her, making promises she knew she could trust. "It won't be long now."

Aggie couldn't wait, but she'd have to. The money she'd saved wasn't enough. Yet. She'd counted it under the dimmed light of the oil lamp in her bedchamber before coming to work this morning. It was the only time she could do it, and even then, she risked waking Orla. But he'd assured her he'd almost got enough, and with the upcoming golf tournament, he would be getting more soon.

The boiler rumbled, emitting a loud clang, calling Aggie back to her tasks. She adjusted its temperature and added another log to the fire in the drying cupboard before tackling the mound of unsorted dirty clothes. She was setting aside one of Mr. Stevenson's shirts with ink spots on the cuff when the clattering of golf clubs alerted her that someone was passing nearby. Aggie peeked out the window. The path in front of the laundry house led to the stables and the golf course and many an interesting guest and golfer frequently came this way.

Not spotting anyone, Aggie straightened her cap and went back to work, sorting the clothes by color and fabric, checking each item for wine stains, fruit stains, ink spots, or blood. The doorknob suddenly rattled vigorously, and Aggie dropped one of Mrs. McEwen's lacy petticoats into the wrong basket.

Who could that be?

She bent to correct her mistake, but whoever it was began pounding on the door. But it wasn't locked. The humidity often made the door stick, and any staff who frequented the laundry house would know to give it a little shove.

Aggie dropped the petticoat again as the door burst open, and a man strode through. Distracted, he slipped a cloth into his trouser pocket but missed as he closed the door behind him. It fluttered to the floor. He didn't notice, busy as he was sizing up Aggie as if she were a prize cow, his eyes lingering on her curves, evident even beneath her corset and apron.

"Can I help ye, sir?" she whimpered, backing up as he drew closer until she met with the hard, damp wall.

He said nothing, but the glint in his eye spoke volumes. Aggie searched the room for a way to escape, but she knew better than anyone she had nowhere to go.

*   *   *

Stella swatted the plumes of ostrich feathers that tickled her temple every time a gust of wind blew through the open carriage window.

"Quite the distance to travel to visit strangers, wouldn't you say?" Lyndy, his casual straw boater a contrast to his impatient posture, shifted in his seat beside her, tugging on the sleeve of his light-gray linen jacket.

They rumbled through a verdant, bucolic landscape of rolling checkerboard farmland dotted with grazing sheep. The sheep reminded Stella of the fluffy white cottonwood seeds that peppered the paddocks in Kentucky this time of the year. Nowhere were the wild, dramatic peaks of the Scottish Highlands she'd read about. But even from here, she could smell the sea.

"Hamish and Virginia McEwen aren't strangers. They're my grandmother's cousins. They're family."

"On your father's side."

Lyndy had a point. If these Scottish cousins were anything like her father . . .

Hitting a rock in the road, the carriage jolted, and Stella's muscles clenched in protest. She'd been so eager to meet them, embarking on this journey with unwavering enthusiasm. But now? Stella was tired and plagued by trepidation and nervous anticipation. Was it the nearly two days of traveling by train? Or was she having second thoughts? Until recently, she didn't even know the McEwens existed. She'd been thrilled to learn of Scottish kin, immediately forming an ideal vision of them in her head. But Lyndy was right. What would these new family members really be like? Friendly? Curious? Snobbish? Opportunistic? Moneygrubbing?

Was that what had been nagging at her? It was no secret Stella had come to her marriage, not even a year old, with a vast fortune. But surely the McEwens wouldn't invite her all the way here just to ask for money? She said as much.

"It's something your father would've done," Lyndy said, slumped despondently against the carriage wall as Stella braced for another jolt. "So why not his cousins? Why else would they have invited us?"

Lyndy was always skeptical about others' intentions, having been raised to do his duty but with little love, praise, or attention. Stella, on the other hand, had grown up surrounded by kind, hardworking servants and stable hands—and horses—who, despite her father's negligence and abuse, instilled in her the opinion that most people were well-meaning.

Then why was her mind filled with doubt?

"As I assured you before, Lyndy, I know something of the McEwens." Perched on the edge of the seat across from them, Freddy Kentfield tossed and caught the golf ball in his palm as he had done dozens of times since they left the train station. He held the ball briefly to smooth his tidy blond mustache before beginning again. "Hamish McEwen is a very wealthy man and has no need of your money."

Lyndy's sister, Alice, laced her arm with Freddy's between ball tosses, careful not to disturb his game. Animation colored her cherub cheeks as she spoke, the pink blush of her skin complementing the well-tailored gray traveling suit that fit her like a glove. Stella had never seen Alice this excited.

"Freddy says they have quite the reputation as a sporting family, Lyndy. They adore all things related to sport and games. You, of all people, should love it here."

"And wasn't it your mother who suggested we needed a *change of climate*?" Stella reminded him.

Lyndy bolted upright, pressing a finger to his dimpled chin. A hint of a smile spread along his lips and across his chiseled features to shine from his eyes. They both knew what a *change of climate* meant—freedom from the new, oppressive rules reigning at Morrington Hall.

Though that was not how Lady Atherly had intended it.

They'd been trying for a baby for months, yet Stella was still not pregnant. She'd been put on rigid dietary restrictions—no fatty foods, sweetmeats, or nuts—told what to wear, and forced to curtail her riding to once a week. The latter because Lady Atherly, with Dr. Hale's concurring medical opinion to support her, felt it too jarring. At least Stella was allowed to visit her beloved Thoroughbred, Tully, every day until that, too, was frowned upon. As if visiting the stables was the cause of Stella's infertility. Yet, worse than that, the doctor insisted she and Lyndy refrain from intimacy, as too much was *detrimental*, Stella's organs *needing time to recover*. Stella hated it. Lyndy hated it. But it was for their own good. Or so Lady Atherly and Dr. Hale said.

But so far, nothing had worked.

Needless to say, when Dr. Hale mentioned that many women found themselves pregnant after a *change of climate*, Lady Atherly more than encouraged this trip to Scotland. She insisted.

"What quality of stable does McEwen keep?" Lyndy leaned forward, his elbows on his knees.

"I don't know," Freddy said, "but after he made his money in textiles, Hamish McEwen bought Glenloch Hill to transform it into a pastoral playground. He has lawn tennis courts and a cricket pitch. He even owns a nine-hole golf course."

"Which is why he invited us," Alice said, squeezing Freddy's arm as she drank in his boyish, handsome features, unmarred, if not enhanced, by the scar through his left eyebrow. One couldn't slide a piece of paper between them. "Not only will they get acquainted with Stella but they'll be able to boast they hosted this year's Open Champion at Glenloch Hill."

The McEwens had reached out when they'd read of Alice's upcoming wedding to Freddy, a renowned golfer. In the announcement, Stella had been described as the Right Honorable Viscountess Lyndhurst, Stella Searlwyn née Kendrick, for-

merly of Kentucky. Hamish McEwen had written Great-Aunt
Rachel, Daddy's maternal aunt whom Hamish had known as a
child. Confirming Stella was indeed Elijah Kendrick's daughter, Hamish McEwen had invited Stella and Lyndy, Alice, and
Freddy to stay at Glenloch Hill for the long weekend while
Freddy played in the famous golf tournament in nearby St. Andrews.

Freddy chuckled, smiling lopsided at Alice. "I'd certainly
win if your faith in me was enough." He kissed Alice's cheek.

Alice shied away, her cornflower-blue eyes flickering from
Stella to Lyndy to size up their disapproval. When it didn't
arise, a sheepish smile hovered on her lips. How good it was to
see Alice this happy. So why were she and Lyndy out of sorts?

"It's a bloody good thing you carry those clubs around with
you," Lyndy said, "or this blasted mix-up with the luggage
could've jeopardized the whole thing even before you teed off
on the first hole."

"You aren't wrong there." Freddy patted the well-worn
leather caddie bag leaning against the seat beside him. "Why do
you think I do it?" The wooden club heads clattered against
one another as the hired carriage hit another bump.

They'd discovered at the train station that not all their luggage had arrived with them. Stella loved her pink traveling suit,
with its pink lace collar and pink ribbon trim, but she hadn't
planned to wear it all day, every day. *And this hat is driving me
crazy.* She swatted the feathers away again. She hoped the missing luggage would arrive soon or she'd have to send Ethel back
to St. Andrews on a shopping spree soon after her lady's maid
arrived.

"At least the weather's nice."

Stella stuck her head out the window, hitting the brim of her
hat on the frame, the sun's glare forcing her to squint. She'd
heard tales of Scotland's famously finicky weather, and after
two days of traveling in the rain, she was relieved to see blue

skies. But as they rounded the last bend of the hill that gave the McEwens' estate its name and the carriage made its way up the long drive, they entered a deep shadow. Decades ago, someone had planted a row of Scots elm on either side, and the tall, mature trees now obscured both the sky and the view of what was waiting for them.

Stella's stomach clenched as she craned her neck, hoping to catch sight of the house, the grounds, and her distant Scottish kin. Had she been reckless in coming here?

The sudden thought surprised her. Yes, they were desperate to get away and could've easily found a *change of climate* closer to home. And yes, she'd traveled hundreds of miles, dragging Lyndy away with his Thoroughbred Knockan Crag's debut at Ascot a few weeks away. But why not? What had she to lose? Wasn't she always one to indulge in her sense of adventure? At Glenloch Hill she'd meet people who shared a common ancestor, who might help her understand her father and welcome her as one of their own. As a child with a missing mother, a distant father, and no siblings, she couldn't have imagined the extended family she could now lay claim to, let alone all the kin she'd been reacquainted with back in the States. But how could it be greedy to want more? Especially when loved ones had a habit of leaving her or dying.

But that wouldn't ever happen again. Not now that she had Lyndy. *Or would it?*

And there it was.

How easy it had been to blame her apprehension on the upcoming meeting and the unknown nature of the McEwens. But Stella now knew better. Rumbling up the drive toward the obscured manor house had brought to mind the day she'd roared toward Morrington Hall to meet Lyndy and his family and an unknown fate. She wasn't that naïve girl anymore but faced an unknown future again. Lady Atherly wasn't the only one anxious about Stella's health. Stella refused to confront or talk about the concern, not even to Lyndy. Coming to Scotland, she'd hoped to outpace it.

But what if she couldn't give Lyndy an heir? What then?

With the edge of the open window biting into her gloved palms, Stella pressed harder as if banishing the unspoken fear to the sill and the dust lodged along its cracks. During her fretting, the manor house came into view.

Wrapped in a white, stuccolike exterior and fashioned with more windows than wall, the two-story square stone building flanked on the back with three-story wings gleamed in the sunshine. Nestled between terraced gardens, the hillside, and sunken gardens that followed the slope on the other side, the house was a sturdy beacon among the meticulously landscaped parkland. Pink and white roses climbed two-story trellises on either side of its entranceway. Stella's natural optimism rose with them.

"Isn't it lovely?"

"I'd say," Freddy said.

"It's quite charming," Alice agreed.

"It does have a welcoming aspect about it, doesn't it?" Lyndy conceded, not looking at the house but at what appeared to be the stable block peeking through the trees down the hill.

Stella was the first to leap from the carriage without waiting for the coachman or attending footman to help. She landed with a satisfied crunch on the gravel drive, her eyes still riveted on the house and the expansive gardens and grounds stretching up the hill and down the slope. Lyndy joined her, looping his arm around hers, gently brushing a knuckle across her cheek. His skin was cool to the touch.

"Ready to meet your Scottish cousins?" he whispered as the wide entrance door swung open, the shaded interior revealing nothing of the person lingering on the threshold.

Stella took a deep breath in anticipation, willing the trepidation about meeting her Scottish family and her fear of losing her English one to not show on her face. She forced a smile, stepped forward to greet her cousin, and all other concerns fled from her mind.

"What the devil are you doing here?" Lyndy seethed. Stella had been wondering the same thing.

Instead of a stranger whose features, in the right light and at a certain angle, might regrettably recall Stella's dead father, the very familiar Sir Edwin Kentfield greeted them with the theatricality of a ringleader at a circus, arms stretched out as if he were their host and not the usurper he was.

As if it were all the answer that was needed, he crowed with a lopsided grin, "Welcome to Glenloch Hill, my boy!"

CHAPTER 2

"You didn't answer Lyndy's question, Father," Freddy said, shoving the golf ball deep into his jacket pocket before helping Alice from the carriage.

"I met your caddie, my boy," Sir Edwin said. "Birdwell, isn't it? He arrived on the same train."

"That's all well and good, but what are you doing here?"

Stella looked past the baronet toward the still-open doorway. Of course she was curious why Sir Edwin was here but cared more about the missing McEwens. Hints of the warmly stained mahogany wall paneling of the inner hall outlined the manor's formidable butler, in a black suit and tie, who blocked the entrance with his demeanor as well as his size. A soldier whose sole weapon was his stony stare, he guarded his master's keep like a brick wall. But where was the master of the house, and why wasn't he here?

Stella voiced her questions as Freddy fervently repeated, "What are you doing here, Father?"

Whisking the fedora from his head to rake fingers through his full head of hair, Sir Edwin chose to answer Freddy's question instead. "I'm here to see you win the Open Golf Championship, of course." With the artistry of a magician, he deflected Freddy's attention and any further inquiries by slapping his hat back on and paternally cupping Alice's cheek. "Delighted to see you again, my dear."

He took Alice's offered hand and kissed it. She smiled shyly at her future father-in-law, a graying, bearded, but equally handsome copy of his son. Even standing still, Sir Edwin exuded an electric vitality that put his juniors to shame. He'd changed little in the time since Stella had seen him last.

"You too, Lyndy, my boy," he added, shoving out his hand, a lopsided grin on his face.

"Sir Edwin." Lyndy returned the gesture reservedly. "Is your wife with you?" Lyndy had mixed feelings about the man who, this past Christmas, was revealed to be his mother's former lover, but he had no ambiguity about his feelings for Lady Isabella Kentfield, Sir Edwin's wife. He loathed her.

"But you never attend my golf matches," Freddy said, his face scrunched up in confusion. Sir Edwin ignored him.

"Alas, my wife did not accompany me," he said with mock regret. "As Freddy well knows, Isabella is spending the Season in London with our daughter, Maude." He sounded almost giddy at his wife's distant preoccupation. Everyone knew there was no love lost between them. "She will indeed miss seeing you again, Lady Lyndhurst." *And horses have wings.* "As always, it's a great pleasure, my girl."

"Nice to see you, too, Sir Edwin." Growing impatient to meet her new relatives, Stella sidestepped Sir Edwin. "Are the McEwens—?" As she passed, Sir Edwin, the dusty scent of the road still on him, reached down and snatched up her hand. Her throat tightened, cutting her question short.

Sir Edwin had kissed her hand before without asking and she hadn't resisted. As he put her hand to his lips this time, she tugged it back, the whiskers of his silver-streaked beard scratching against her glove. Lyndy took a step forward protectively. Surprised, Sir Edwin let go.

"Still touchy about that incident at Christmas, are you, my boy?"

Stella had tried to forget the *incident* at Christmas, when someone mistook her friendliness for affection and forced a kiss upon her. But like Lyndy, she was now averse to any unwanted physical attention toward her, well-intended or not. Thinking about the missing McEwens had caught her off guard. She should've expected Sir Edwin to be so bold.

"As you would be if someone attacked your wife," was Lyndy's retort.

Knowing Sir Edwin's dislike for his wife, Stella couldn't stomach hearing his inevitable, thinly veiled denial. Instead, she asked again, "What's going on, Sir Edwin? Where are Hamish and Virginia McEwen? They knew we were coming. Why aren't they here to greet us?"

Sir Edwin shrugged. "I haven't the faintest idea. They were out when I arrived as well. Stevenson," he pointed to the butler, who stood twisting the tip of his handlebar mustache, "says they're somewhere on the property but couldn't be more precise. I went out looking for them earlier and was about to have another go at it when you arrived. Would anyone care to join me?"

"Have the sporting papers arrived yet, Stevenson?" Lyndy asked the butler, who had stepped forward.

"Aye, they have, my lord. They are at yer disposal as Mr. McEwen has finished with them."

Lyndy loosened his tie in anticipation. "Then no, Sir Edwin. I've got some catching up to do."

"Oh, dear, I am sorry, Sir Edwin," Alice said, "but if our rooms are ready," she looked for confirmation from the butler, who nodded slightly, "I really could do with a lie down. It's been quite the journey."

Freddy agreed with Alice. "And I need to rest up for to-morrow."

"Tomorrow?" Sir Edwin said.

"The Open Championship?" Freddy said, raising his scarred eyebrow. Alice had told Stella that the scar had resulted from a childhood fall and that Freddy hadn't climbed a tree since. "Have you forgotten already? It is the reason you came, after all. Isn't it? To see me play?"

"Yes, of course. The golf match." Sir Edwin recovered from his slip in memory and slapped his thigh.

Stella caught Lyndy's eye and silently mouthed, *What's that about?* Casting a suspicious eye over at Sir Edwin, Lyndy shook his head slowly.

"No need for me to rest, though," Sir Edwin was saying. "Just the opposite, I'd say. My legs could do with a bit of a stretch."

Stella silently agreed. With the McEwens inexplicably else-where and having sat for two days, Stella was restless and needed to get some energy out. But not with Sir Edwin as a companion.

"What say you, my girl? Are you game?"

Stella bit her tongue. She wanted to remind him in no uncertain terms she wasn't *his girl* but instead replied, "No, thank you."

She had no intention of wandering the grounds in search of the missing McEwens with Sir Edwin.

Sir Edwin shrugged nonchalantly. "Until later, then."

As Sir Edwin ambled away, Stella took in the sweeping land-scape that was spread out before her: the terraced lawns, the sunken walled rose garden, the tree-lined drive, and the golf course on the other side of a gently sloping valley. On the clos-est hole she could see, a single golfer, his back to her and a bag of clubs on the ground by his feet, was taking a swing. Could that be Hamish McEwen? Then he turned, and the light caught on the man's beard. It was the color of Mrs. Downie's copper pots. It couldn't be her cousin. From Aunt Rachel's description, Hamish McEwen's hair was a shade darker brown than Stella's.

Stella slowly circled around. Behind the manor house, the forested hillside swept steeply to its obscured summit. Winding away and down from the house, a flagstone path disappeared into the wooded, brushy area surrounding what they'd assumed were the stables.

The McEwens could be anywhere.

The *clip-clop* of horseshoes on gravel and the creak of a heavily laden carriage announced the arrival of Ethel Eakins, her lady's maid; Harry Finn, Lyndy's valet; and what luggage hadn't been misrouted. As it emerged from the shadowy drive and rumbled up beside them, Stella made her decision.

Brushing away her hat feathers again, Stella kissed Lyndy on the cheek. "You go on without me. I'm going to look for the McEwens." When concern clouded his countenance, she added, "In the opposite direction from Sir Edwin."

Lyndy returned the kiss. "May you find them soon enough. It is quite odd of them not to be here. It makes me a bit uneasy."

Stella couldn't have said it better. But Lyndy was calling out to his valet when she turned her back on the commotion in the drive as the luggage was unloaded. From the timbre of his voice, he'd already put his concern out of his mind. Then he cursed. A travel trunk was still missing.

Stella increased her pace.

Stella chose the flagstone path that snaked around to the side of the house, past a kitchen garden alive with buzzing bees and smelling strongly of lavender, rosemary, and chives, down a series of broad steps to an expanse of lush green lawn. The path branched into a simple gravel trail leading back to the servants' entrance and a widened paved walkway toward the stables. If her Scottish cousins were like her, they might be enjoying the sunshine on horseback. Stella headed for the stables.

The path led her through a mix of tall woodland trees, dappled sunlight streaming through the broad canopy of leaves. Out of sight of the others, she unpinned her hat, relieving herself of the pesky tickling feathers, and deeply inhaled the humid air. All was hushed and still, and Stella slowed her pace to relish the calm. Her mind had been swirling, the fear that had consumed her on the carriage's approach pushed to the background. Between the apparent dishonesty behind Sir Edwin's unexpected appearance and the McEwens absence, Stella had a more immediate foreboding she couldn't shake. Even Lyndy had felt it. Why weren't the McEwens there to greet them? They knew when Stella and her party would arrive. Had she opened herself up to be disappointed by a family member yet again? Or was something more sinister going on?

A year ago, such dark suspicions wouldn't have entered her mind, but after encountering multiple unnatural deaths, including her father's, she was wise to the possibility. Heinous things happened.

A flash of color and motion among the trees caught Stella's attention. Had she seen eyes in the undergrowth? There! A peacock butterfly fluttered past, its orange-brown wings with distinct azure "eyes" glimmering as they caught the light. Stella chuckled in nervous relief. She and Lyndy had enjoyed blissful matrimony for six months without one menacing incident. Not a soul had died of unnatural causes. Not a single fight had broken out, unless she counted the initial encounter between Mack, their stray mutt, and Mr. Gates's new mouser, and even the animals worked out their differences in the end. Nothing of theirs had been stolen or destroyed. Not even a poison-pen letter had been slipped through the letter box. But still, Stella kept her guard up. The McEwens' absence saw to that. Renewing her brisk pace, she continued down the path.

The scent of damp laundry reached her before she saw the small squat building with the same white stuccolike walls and slate roof as the main house, tucked discreetly into the woodland's overgrowth. A narrow path of hard-packed earth cut through the brush toward it. Without straying from the main walkway, Stella filled her lungs with the fresh scent as she passed.

"No. No. Please, stop. Please, go away. No!" The woman's strained whimpers, originating somewhere behind Stella, pierced the serenity of the woodland like a serrated knife into a tin can.

Goosebumps prickled at the nape of Stella's neck. Something heavy and metal clanked as it fell hard. Stella hurriedly retraced her steps.

"Stop! Please, stop! No!" The protests grew in volume and desperation. They were coming from the laundry building.

Shrubbery branches swished and flicked against Stella's pink skirt as she bounded down the narrow dirt path to the closed wooden door. The scent of a musky cologne mingling with fragrant soap lingered on the threshold. The protests had stopped, but Stella didn't desist. She grasped the knob, tugging and rattling it with all her strength. All her efforts were in vain.

The door wouldn't budge.

"What's going on in there?" Stella pounded. "Open this door!"

A muffled cry and a deep menacing voice whispering something Stella couldn't make out through the door was all that answered her. Shoes scuffled erratically across the floor. A metal scraping followed. Stella peered through the windows but, being fogged up, they revealed nothing more than vague shapes within.

"Open the door!" She rattled the knob again.

It was useless.

Stella stepped back, raised her foot, and kicked with all the power she could muster. The door, giving little resistance, flung open and bashed against the wall. Stella stumbled forward, her arms flailing to keep her balance. The damp steamy heat immediately engulfed her.

Only steps out of harm's way stood a squarely built young woman in the light gray dress and starched white apron of a maid. But her cap was askew, large swaths of her dark brown hair had come loose from her bun, and her freckled face was splotched with red. She hugged herself, the muscles in her arms tight against her sleeves.

"Where is he?" Stella said.

The square room was dominated by two massive built-in eight-foot tall vertical drying cupboards pulled out toward the middle of the floor. Piles of unsorted clothes covered the wood tables and half-empty wicker baskets lined the walls. Weak sunlight filtered through the fogged-up windows left the whitewashed room dimly lit, yet there was nowhere to hide.

"Who, ma'am?" The maid brushed away tears from the corners of her eyes with the tips of her pinkie fingers. "I dinnae ken who ye mean."

Stella stepped under the archway and peered into the next room. Clothes soaked in half of the line of sinks set beneath the windows. A large laundry press, several mangles, and two empty washtubs were scattered around. With its white ceramic-tiled fireplace, the active barrel-shaped metal boiler dominated the room's far corner. It clanked loudly.

Stella returned to the woman's side as the maid was replacing a flatiron on the table from the floor. Was that the metal crash Stella had heard?

"Are you okay?"

The woman dropped her gaze, fiddling with the ends of her apron. "I'm fine, ma'am."

"Are you?" Stella pointed to the maid's swollen and red lip. Had someone hit her, forced kisses on her, or bitten her lip? Stella couldn't tell. "Then what caused that?

"Thank ye for yer concern, but I'm fine, ma'am."

"What's your name?"

"Aggie Neely, ma'am."

"I heard your cries, Aggie. I know someone was attacking you."

"Ye must be mistaken, ma'am."

Stella, hoping to draw her out, sought inspiration in the room. It was simple, well-ordered, and immaculately clean. The walls were unadorned but recently painted. The sorting tables were in perfect symmetry. The cement floor was swept of any trace of soot or tracked-in dirt. Except . . . Clutching her hat, Stella knelt beside the closest table and, reaching beneath it, retrieved a muddied cotton cloth, thicker than the average handkerchief, from the floor. A family crest, dominated by a falcon clutching two arrows in one corner and three keys in another, was tightly stitched into it using fine red, orange, and black thread. Fresh mud and sand clung to Stella's gloved finger as she picked it up.

"This must've fallen out of a basket." Stella held out the cloth toward the maid.

Forced to lift her gaze, Aggie reached for it with trembling fingers. She snatched the cloth from Stella and shoved it into the deep pocket of her apron. "Thank ye, ma'am. Sorry tae trouble ye, ma'am."

Stella sighed at the rote response, climbed back to her feet, and brushed her skirts of what little was there. "Aggie, I know I'm a stranger, but I'm also someone who wants to help."

Aggie threaded her fingers together and held them up in supplication. "Please, ma'am. Leave it be. Nothing happened. Not really."

"Even if it could've been worse, something happened, Aggie. I can't just leave it be. At the very least, Mrs. McEwen should be told of your mistreatment." Stella turned to leave.

"Please, ye mustn't tell anyone." Aggie grabbed Stella's arm to stop her. Suddenly worried about the impropriety of what she'd done, she quickly let go and took a step back. "I'm so sorry, ma'am. I dinnae mean tae—"

"It's okay, Aggie." But the maid began shivering despite the oppressive heat, and Stella feared she might collapse. She guided Aggie to the sole chair in the room and pushed her into it. Stella knelt before her, resting her hand on top of Aggie's clasped in her lap. "But why can't I tell anyone?"

Stella waited patiently. Silence loomed between them. In the other room, a faucet dripped, a rhythmic *plop-plop* into a porcelain sink. How had Stella not noticed it before?

Aggie's knuckles turned white as she clenched her hands tighter. With a tremble in her voice, she said, "I could lose me position, ma'am. And I cannae afford tae dae that."

Stella groaned at the truth of it. The maid was attacked, but depending on the attitude of her employers, she could bear the brunt of the blame for supposedly provoking it. Stella swallowed hard, reminded of her own father's abuse and a recent brush with a violent admirer. How trapped this woman must feel.

"I can't promise I'll never say anything, but it will be between us for now. I haven't even met the McEwens. So, you're right that I can't know how they'll react to the revelation."

The *click* drew both women's attention to the next room. It sounded like the fastening of a door latch. Aggie's head and shoulders drooped in relief.

"He's gone."

"Your attacker has been hiding in there the whole time?" As Aggie silently nodded, hiding behind closed eyes, Stella stared in disbelief at the beads of remnant tears clinging to the maid's thick eyelashes. Stella had searched both rooms. How could she not have seen him? Where had he been hiding? "Why didn't you say?"

Stella leaped from the floor, ran through the next room,

snagged her skirt on a chipped edge of fireplace tile, and threw open the back door onto the shrubby woodland behind the building. An overgrown dirt path, more suited to deer than people, worn into the grass, was clear of anyone, but the still bobbing branches marked the man's passing. He couldn't have gotten far. Stella sprinted down the path, following it to the front of the building, but saw no one.

Stella threw her hat in frustration. Aggie's assailant had gotten away.

CHAPTER 3

What a disaster!

His arms straining under the weight, Harry Finn hoisted the russet bridle leather suitcase onto the bed and grunted. With a footman's help, he'd already hauled two travel trunks up three flights of steep narrow stairs in the servants' wing, and his muscles burned.

When they'd disembarked at St. Andrews, he'd been more distressed than Lord Lyndhurst that not all of the luggage had arrived with them. He'd overseen himself the many carefully labeled trunks, cases, and hatboxes loaded into the railway baggage car in London. So how had any of it gone missing? Finn arranged for the displaced luggage to be delivered to Glenloch Hill when they arrived. Less than a half hour later, all but one travel trunk had been on the next train, thank goodness.

But what a state they were in! Newly polished brass corner bumpers and clasps on the trunks were scuffed or caked in mud. The leather suitcases were banged up and dirty, one with nicks and scratches so deep it was as if cats had used it for scratching. They smelled less of well-oiled leather than of stale tobacco and coal ash. It left an off-putting, smoky taste in Finn's mouth. Where had they kept these then, near the engine? Several pieces of luggage had labels with ripped edges. Of Lord Lyndhurst's trunk that was still missing, Finn wondered if the nameplate had come clean off. Would they ever see it again?

Finn snapped the brass latch on the front of the suitcase, and the lid sprang open. He wasn't certain where this case had come from. Oddly, it had already been brought up to the guest bedchamber Lord Lyndhurst was sharing with Her Ladyship before Finn arrived with the first travel trunk. It had no identifying label beyond a *Grand Northern Railway* sticker, and he hadn't packed this one for His Lordship this trip. Yet it was nearly identical to one he'd used multiple times before.

Good Lord! Would this debacle ever get straightened out?

Clearly, the case belonged to someone else. And based upon the slapdash effort, that someone's valet should be sacked. Shirts had been hastily thrown in, with no regard to creases or collars, and stacked among unwrapped waistcoats that could snag unrolled stockings with their buttons. Besides, Lord Lyndhurst would never wear lavender-colored suspenders. As Finn shifted disdainfully through the shambles for some inkling of ownership, his eyes lit on the sullied corner of a thick white postcard poking out between the undershirts. Finn slipped it free.

"Well, I'll be . . ." He chuckled.

Despite being alone, Finn glanced around the room—it wouldn't do to be found gawping—before returning to appreciate at more length the French postcard in his hand. Lounging provocatively on a stud-backed leather chair against a dark backdrop in an otherwise empty setting was a sultry, curvaceous, and, but for the feather boa around her neck, naked young woman. With such alabaster skin, she was the stuff of

ancient legend, the statue of a Greek or Roman goddess come
to life. Finn had seen a few of these passed around his local pub
by stable hands and farmers but had never held one. He raised
the postcard to study it closer.

At the sound of a nearby door closing, Finn started like a
hall boy caught staring at the scullery maid's ankle, which was
inadvertently exposed as she scrubbed the floor. He immediately tucked the postcard back among the undershirts and
continued his search for the owner's identity. At the bottom
of the case lay a small purple velvet box. Finn flipped the lid.
Silver cuff links etched with the initials *EK* reflected the afternoon sunlight. Satisfied, Finn returned the velvet box, closed
the suitcase, and removed it from the bed. He smoothed the
wrinkles from the woolen tartan coverlet, a checkerboard of
forest greens, dark blues, deep red, and yellow, nodding in
self-congratulation.

"At least one mystery solved."

The suitcase and the French picture postcard belonged to Sir
Edwin Kentfield.

Stella could hear them as she headed back up to the house.
Leisurely strolling toward her on a path originating in the
woods that dominated the hill's summit were two women and a
man, all of a similar age to Stella and Lyndy's parents and
dressed in tweed. None of them had spotted her yet. The pale
willowy woman, clutching the man's arm, scrutinizing the
ground ahead as she walked, tucked a strand of shiny black hair
behind her ear. The other, of fairer hair and plump skin bronzed
by the sun, strolled carefree, admiring everything and nothing
in particular. Though past their youth, both were elegant, athletic, and handsome. The man, their aesthetic equal with a well-
manicured black mustache peppered with gray, swung a
walking stick in circles as he spoke. He seemed as comfortable
in his skin as in his surroundings. Did he remind Stella of her

overbearing, portly father? Not in the slightest. But in the tilt of his head and the slight rise of the corner of his lips, perhaps she could see a resemblance to her Uncle Jed. She liked him immediately.

"Ah was noot but a bairn," the man said with a laugh.

Stella didn't know what she'd expected—her cousin in a tartan kilt with his bare knees showing or the ladies with freckles and flaming orange hair—but besides the man's thick, singsong accent and incomprehensible speech, nothing about them deviated from every other member of British high society. Maybe these weren't even the McEwens.

"Ah dinnae ken when the wee lassie will arrive," the man continued.

Stella recognized "wee lassie" and "arrive." Were they talking about her?

"Mr. McEwen?" she guessed.

The party came to a halt as one. The man's stick swung like a pendulum from his stilled hand. As a broad smile spread across his face, his voice boomed with amusement. He shoved his thumbs on either side of his tweed vest. "Aye, lassie, I'm yer cousin Hamish. And I'm pleased as punch tae meet ye. And ye a lady too, eh?"

"I am Lady Lyndhurst, formerly Stella Kendrick, and I'm sorry, but I have no idea what else you just said."

The fair-haired lady rolled her eyes and reached behind the other woman to playfully tug on the man's shirtsleeve. He wasn't wearing a jacket. "Ye must forgive Hamish, my lady. He was speaking Scottish. Of course one from America wouldn't understand."

That, Stella understood. It was said airily, with only the trace of a Scottish burr, but with an undercurrent of an insult. Stella had endured countless comments and criticism, both subtle and blatant, about her nationality. She was so used to it that she immediately brushed it off.

"So yer the wee lassie arrived at last," Hamish said, thickly rolling his *r*'s but much more comprehensible. "Welcome tae Glenloch Hill." He swept his arms about to encompass the landscape around them. "May I introduce my bonny wife, Virginia." Without diverting his gaze from Stella, he patted the dark-haired woman's hand holding his arm.

Who introduced themselves by Christian name to strangers, kin or no kin? No titles, no pretense, no pre-held judgment on display? Hamish was like no other British person she'd met so far.

How refreshing it was to find him warm and welcoming. *And so unlike Daddy.*

With an effort of one exhausted, Virginia McEwen raised her deep brown eyes, her smile reflected in them. "So pleased to finally meet you, Stella. Your Auntie Rachel didn't do your beauty justice." Her gentle breathy voice couldn't have contrasted more with the other woman's surprisingly deep tone. And her accent was English.

"Indeed, my lady," the fair-haired woman said, clinging to a bit more formality. "Yer quite the stunner." She waited in vain for Hamish or Virginia to introduce her. "I'm Mrs. Jean Agnew, Ginny's chum, by the way." She wrapped her arm through Virginia's free arm and squeezed. "But all my friends call me Jeanie."

Was she inviting Stella to call her Jeanie? Stella couldn't tell.

"We're so sorry not tae have been here tae greet ye, lassie. The weather was so grand we just had tae nip out and enjoy it." Hamish pointed back up the path he and the ladies had come down with his walking stick. Up close, the stick appeared to have been whittled by hand. "It leads tae the top. Have a mind tae go up there while yer here. It has an ancient monument and a commanding view of the sea."

"I would've waited for you, but Hamish insisted I join him," his wife said with a hint of admonishment.

"Fresh air is guid for ye, hen. Shall we?" Hamish began twirling his stick with the natural ease of a man without a care as he proceeded toward the house. Virginia smiled fondly at her husband and nodded.

Stella fell in alongside them, relief easing the tension she'd held since arriving.

"I take it your journey was a good one, and Stevenson and Mrs. Graham saw you all settled in?" Virginia asked.

"Honestly, I was too eager to meet you to do anything but set out looking for you." A flash of Aggie, disheveled and shaking, came to mind. *Instead, I found violence.* "I haven't even been inside the house yet. By the way—"

"Ye did bring Lord Lyndhurst with ye, I hope?" Mrs. Agnew interrupted. "And that buck, Freddy Kentfield?"

"Of course," Stella said. "My sister-in-law and Freddy's fiancée, Lady Alice Searlwyn, came with us too."

"Shame on ye, Hamish," Mrs. Agnew said, playfully swatting his back with a fir bough she'd picked up. "Ye didn't tell me young Kentfield was engaged."

"Isn't he a bit young for you, Jeanie?" Virginia teased.

Mrs. Agnew shrugged, an impish grin spreading across her face.

"Speaking of the Kentfields," Stella said, trying to keep from blushing. She was a married woman, yet she'd never met a woman quite as forward as Mrs. Jeanie Agnew. Stella assumed she was a widow. Or did Mr. Agnew, or anyone else, care so little about his wife's flirtation? "I didn't know Sir Edwin would be here."

Hamish dropped his walking stick. "Sir Edwin Kentfield?" Hamish strained to sound nonchalant as he retrieved the fallen stick. "Here? I wouldnae have thought so. Virginia?"

His wife shrugged noncommittedly.

"He greeted us in your stead," Stella said. "He's out looking for you right now. Weren't you expecting him?"

"Edwin? Really?" Mrs. Agnew's impish smile broadened. "How long has it been, Ginny? Twenty? Twenty-five years? It was most definitely before Dougal died." So, Mrs. Agnew was a widow after all.

"Something like that." Virginia nibbled on a thumbnail.

Mrs. Agnew knew Sir Edwin too? Well enough to drop his title? Or was that more of the informality that prevailed at Glenloch Hill?

"Yet another thing ye forgot to mention," Mrs. Agnew lightheartedly chided her friend.

"Really, Jeanie. I had no—"

"Ginny?" Jeanie Agnew asked.

Virginia suddenly swayed, releasing her husband's arm to seek the stability of the dry stone wall lining this part of the path. Stella instinctively reached toward her but was waved off by Hamish. Virginia's inhales were short and shallow as she bent over, her gaze aimed at the leaf litter collecting at the base of the wall. Mumbling reassurances, Hamish rested his hand on the small of her back. When her breathing steadied, she threaded her arm through Hamish's again. Virginia caught Stella's eye and attempted a feeble smile, her heart-shaped face the color of ash.

What just happened?

"Virginia, are you all right?" Stella asked.

"Alasdair, how were the links?" Mrs. Agnew called, diverting everyone's attention away from her friend.

A broad-shouldered gentleman of robust physique strode across the grass toward them, golf clubs tucked under his arm. With a tartan tam of dark green, dark blue, and bright red flopped to one side of his head and the sun catching the reddish-brown hues of the unshaven whiskers dotting his chiseled cheeks, he looked more the part of the mythical Scotsman that Stella had read about in Jane Porter's romance book,

The Scottish Chiefs, except for the lack of height. Stella was nearly his equal.

"Too slow, at least compared with what I expect to find at the Old Course tomorrow." He eyed Stella with curiosity while addressing Mrs. Agnew's question.

"Well, Virginia and I found the course quite up to par this morning." She laughed at her pun, a surprisingly high-pitched barrage of short fast giggles shooting out of her mouth like bullets from a Gatling gun.

The gentleman flashed Jeanie an amused smirk but quickly set his attention back on Stella. "I think introductions are in order, are they not, Virginia?"

Still not fully recovered, Virginia dug her fingers deeper into her husband's arm, struggling to remain upright, let alone say anything. "Hamish?" she pleaded quietly.

Hamish patted his wife's hand, concern crinkling across his forehead, before obliging. "Alasdair McCormack, this is Lady Lyndhurst, my second cousin's daughter from America."

"Pleased to meet ye, my lady." His Scottish lilt was almost musical.

"And you, Mr. McCormack. You're friends with my cousins too?"

"He's more than a friend, aren't ye, Alasdair," Mrs. Agnew cooed, dropping her fir bough and slipping her arm through his.

"Alasdair and Virginia have been acquainted since their school days," Hamish added.

"And it's our good fortune that he's staying at Glenloch for the duration of the tournament." Smiling coyly up at him, Jeanie walked her fingers up the checkered tweed sleeve of his jacket to his shoulder. "For Alasdair, here, is not only the younger brother to the Viscount Camgossie but the future Open Champion." She lightly tapped the tip of his nose. "Aren't ye, dearie?"

Mr. McCormack snatched Mrs. Agnew's finger and kissed it. The woman's head whipped back, piercing the sky with her high-pitched giggles before taking her hand away and wagging her finger at him like a naughty child. Hamish cleared his throat, swinging his walking stick again, urging them all forward.

Mrs. Agnew slipped her arm through the redheaded golfer's again as he took the lead and sauntered beside him along the path. "So, Alasdair, when are we going to play together?" When Alasdair laughed, Jeanie glanced back to see Virginia recovered and following beside Hamish. "Ye know, I meant golf, didn't ye?"

"Aye, right."

Grateful to be moving back toward the house, Stella strolled beside her cousins. "Then you should know my sister-in-law's fiancé, Mr. McCormack. He's also playing in the tournament. Mr. Kentfield?"

Her question had a chilling effect, and the group came to a standstill again.

Mr. McCormack's face, warmed by Mrs. Agnew's administration, slackened. "Did ye say Kentfield?"

"Freddy Kentfield," Hamish added. "Of course ye ken him, Alasdair. He's that promising young amateur we invited tae stay at Glenloch."

"Young Kentfield, eh?" Alasdair said with noticeable relief. "Aye, I do know the young man. He's quite the competitor. Though this is his first Open, I believe. We'll soon learn the true mettle of him."

"Edwin's here too," Mrs. Agnew said, watching as closely as Stella for the golfer's reaction.

"Is he?" Mr. McCormack, with an apologetic smile, removed Mrs. Agnew's hand from his shoulder and busied himself with straightening the clubs in his bag.

"And from what I gather," Mrs. Agnew continued conspiratorially, her hand held to one side of her mouth, "he came un-invited."

"Come now, Jeanie," Hamish said. "Dinnae trouble trouble till trouble troubles you."

"Ye obviously don't know me, Hamish McEwen, if ye think I'm going to heed that advice." Jeanie winked at Stella.

"Too true," Hamish admitted good-humoredly. "Either way, we mustn't leave the wee lassie's husband and friends waiting. Besides," he pointed with his walking stick to a gray stone obelisk sundial barely poking up through the middle of a circular planting of boxwood, "according tae that, it's time tae dress for dinner."

Stella had never been so far north before and still wasn't used to how high the sun was at this hour. But it wasn't Hamish's urging or the need to change that compelled Stella to quicken her pace as she followed the others back toward the house. So many awful and odd occurrences had happened since she and Lyndy parted: the incident with the maid—Stella could give him the gist of what she'd thought happened without betraying her promise—Virginia's spell, the strange reaction to Sir Edwin. Stella couldn't wait to tell him.

"And maybe at dinner Sir Edwin will be able to tell us why he's here," Stella said, voicing the question no one else was willing to ask, but everyone wanted to know.

CHAPTER 4

Alasdair strode along the hall lined with Hamish's collection of paintings depicting golf, the letter crumpled in his fist. On other occasions, he'd stop to study one or two, whether it be a Dutch artist's rendering of the sport played on a frozen pond or Chalmers's portrait of William St. Clair in his bright red coat, black tam, and club in hand. But tonight, he kept his feet moving and his eyes before him. The doors to the dining room, drawing room, and library were wide open, and if Edwin Kentfield was loitering about in any of them, Alasdair had no desire to encourage any exchange.

The impertinence.

To arrive unannounced and, from the widow's implication, uninvited. Of course, Hamish would say he'd welcomed him to visit. He wouldn't air their dirty linen in front of a stranger. But even Lord Lyndhurst's American wife had questioned Kentfield's unexplained presence. It was a vulgar thing to do. But Alasdair wasn't beyond admitting he wanted to know what the baronet was doing here as well.

But all that would have to wait.

He resisted the urge to lengthen his strides as the din of conversation in the library eclipsed the echoed clicking of his golfing shoes on the wooden floor and the rattle of his clubs under his arm. He would've had an excellent round today if it hadn't been for the dastardly slow greens. He'd have to speak to McEwen's groundskeeper to see them mowed and rolled more. Thank God the Old Course won't be so neglected.

Alasdair was eager for tomorrow's challenge. And as was his usual routine before a tournament, he'd opted to eat alone in his room. It gave him time to distance himself from distractions and mentally focus. Tonight was no different. If anything, he needed the solitude more than usual.

First, there was this from his wife, the right old hag. He regarded the letter in his fist and squeezed tighter. What timing that woman had, writing him from Inverness, where she was staying with her sister, threatening him the day before he was to play the Open. Either pay for a separate residence in Edinburgh for her or she would seek a divorce. As if she weren't the unfaithful one. Were all women so heartless? Alasdair was inclined to think so. Virginia, with her dark beauty and liquid eyes, was distant, cold even, and the lovely Jeanie Agnew was rumored to be recklessly fickle. Alasdair hadn't met Lord Lyndhurst yet, but surely his lady wife hadn't traveled the ocean for love. Alasdair massaged the side of his neck. He wouldn't give his wife another thought.

And then there was that bloody Kentfield's arrival. Despite his earlier attempts to restrain himself, Alasdair picked up his pace. It wouldn't do to see that miscreant now. It might throw off Alasdair's game.

With his hand reaching for the banister, Alasdair heard a door close and footsteps approaching the blind side of the stairwell. He burst up the stairs, taking two steps at a time, and was peering from the top of the balustrade when a wee, thickset lad came into view. It wasn't Kentfield.

"Calm doon, McCormack. Get a haud of yersel'," he muttered, his palms slick as he clutched the railing. It had been years. Why should he care if Kentfield accosted him in the hall? Who was he, anyway?

Alasdair squared his shoulders and, seeing that the lad had come from Hamish's study, glared disapprovingly as the brass bird button stitched on top of the lad's brown-and-white-checkered golf cap caught the light of the hall's chandelier. It was the English caddie, Billy Birdwell. Alasdair had seen the henchman many times over the years, traveling about with various players. Why anyone would prefer one caddie over another, Alasdair could only speculate. To him, any boy could carry clubs. But what was the Englishman doing here? Had someone engaged his services? Young Freddy Kentfield, perhaps? Even so, what business had Birdwell in the house, let alone coming out of Hamish's study?

The caddie quietly whistled an indistinguishable tune as he ambled toward the front door. Alasdair considered shouting at Birdwell, rebuking him for the impropriety of his being in the hall, and leaving by the front, but Alasdair's mind and routine had been unsettled enough. Best to continue to his room where, hopefully, a hot tray had already been delivered. He had, after all, a golf championship to win.

The soft breeze enveloped them with the scent of honeysuckle as Lyndy strolled arm in arm with his wife. A few dozen yards ahead, Freddy and Alice, in a pretty, shimmering green gown two shades lighter than Stella's, mirrored them. The two couples had climbed the stone stairs that connected the lawn terraces to reach the wide path at the top of Glenloch's extensive hillside garden. From there, they could see a sweeping vista that stretched for miles. A faint blue shimmer on the horizon beyond the rolling hills hinted of the sea. Closer at hand, colorful flower borders lined the brick wall that separated the garden from the woodland beyond. How strange to see hydrangea and hollyhock thriving not feet away from cycads and exotic trees Lyndy couldn't name.

Lyndy had never been further north than the racecourse in Newcastle. He'd learned of the rugged Scottish Highlands, the country's enviable number of lochs, and the brutal winds, but never envisioned Scotland as such a mix of familiarly lush and exotically alluring landscapes.

Neither had he ever imagined his sister comfortable on a man's arm, head held high, with not one of her coveted American magazines clutched to her breast. Alice had hidden behind them for years, admiring the fashions and reading the intriguing stories. She'd lived vicariously through the words, leaving others to adventure beyond the pages. Yet here she was, chatting effortlessly, though her comments at this distance were indistinguishable, eliciting eager banter from Freddy.

What was it that drew Alice from her shell? Could it be—?

"I can't believe how quickly Alice has blossomed now that she's out of your mother's shadow," Stella said, answering his thought. Too often for Lyndy's comfort, his wife knew precisely what he was thinking. "Just look at her: the color in her cheeks, the easy laughter, and . . ." Stella placed the palm of her hand on Lyndy's shoulder as she paused. "Did you know that she didn't pack a single one of her magazines?"

"That is quite extraordinary."

Stella bent to pluck a bloodred cranesbill geranium flower. "It's either your mother's absence or Alice is in love."

She crushed the petals beneath her nose, releasing a faint but calming scent. Lyndy breathed it in. He wouldn't admit it, but he loved any flower arrangement that included his mother's geraniums. At Morrington, Mother grew several varieties.

"Or a little bit of both," Stella concluded.

"Freddy's a good chap, but I believe you were right the first time." Once, last summer, Alice formed an attachment to a man, who, as it happened, turned out to be a fraud and unworthy of her affection. However, throughout her infatuation, she'd persisted in clinging to her issues of *Life* and *Ladies' Home Journal*. "Mother tends to have a stifling effect."

"She can, I agree, but even the Countess of Atherly has been humbled by love." At Christmas, when Sir Edwin was suspected of murder, Mother swallowed her pride and sought Stella's aid. "That's what love can do. It changes us."

"Are you referring to you or me?" Lyndy quipped, lifting her hand to his lips. It still hinted of geranium.

Stella's laugh mingled with the breeze. It had been little more than a year since she'd roared up his drive in her motorcar and into his life. In a wife, he'd desired nothing more than a beauty that didn't bore him like all the indistinguishable women he'd been entangled with before. How could he have known she'd steal his heart and make him a better man?

A pine cone lay on the path, and Stella spiritedly kicked it down the terrace, smiling at her achieved distance.

But it wasn't just him that had changed, was it? Hadn't his whole family been touched by this incredible woman's adventurous, loving presence?

Ahead of them, Freddy pulled a branch of one of the exotic trees within Alice's reach. Alice, who'd barely lifted her nose out of her magazines last year, rose to her tiptoes to strip off a leaf to add to the collection she clutched in her fist.

Was it a coincidence that Alice was becoming more confident? Certainly, Mother's absence freed Alice to express herself, but would Alice even be here, with this man, sans *Maman*, joyfully engaged, if Stella hadn't shown her what a woman could do? And what of Papa, who shared nothing of his passion for fossil hunting with his family and who'd prohibited everyone from the inner sanctum that was his study? Hadn't he been charmed by Stella's genuine interest and now readily opened his heart, mind, and the doors of his study to anyone genuinely interested because of her? A year ago, would he have embarked on his great adventure, accepting Professor Gridley's invitation to visit the fossil fields of Wyoming? Of course not. When he'd left last week, instead of the usual goodbye, he'd thanked Stella for her unflagging encouragement to brave the wilds.

And then there was Mother, who'd objected to Stella from the first, scoffing at her *American ways*, who'd tried to sabotage their engagement and trusted no one but herself to protect Morrington and the family. Wasn't she now one of Stella's staunchest defenders?

At least against those outside the family.

Lyndy's quiet chuckle quickly died as thoughts of Mother's latest campaign, to help them conceive a child, sullied his humor. After a happy truce between them, she was again proving intolerable.

"For whatever reason," Stella said, a warm smile aimed at Alice and Freddy's backs, "I'm happy for her." A flicker of uncertainty dimmed her bright countenance. "And Freddy doesn't seem to have his father's pretense."

"So, you still don't believe Sir Edwin came here to watch Freddy play golf?"

Stella had told him about her first encounter with the McEwens and their guests. Although he agreed Sir Edwin's motives could be suspect, Lyndy hadn't sensed any of the awkwardness or tension she'd described between the McEwens and Sir Edwin when the latter returned to the manor house from his search of the estate, or at any time afterward.

"I don't. There's just something not right there." Stella tucked a strand of hair behind her ear, then began gnawing on her bottom lip. It wasn't like her.

"You're thinking of the maid?"

Stella nodded. "I don't know what to do."

Lyndy tugged sharply at his dinner jacket. The account she'd relayed of the maid's distress recalled too closely what Stella had been forced to endure last Christmas. The thought of it alone was enough to quicken his breath. But it wouldn't do, involving themselves in the domestic affairs of their hosts. They were strangers, after all, Stella's kin or not.

"You've done all you can," he said. But she hadn't, and they both knew it. Lyndy just hoped it would end here. "At least the McEwens seemed pleasant enough." From the gaiety and easy conversation at dinner, they'd had nothing to worry about on that score. "Mrs. McEwen was quite reticent. I don't think she took more than a few bites." Lyndy could still taste the succulent mushroom and salmon pie. "But she was amiable when I engaged her in a conversation about her stables, and Hamish McEwen is nothing like your father. Quite the opposite."

"That's true," Stella conceded, resting her head on Lyndy's shoulder. "Mrs. Agnew is a bit of a flirt, though, isn't she?" She chuckled. "First with Hamish, right in front of Virginia, then with Alasdair McCormack, and then Sir Edwin. She even started in with you."

Lyndy coughed into his hand. Stella laughed. "Right, well. Jeanie Agnew and Sir Edwin were quite chummy, weren't they?"

As the widow was with all the men, including Freddy and Lyndy. Neither her being old enough to be his mother nor his obvious marital state had stopped her from winking and commenting on Lyndy's dimpled chin. She'd even straightened his cravat when Finn, his valet, had previously tied it with his usual perfection. Lyndy didn't care for such fickle women.

He gazed at his wife's profile. *There's only one woman for me.*

"You think that was chummy. You should've seen her earlier with Alasdair McCormack." Stella laughed.

"A bit odd, that golfer, don't you think?" he said. "Dining alone in his room when there's a house full of guests."

"From what Freddy told me, it's his usual routine before a golf tournament."

"And I thought Freddy's habit of carrying golf clubs around was strange."

The first time they'd met, Freddy had disembarked from his motorcar with a bag of golf clubs hanging from his shoulder. There'd been snow on the ground.

"He doesn't carry them everywhere. He just makes certain he has them wherever he goes."

"My love, that doesn't make sense."

"See, he doesn't have them with him now, does he?" Lyndy acknowledged he didn't. "But we know he's brought them to Glenloch." Stella smiled mischievously. "So, he has them, but he doesn't."

Lyndy reached up and tickled the soft hairs at the nape of Stella's bare neck. She giggled, scrunching her shoulders up to her ears. When their eyes met, not a trace of Stella's apprehension remained. Lyndy congratulated himself on successfully driving the unfortunate incident with the maid from her mind. Now, if only he could do more than tickle her neck.

"I hope we don't have to chaperone too much longer," Stella said wistfully. "The chill in the air seems just the *change of climate* we were hoping for when we came north." Stella feigned a shiver, for the evening was unseasonably warm. "It would be such a shame to miss an opportunity to warm each other up."

She'd read his mind again. *How did she do it?*

Lyndy stared longingly at the knowing smile spreading across her lips, anticipating their taste, even as he shouted after his sister that it was time to return to the house.

CHAPTER 5

Sun streamed through the wall of paned glass and the feathery fronds of tree ferns outside just beyond and into the brightly painted room. The McEwens didn't stand on ceremony, having their guests gather in the dining room, but insisted they join them in the family's more intimate breakfast room adjacent to the conservatory. The lace-covered table had been set for five: the four men and Alice. As was the custom, all the married— or in Mrs. Agnew's case, widowed—women were given the honor of having trays taken up to their bedchambers. Lyndy had been more than reluctant to leave Stella's side this morning, and the sight of haggis on the sideboard made him regret it all the more. If the scent of bacon wasn't making his stomach rumble, he'd return to bed at once. Freddy and Sir Edwin were already seated on opposite sides, a simple bouquet of pink and white roses between them. They'd exchanged a few pleasantries with Lyndy before Sir Edwin had returned to his newspapers, and Freddy pushed food around his plate, the strain of uncomfortable silence between them.

Odd. It wasn't like either man to be reticent.

Lyndy was spooning eggs next to the potato scone and bacon on his plate, contemplating the platter of black pudding his mother had banned from Morrington years ago—*Black food doesn't belong on a plate at any time of the day, month, or year*, she'd insisted—when Hamish McEwen arrived, accompanied by a man Lyndy didn't know but whose identity he could guess from the checkered golf trousers he wore, just below the knee.

"Lord Lyndhurst," Hamish said, "may I introduce Mr. Alasdair McCormack, oor resident golf champion? Alasdair, Lord Lyndhurst is the son of the Earl of Atherly and," he indicated Freddy with a jut of his chin, "that wee lad's soon-to-be brother-in-law."

McCormack? When Stella had mentioned the golfer, the name hadn't struck a chord. But the sight of him called to mind an amiable fellow he'd become acquainted with a few years back. Now, what was the man's Christian name?

"What a pleasure it is to meet ye, my lord."

As Lyndy returned McCormack's firm handshake, he mentally sifted through names of men he'd been acquainted with.

"Any relation to Jamie McCormack, Lord Travit?" Lyndy and Lord Travit had sat together at the racecourse in Newcastle a few years ago. Lyndy remembered he'd been a Scotsman.

"Aye, my elder brother," McCormack said. "The Earl of Camgossie."

"Is that so?" Sir Edwin said, as if reading something of interest in the newspaper. "I hadn't heard of your father's death. He was a lovely man. I am sorry."

"You have my sympathy," Lyndy said. Freddy added his condolences as well.

"Thank ye." McCormack flashed a strained smile. "We weren't close. Are ye as fond of the turf as my brother, Lord Lyndhurst?"

"Indeed. If I remember, Lord Travit was vying to buy Osbech, winner of that year's Northumberland Plate," Lyndy said. "And do call me Lyndy."

McCormack, pleased, revealed a set of perfect white teeth.

"Do ye enjoy golf as well, Lyndy?" he asked, retrieving a plate and piling it high with everything from bacon to oatcakes. Beside his late father-in-law, Elijah Kendrick, Lyndy had never seen anyone eat so much. Golf never struck Lyndy as a very athletic pursuit. How did McCormack stay so lean?

"Not particularly," Lyndy said. "Bit pedestrian for me, I'm afraid."

"But you're willing to give it a shot, aren't you, old chap?" Freddy said, slathering his toast with honey.

"As promised. I will attend today's tournament with an open mind. I have to say, McCormack, it does improve my perspective, having a champion of the sport at the breakfast table."

McCormack's smile widened and Freddy chuckled, but Sir Edwin's indifference as he continued to read and ignore the others dampened the effect of Lyndy's lighthearted quip.

"And a future one as well, don't forget." Alice charmingly countered as she crossed the threshold. "And he's soon to be family."

Dressed in a white linen and lace dress with her blond hair mimicking Stella's fluffy bouffant style, she'd never looked prettier. Or was it her relaxed manner and the shy smile she shared with Freddy that was so becoming? The men stood as one, Freddy quickly pulling out the chair beside him for her. She filled her plate before settling in.

"No disrespect to you, Mr. McCormack," she continued, "but I'll be rooting for Freddy to shoot the lowest score."

"Hear, hear, my dear," Sir Edwin said, laying his broadsheet beside his plate and toasting Alice's sentiment with his teacup. Not wearing cuff links, his sleeve slipped down his arm. "May the best man win."

"Noo jist haud on, Edwin," Hamish said, pointing to Mc-

Cormack with his fork, its tongs spearing a slice of black pudding. "Have ye seen Alasdair play?"

"I have," Alice piped in. "At the Matchplay Championship in Richmond last October."

Lyndy had no recollection of Alice attending a golf tournament last year. "Was that while you were with Mother in London?"

"And you were on your honeymoon."

"I won at Royal Mid-Surrey, if I recall," McCormack said casually between bites.

"You did," Alice conceded.

Sir Edwin set down his teacup with a hard *clank*, his loose cuff catching the handle of his knife and flipping it off his plate. It stuck to the tablecloth, butter side down.

"Any word when we're to get our luggage, Hamish? It's been a blasted inconvenience, not having my suitcase." He held up his sleeve to exhibit his lack of cuff links.

"I dinnae realize the mix-up hadnae been resolved." Hamish shot a questioning glance at Stevenson, who lingered unobtrusively at the far end of the sideboard. The butler appeared to ignore him. "Is anyone else missing their wee luggage?"

Lyndy wiped his mouth with his napkin and confirmed he, too, was affected. Before breakfast, Finn had informed him that he was still missing a travel trunk.

"I have all of my belongings," McCormack said.

"Me too," Alice agreed.

Freddy, having just taken a bite, mumbled something and nodded.

"I'll get it sorted. I promise ye," Hamish said. "I cannae imagine whit could be hauding it up."

"I do hope so."

"There isn't anything irreplaceable or of high value in your case, is there, Sir Edwin?" Alice asked.

With his eyes still on Hamish, who was scratching his mustache as he reached for the newspaper Sir Edwin had abandoned, he answered, "It all depends, my dear girl. It all depends."

Before Lyndy could insist he elaborate, Sir Edwin pushed back in his chair, threw down his napkin, and said, "See you on the first tee, Freddy. As I said before, 'May the best man win,'" before strolling from the room.

Stella stood on the steps of the gray three-story stone Royal and Ancient Clubhouse, a model of indestructible architecture with its sturdy gables and chimneys and large round built-in clock, as crowds were beginning to form lines along the edges of the first fairway. If Stella squinted, she could see a flag flapping on the end of a pole in the distance.

"Let us check with the starter," Alasdair McCormack was saying.

Stella, Lyndy, and their party, minus Virginia, who hadn't felt up to attending, followed him toward what looked like a Victorian ladies' bathing hut on wheels positioned near where players were teeing up. A little hatch cut into the box allowed the man inside to communicate with golfers waiting for their names to be called. Taking in her surroundings, Stella purposely lagged.

She hadn't known what to expect of the Old Course, as everyone called it, but the expanse of treeless linear lawns stretching away beyond where she could see, punctuated by deep sandy craters and cradled by the rolling sandy dunes of wild grasses and stunted gorse endemic to the seaside, wasn't it. The first hole, though a straightaway from tee to the green, was several hundred yards long and crossed by a narrow road and a sinuous creek that snaked its way past the green on its way to St. Andrews Bay. Stella had driven by golf courses before in the States, but these were artificial swaths of highly manicured green cut through forest. This, on the other hand, was far windier and wilder and open than she could've imagined of a landscape where the intent was to hit a small ball through the air and into a tiny hole in the ground. She loved it.

When Stella caught up, Jeanie put her finger to her lips. They waited while a group of golfers teed off one by one.

When the players headed down the fairway, Lyndy leaned in to explain. "Seems it's proper etiquette not to talk while the players are hitting."

"Not only that," Alasdair expounded, "the rule states that 'while a stroke is playing no one of the party shall walk about, make any motion, or attempt to take off the player's attention, by speaking or otherwise.' Can't have anyone distracting us from playing our best game, now can we?"

"I'm surprised ye didn't ask me to leave, then," Jeanie said, a glint in her eye. "My beauty alone would distract any man."

She winked at Stella when Alasdair rolled his eyes. She then stood on her tiptoes and placed her cupped hand and mouth against his ear. What she whispered brought a smile to Alasdair's lips.

During the next gap between players, Hamish called "Tom!" in a low voice.

A well-built weathered old man with a long white beard and crook cane left his conversation with a gentleman in a high-domed black bowler hat to join them. Only the top button of his jacket was fastened.

"Fine day for some golf, eh, Hamish, lad." Tom lifted his tweed cap at Jeanie. "Lass."

"Nice to see you still keeping an eye on things, Tom," Alasdair said, peeling Jeanie Agnew from his arm.

"Aye, couldnae keep me away, Mr. McCormack."

"Tom, ye must meet my guests." Hamish swept his hand to encompass their whole party.

After the string of introductions, he finished with a flourish, "And this, to we who ken and admire him, is Old Tom Morris."

Hamish waited expectantly, as if he deserved applause for

the coup that was this grand introduction. Was Stella supposed to know who the elderly gentleman was? From Lyndy's blank stare, he didn't have any more of an inkling than she did.

"*The* Tom Morris?" Freddy said, his eyes wide with awe, giving Hamish the pleasure of the expected reaction. Freddy shoved his hand out in greeting, pumping the old man's hand like a well handle. Mr. Morris's weathered cheeks colored either from the sudden exertion or embarrassment, Stella couldn't tell. "It is indeed a pleasure to meet you, sir."

"Really, Freddy." Sir Edwin laughed. "You'd think he was the Prince of Wales."

"He's better," Freddy declared. "He's 'the Grand Old Man of Golf.'"

"Ach, laddie. St Andrews bairns are born wi' web feet an' wi a gowf club in their hands. Will ye soon be calling me 'Grand Old Man of the Sea'?" He winked at Stella.

She hadn't understood every word but returned his playful smile.

"Freddy says that you won the Open Championship four times, Mr. Morris," Alice said once Freddy sheepishly stepped back, giving the others a chance to address him.

"Aye, lassie. As did me son, Young Tommy, Willie Park, and Harry Vardon, there." He pointed to the player who'd just teed off.

"Old Tom was keeper of the greens here for many years," Hamish added. "Much of whit ye see is a credit tae him."

"Then I'll know who to blame when my ball finds the rough," Alasdair quipped.

Their shared laugh died in their throats as another player readied to tee off. Again, they watched and waited in silence until the golfers had moved on. While the others were preoccupied with the golfers, Stella followed the approach of a short stocky man with a wild bushy mustache, a bag of golf clubs slung from his shoulders, and a heavy leather band with a cumbersome brass plate encircling his right arm. Stella had seen all the caddies wearing them.

The sun peeked out from behind a line of threatening clouds and lit on the brass button stitched to the top of the man's brown-and-white-checkered flat cap as Freddy and the caddie acknowledged each other with a silent nod.

When it was safe to speak again, Freddy said by way of introduction, "You all know Billy Birdwell, don't you?"

Alice greeted him like a familiar acquaintance.

"I've seen ye aboot, Billy," Old Tom replied. "Been learning the lay of the land, havenae ye, laddie?"

"Wouldn't be worth my salt if I didn't. Nice to finally meet you, Sir Edwin, though haven't I seen you at Freddy's tournaments?"

"No, I've never been," was Sir Edwin's tart reply before turning his attention to two passing seagulls. In midflight, one stole a fish from the other's beak.

"My mistake, then."

"Ach, no. A caddie with poor eyesight is quite the liability." Alasdair McCormack laughed.

Billy Birdwell shifted the weight of the clubs with a jerk of his shoulder. As the clubs clattered against one another, he glared at the champion golfer from beneath hooded lids. He didn't find anything funny about it.

Freddy frowned. "It's true it couldn't have been him, Birdie. He's never been interested in golf, whether I'm playing or not. Which is why it's so odd you're here now, Father.

Stella leaned in in anticipation. Would Sir Edwin finally tell them why he was there?

Instead, Sir Edwin said, "Perhaps I might find some interest in the game if you cared to educate me, Mrs. Agnew. I hear you're quite handy with a club." He was rewarded with a torrent of Jeanie's giggles.

"Time to get on, I should think." Old Tom Morris compressed his lips in disapproval, tipped his hat, and strode away. Billy Birdwell quickly drew alongside him, peppering the old man with questions.

"Seems you know everyone, Hamish," Sir Edwin said, staring at the old man's back.

"Hamish likes to claim he's friends with everyone who is anyone in any British sport," Jeanie answered. "Be it polo, football, or golf."

"Then you must've known my uncle Richard," Freddy said, tracing the scar that crossed his eyebrow. He chuckled to himself. "He was a renowned cricket champion."

"Aye, we kenned your uncle Richard. Virginia, in particular, kenned him quite well. Oor condolences, laddie."

As the approach of another golfer teeing up demanded silence, Stella leaned into Alice and whispered, "What happened to Freddy's uncle?"

In a voice barely audible, Alice whispered in Stella's ear, "He died about two years ago. Drowned in the River Great Ouse."

Freddy was shaking his head, but not to deny what Alice had said. He couldn't have heard. He backed away but stepped forward again, his features crinkled with consternation and indecision. When the player had hit his drive, Freddy grabbed Sir Edwin's arm and drew his father aside.

In a rough whisper, he demanded, "If Hamish knows you and Uncle Richard, how is it that it took an invitation to me through Lady Lyndhurst for me to meet them? Why have you never mentioned the McEwens before, Father?"

"Ye'r up next, Young Kentfield," Alasdair called, cutting through the invisible tension. "Ready, laddie?"

"Of course." Freddy's face said otherwise.

"Good luck, my boy." Sir Edwin added his comment to a chorus of others' well-wishes, slapping his son on the back. He hadn't answered Freddy's question.

"Frederick Kentfield, London," the starter bellowed.

"Better skedaddle, Young Kentfield," Alasdair said. "I don't want to beat ye by forfeit. Takes the fun out of it."

"You won't win that easily, McCormack," Freddy said, a forced mirth to his tone as he shot his father one last questioning glance before catching up to his caddie and yanking out a club from his bag.

"What was all that about?" Lyndy said before Stella could. She still shouldn't be surprised by his open curiosity, but she was.

"Oh, that," Sir Edwin said, shrugging it off. "Freddy will learn one day when he has children." He looked first at Alice, who blushed and dropped her gaze, and then at Stella, who met his stare with a challenge. She couldn't let him or anyone else suspect the fear blazing like the rush of heat throughout her body. "Children don't get told everything," he continued. "Solely what they need to know."

"Shhh," Jeanie hissed as Freddy positioned himself beside his ball and swung with a ferocity Stella had never seen.

The ball soared down the fairway and the crowd cheered, but Stella lost it in the sky and didn't see it land. When she turned to see Freddy's reaction, he and Billy Birdwell had already moved on.

He was gone. At least for a few hours. Virginia could finally relax!

She shifted the clubs on her shoulder and hiked up the hill to the next hole. The fresh air, the exercise, and the solitude were doing her good. How could it not; this was one of her favorite spots on Earth. Let the others go to the Old Course. She'd rather stay and play here. But as she chose her brassie from the bag and set up her tee shot, she couldn't avoid the expansive view of Glenloch Hill looming large on the opposite side of their little valley. Her beloved house, surrounded by its cozy cottages, game fields, and gardens, had been her haven for so long.

Until now.

Impatient and unsettled, Virginia took her stance and whacked at the ball, slicing it off too far to the right. It landed in a strip of ungrazed grass—out of bounds. No matter. With no one in sight—Colonel McCloud, who enjoyed golfing privileges as their nearest neighbor, had finished his daily round an hour earlier—she retrieved a second ball, set up to take another shot, and whiffed.

Virginia righted her straw hat and chewed on her thumbnail.

She was a decent golfer; not as accomplished as Jeanie, but this was her home course, literally. She and Hamish owned it, and she'd played it countless times. She'd never whiffed a ball before. Perhaps she'd been too off-balance? Forcing herself to concentrate, Virginia waggled the brassie over the ball, one, two, three times, before finally swinging at it with all the force of a scythe cutting through hay. And missed again.

Virginia slammed the wooden club's head into the ground in frustration.

Why did he have to come here, stirring it all up again? She couldn't sleep. She couldn't eat. She couldn't even play golf. How humiliating it was to nearly faint yesterday. What must Stella, Hamish's cousin, think of her? Virginia hated how jittery and helpless she'd become. She'd believed she'd moved past it. But seeing him again . . . It was as if it had been yesterday, not decades ago.

And now he was making himself at home, in her home, as if nothing had happened. But what could she do? How was she to be rid of him? She couldn't just send him packing. Not without having to explain why. And that she'd sworn she'd never do. Not to Hamish, not to anyone. She couldn't endure the shame.

Virginia was trapped.

She tried to settle her fears, her rising hysteria, and swung at the ball again, but the tears welling in her eyes blurred her vision, and she missed again.

Damn it!

She cracked the hickory shaft of the brassie across her knee in an attempt to break the club in two, but the wood was too strong and the impact sent pain shooting through her leg. She barely noticed. Double fisted, she slammed the club into the ground, over and over, kicking up dirt and grass, hoping to make the biggest, most hideous hole in the grazed turf she could. A speck of dirt flew into her eye, and as she wiped it away, the earthy scent of the soil she loved so much brought her to her senses.

"Oh, no, what have I done?"

Her anger spent, her head spinning, she dropped the brassie and sank to her knees beside it. Oblivious to the grass stains on her white skirt or the dirt lodging beneath her nails, she gathered up clumps of sod, trying to repair the hole she'd made. But, as with her, the damage was done.

CHAPTER 6

Leaving the McEwens and Mrs. Agnew to follow Alasdair, Stella and the others followed Freddy from tee to tee. He'd been paired with two players Stella had never heard of. She enjoyed the whack of the ball as it was struck by the club, splitting the silence, the rush of excitement as it flew through the air, anticipating where it might drop and settle, the odd hush that descended as everyone clustered around a green, a patch of grass either mowed—or, if the sheep they'd passed on the adjacent hole was any indication, grazed—shorter than everywhere else, vying for the best perspectives to watch the golfers putt the ball softly toward the hole cut in the ground. But after this was repeated time and time again, she found herself distracted, gazing toward the gray-stone buildings that marked the border of the course and the beginning of the town of St. Andrews, dwindling farther and farther in the distance or following the flight of the seagulls gracefully riding the wind. Alice and Sir Edwin were utterly engaged with every move Freddy made. If he hit the ball far, they cheered and clapped. When he missed a putt, they added their groans to the crowds. Surprisingly, Lyndy was also caught up in the game.

"Do you want to see if we can find the beach?" Stella once whispered after watching the same three players tee off for the fourth time. It was just a short walk away. Stella could smell the salt in the air.

"And miss this?" Lyndy said, not taking his eyes off the golfer whose turn it was to strike.

Hadn't Mark Twain defined golf as *a good walk spoiled*? Stella was starting to think he was right. But had she given the sport a chance? Perhaps if she knew more?

With her mind made up, Stella snuck in her questions whenever the demand for silence lifted, first of Alice and Lyndy, who, between them, knew a little, and then of their fellow spectators, a jolly dedicated bunch. Why are there eighteen holes? Why is it better to get a lower score than a higher one? How do you know which club to use? How pleasant it was to find many Scots willing and eager to educate her. One older gentleman, a Mr. Campbell, imbued golf with a mysticism that captured Stella's imagination. In between swings, chips, and putts, he liberally offered up anecdotes and factual tidbits that enriched the play. Thanks to this friendly fellow in a tan tweed suit, Stella learned how the course was designed to follow the land's natural contours and had been played upon for hundreds of years before America was founded, the first bunkers being sheep wallows in the sandy soil. He explained how the Ladies' Course was one large putting green, that the name of the creek that cut through the course was Swilcan Burn, and the small six-hundred-year-old stone bridge crossing it was initially built to help get livestock across. Golf wasn't just a game to him; this wasn't just a golf course but a connection to the land and his ancestral past. With his friendly, almost paternal demeanor, he and Stella soon made fast friends.

"Dae ye ken why that hole is called the Ginger Beer Hole, lassie?" he'd asked after explaining that all but the tenth hole had a name and a number. Why the tenth was never named, he didn't know. "Because years ago, Old Daw Anderson used to have his refreshment stand just there. As ye can guess, he sold ginger beer and," he smiled and tapped the side of his nose, "for those of us in the know, something a wee bit stronger."

As they hiked up an eroded and crowded grassy dune to get a better view of the fairway, a train chugged along the tracks, demarcating the far boundary of the course. Mr. Campbell pointed toward it as it spewed smoke into the sky.

"Last year, on the last round at sixteen, I saw Braid hit his ball off the railway tracks. Wasnae allowed to move it without penalty, so he played it where it lay. Wouldnae ye ken, he thinned it tae the back of the green and, after a delicate chip, saved the hole."

Sometimes Stella had no idea what the Scotsman was talking about, but she appreciated his enthusiasm. It lent excitement and glamour to the seemingly slow-moving game. And all the while Mr. Campbell was educating and entertaining Stella, Lyndy was listening too.

"Isn't that Braid over there?" Lyndy indicated the tall lean player crossing the enormous almost acre-sized green nearby. Mr. Campbell affirmed it was. To Stella's unspoken question, Lyndy added, "James Braid is another Open champion. Last year's winner, from what I gather."

"But isn't that the green for this hole? Mr. Braid isn't in Freddy's party, so why is he already on the green?" Stella was again confused.

"Here at the Old Course, all but two are double putting greens, one hole for outgoing parties and one for the homeward bound. Braid there is playing the thirteenth. Puzzling, aye, but all part of the charm."

As the players stopped at their second shot, Mr. Campbell and the rest fell silent. Aiming toward the green, the first golfer swung hard, but instead of flying straight, his ball curved to the right. The ball landed with a muted thud, spraying up sand at the bottom of what Stella had learned was called a pot bunker. This one looked several feet deep. The crowd groaned.

"Bloody slice!" the player cursed, smashing his club at the ground.

"That's unbecoming behavior if ye ask me," Mr. Campbell muttered beside them.

"Yes, quite," Lyndy readily agreed.

"Lose one's temper and one may very well lose the game," Sir Edwin snickered. "Much like life, eh?" He shot a meaningful look at Lyndy, who was known to be a little hotheaded.

"Shhh," was Lyndy's retort.

It was Freddy's turn to strike his ball, which sat in a deep patch of tall windswept grass. He studied his predicament and then, after a whispered consultation with Billy Birdwell, selected a club from his bag. Freddy was the only one of the three players Stella had seen do this. The others had the caddies hand them their chosen club.

After Freddy successfully hit his ball next to the green, Stella asked, "Why doesn't Freddy's caddie hand him the club like the other caddies do?"

"That's just how they always do it," Alice said, shrugging.

Mr. Campbell indicated for Stella to linger behind when, after the third player hit his ball, the golfing party headed toward the green. "It's a guid question ye asked, lassie. Aboot the young Kentfield's caddie."

"Why? Is it unusual?"

"Unusual? In all me years of playing and watching this glorious game, which is a very long time, I've never seen it done. With that part of the caddie's job, it makes ye wonder why."

Why indeed? When the day's golf was over, Stella would have to ask Freddy.

"Are you settling in okay, Ethel?"

Stella mindlessly flicked the cluster of white lace draping

down her bodice as her lady's maid tackled her unruly hair. The constant breeze off the North Sea at the golf course hadn't made the task easier. The soothing lower tones of Lyndy and his valet's audible but indiscernible voices wafted through the dressing room door. It had been an exciting but exhausting day.

Alasdair McCormack had proven to be as accomplished as everyone claimed, finishing the day second to the top. Still, it was Freddy who surprised everyone, even, Stella suspected, himself, by scoring low enough to be in the top ten. According to Alice, it was his best showing yet. On the carriage ride home, Lyndy and Freddy had swapped keen observations and animated declarations, discussing each drive, each putt, the break of each green as the women looked on fondly. They'd returned from the golf tournament just in time to hear the dinner gong.

"I am, my lady. The staff here is more congenial than I expected. Very welcoming and helpful."

"I'm glad to hear it, Ethel. And I'd have to agree. I don't think I've met an unfriendly Scot yet." However, the McEwens and Alasdair's reaction to Sir Edwin's impromptu arrival had come close. Yet, after they'd greeted him, all that hesitancy seemed to vanish. He was treated as cordially as everyone else.

"The only thing is . . ."

Ethel paused, her concentration focused on piling Stella's hair onto her head and securing it in an elaborate bouffant, hairpins poking from between her pinched lips. When she'd placed the last hairpin, Ethel stepped back to regard her work. Satisfied, she licked the tip of her forefinger and tapped the metal tong of the curling iron. A sizzle said it was still hot. Ethel began applying the heated iron to the loose strands of hair still dangling above Stella's forehead, curling them back from Stella's face.

"The only thing is what?" Stella asked, flinching from the searing heat. Ethel hadn't burned her yet, but Stella couldn't help anticipating that first time.

"I met a maid this afternoon at luncheon who seemed to have been . . ." Ethel bit her lip as she sought the right word. "Injured."

"Oh, no. She's all right, I hope. What happened?"

"I don't know, but she had the strangest bruises on her cheeks, almost like fingermarks. Like someone had squeezed so hard that they left their handprint behind. That couldn't be right, could it?" She set aside the heating iron.

Stella's stomach roiled. She hadn't forgotten about the laundry maid. She'd been thinking about her on and off all day, but having not seen a visible injury on her, Stella had assumed another maid had burned herself in the kitchen or twisted an ankle tripping on the dimly lit back stairs. Working in service could be a dangerous occupation.

"Was the maid's name Aggie?"

Ethel's hands stilled on the diamond tiara she was securing to Stella's head, her fingers casting a shadow across the sparkling gemstones. "How did you know?"

Stella shoved back from the dressing table, her ears burning in anger, forcing Ethel to step aside. "Sorry, Ethel," she remembered to say before stomping out the door.

She yanked open the door at the end of the hall, barely noticing how the brass-headed tacks made an intricate pattern in the green baize lining on the inner side. As Stella pounded down the servant's staircase, a small round-faced woman wearing a serviceable black dress and the tired look of the long-suffering, no doubt drawn by the hard thumping of Stella's heavy steps, awaited her at the bottom, prepared to reprimand the offending servant for causing such a racket. The flicker of stifled exasperation transformed into blatant surprise when she spotted Stella. The matron quickly snapped her gaping mouth shut.

"Where's Aggie?" Stella demanded, sounding harsher than she'd intended. This poor woman hadn't done anything.

"Lady Lyndhurst?" The matron, guessing who Stella must

be from her accent, smoothed the graying hair at her temples, then the white lace on her high-necked bodice.

"Yes." Stella caught her breath at the foot of the stairs. Her heart was still racing. "I'm sorry to intrude, but I must speak to Aggie. Immediately."

"What's all this, then, my lady? I'm Mrs. Graham, the house-keeper. If there's something ye want from the laundry maid, ye can speak to me about it."

Several other servants, a kitchen maid, two footmen, and a hall boy lugging a bucket, scurried past with their heads bowed while stealing glances at Stella as if they'd never seen anyone from upstairs among them before.

Maybe the McEwens aren't as loose with their rules as I thought. Or at least not regarding their downstairs staff.

"No, Mrs. Graham. I appreciate your offer, but this is between Aggie and me."

"Well, if ye insist, my lady." The housekeeper shook her head as if to question Stella's dubious decision. "Aggie is still in the laundry house. But she's expected for supper soon." Stella's mouth watered at the mention of food; the aroma coming from the kitchen was heavenly.

"I can send her up to speak to ye when she arrives if that would suit?" Stella wouldn't wait. She'd passed the house-keeper and turned down the hall before Mrs. Graham called after. "Where are ye going, my lady?"

There had to be a back door. Ignoring Mrs. Graham calling after her again, Stella found what she was looking for and shoved it open onto a lush walled kitchen garden. Paved with crisscrossing flagstones covered with creeping English thyme that released its aroma under Stella's feet, the garden was a haven for the senses. At any other time, she would've lingered, but to speak to Aggie alone, Stella had to catch the maid before she left the laundry house.

Stella spied Aggie through a window, putting up her apron

after what was etched on her face as a long day. Evident, though she'd tried to hide them with face powder, were the bruises Ethel described. Someone had hurt her again. This time, Stella refused to let it go.

But again, the door wouldn't budge. Pressing her shoulder to it, Stella forced it open.

"Aggie?" Stella called in a hushed tone. No response. Where did the maid go? Stepping inside and closing the door behind her, Stella called again. "Aggie?"

"Ach!" The maid, partially hidden behind one of the enormous built-in drying cupboards that had been pulled out, cried out in surprise. Whirling around, she banged her elbow on the corner of the frame.

"Ach, my lady! Ye gave me such a wee fright." She clutched her injured elbow, her hand held to her heart.

Stella held up her hands, palms out. "I'm sorry. I didn't mean to startle you. But I had to see for myself." Stella pointed to the maid's bruised face. "I know you didn't want me to mention what happened yesterday, but these bruises, Aggie . . . What's happened to you is horrendous. You have to tell me who did this."

Stella regretted her strong words as the maid shrunk back from her, covering her bruises with her palms as if ashamed.

"He came back and said . . ."

"That if you told, he'd hurt you even more?" Stella said as gently as she could through her anger. Aggie nodded.

How dare he, whoever he was!

When Stella had refused to marry against her will, her father had crushed her hand so hard she'd thought her bones had broken. At Christmas, Stella had contended with a man's violent attempt to force unwanted affections on her. Both men had been furious at being denied her compliance and hoped to strong-arm her into doing their bidding. Now, the same had happened to Aggie. Stella dug her fingernails into her palms to curb her fury.

"Tell me who it was, Aggie, and I promise he'll never hurt you again."

"But I'll lose me job." With no apron to clutch, she twisted the fabric of her cotton dress in her fist.

"You won't, Aggie. You didn't do anything wrong, and I'll see to it that you don't suffer for being honest." If Hamish and Virginia were as kind as they appeared, they'd be sympathetic to this poor woman's plight. And if not, Morrington Hall could always use a good maid. Just ask Stella's mother-in-law. "If nothing else, I'll—"

Footsteps outside halted the conversation. Aggie skittered back behind the drying cupboard, prepared to hide behind the sheets draping from the racks, but the footsteps continued past. As Stella peered out the window, Sir Edwin's head bobbed by. He struck up a hearty whistled version of "Goodbye Little Yellow Bird."

Where was he going? When everyone else was getting ready for dinner?

Stella turned back to face the maid. "Please, Aggie. Who was it? Who hurt you?"

Aggie closed her eyes, mumbling what sounded like a prayer. She stared at her shoes, the brown leather scuffed and dull, and pointed over Stella's shoulder toward the window. "He did."

CHAPTER 7

Stunned momentarily by Aggie's revelation, Stella steadied herself with the edge of a nearby table. It wobbled under her weight. A clothing iron on the table, set upright on its handle, toppled with a thud.

Sir Edwin? The same man who once wooed Lyndy's mother? Who Lyndy was named for? Who Stella had endangered herself and Lyndy for, to clear his name of murder? He'd forced himself upon Aggie?

How dare he!

The bile in Stella's stomach lurched into her throat, leaving a metallic taste. Her muscles strained like a pair of suspenders stretched to the furthest extent. And then she sprang. Her earlier anger paled compared to the wrath that propelled Stella out the door and onto the path the way Sir Edwin had gone. She barely noted the feeble protests made by the maid left behind, or how the woods were suddenly devoid of sound, including Sir Edwin's jaunty whistling. Stella thought nothing of the snags in her stockings as she picked up her skirts and tore through the thorny shrubs, nothing of what she would do or say when she caught up with the brute, nothing of the dangers of confronting him alone.

Sir Edwin would answer for what he'd done.

"Why didn't you tell me you'd seen Richard?"

The voice's angry demand cut through her roiling emotions, slowing her sprint to a walk, and, eventually, Stella drew to a halt, holding her breath to listen.

"I havenae seen ye in years, Edwin. Why would I tell ye anything?"

Stella crouched and scurried closer toward the tall laurel hedge that enclosed the lower lawn. Tiptoeing along, she found a section where the plants had died back and been partially cut out, leaving a gap she could peer through and, hopefully, not be seen. Hamish and Sir Edwin stood a dozen yards away beside the ivy-covered wall bordering the lower lawn along the northern side. Although the lower lawn, set at the bottom of a series of terraced stone stairways leading from the manor house, was spacious enough to host a village festival or a cricket match, where the men stood wouldn't be visible from the house. It was the perfect place to meet.

Stella pushed the branches slightly wider apart, filling the air with the laurel's scent as the leaves rustled against one another. A puddle of reflected light danced a few feet before her. For a moment, the light caught Sir Edwin's eye. When he lost interest, she snatched the tiara from her head, realizing it was the culprit.

She'd almost been spotted.

Then what would she do? Explain that she'd come to confront Sir Edwin but decided to hide like a sneak thief instead? Her rage, having cooled temporarily, threatened to flare up again. Why was she hiding? She hadn't done anything wrong.

Stella had left the gap in the hedge and taken a few steps toward the gate when Sir Edwin said, "I'm here now, old boy. Tell me what I want to know."

Stella froze. Was she about to find out why Sir Edwin came to Glenloch? Could it help Aggie get some justice?

"Away and boil yer heid, Edwin," Hamish said half-jokingly. What he'd said, Stella had no idea. "I dinnae ken anything ye dinnae ken."

"Then I *dinnae* have anything you want."

Hamish's words were genial, but Sir Edwin's tone was anything but. What had Stella been thinking, intending to confront Sir Edwin alone? If he could violently prey on a maid, who knew what else he was capable of? Once, she'd thought his overly friendly, familiar manner harmless. Yet he'd attacked a maid and was now proven capable of blackmail.

What will Lady Atherly think?

"Be reasonable, Edwin. What's it tae ye, anyway?"

"Information, that's what."

"All I can tell ye is that Richard was alive and well when we left him. Truly, I dinnae ken anymore."

"Bloody hell, Hamish. Why don't I believe you? Until you tell me the truth . . ." Leaving his threat unspoken, Sir Edwin stomped away. From the sound of his heavy footfalls, he was heading in Stella's direction.

"Edwin! Be reasonable, will ye?" Hamish called, a slight desperation to his tone. "Edwin!"

Before Sir Edwin reached the gate, Stella ran back and plunged into the dead foliage. Leaves fluttered to the ground behind her. Sharp, recently pruned branches scratched her bare arms and cheek as she shifted sideways, squeezing her whole body into the gap and wishing the rustling she'd caused would still. As the metal gate creaked open, she tucked the edges of her skirt around her feet, grateful Ethel had chosen her dark green silk gown. Stella held her breath as Sir Edwin stomped past. Whether it was her stealth or his preoccupation, it didn't matter. He didn't seem to notice her. She exhaled, realizing she hadn't paid attention to where Hamish was. When she twisted around and peered through a tiny gap in the branches, he was gone.

"Lyndy!"

Stella sprinted to meet him as he climbed the path from the McEwens' golf course to the house. Before dinner, he'd snuck out to hit a few balls instead of dawdling in the drawing room. Although he'd spent the day studying Freddy's swing, Lyndy was far from mastering his own. He'd try again later.

Shifting the borrowed set of golf clubs from one shoulder to the other, he looped his arm around Stella's waist and plucked several glossy laurel leaves from her hair. She was breathless from running, yes, but the high color on her cheeks was all wrong. And was that a scratch marring her porcelain skin?

"What is it, my love?"

"Not here."

She grabbed his hand and led him back up the path to a small wooden shed set in the middle of the lawn. Designed with large windows, the structure was attached to a circular metal track on the ground that, with the aid of a turning wheel, could be moved to capture the sun as it crossed the sky. Lyndy had heard of such summerhouses but had never seen one.

Ingenious. Perhaps we should have one built at Morrington Hall.

Stella pulled him inside and sat. Lyndy settled in beside her. Hexagonal in shape, it was fitted with benches on five sides, though not large enough for more than a few people. If he could dismiss the scratch and the rent he now noticed in the silk on her shoulder, Lyndy might've fancied Stella had done nothing more than tangle with some bushes and brought him here to shower him with affection in private. But he knew better. Her ears were red.

"What's happened?"

"I knew I should've told you sooner . . ." she began.

Lyndy tensed his jaw until it ached as she relayed the assault on the laundry maid. He clenched and unclenched his fists, attempting to assuage his anger. Not at Stella, though he wished she'd confided in him sooner, but at the ruthlessness of the incident.

What kind of man preyed on innocent women? Men like Stella's father, Elijah Kendrick. Lyndy yanked so hard on the bottom of his dinner jacket that he heard a seam tear.

"I don't know why I assumed it was one of the servants," she said, then hesitated.

"What is it you don't want to tell me?"

"Aggie confided in me who hurt her."

"And?"

"It was Sir Edwin."

"Bloody hell!"

Lyndy exploded to his feet and threw open the door, sending it crashing against the outside wall, rattling the shed's walls of windows. His mind was reeling. His mother's former lover, Lyndy's namesake, for goodness' sake, violently mistreated a maid? Had he hurt Mother as well?

"Bloody hell!"

The golf bag banged against his hip. He snatched the strap and flung clubs and bag rattling to the ground, satisfying some of his need to lash out.

"I was as furious as you were," Stella said, drawing alongside him and reaching out a hand but stopping shy of touching his shoulder. "But there's more."

More? What more could the scoundrel possibly have done?

"He didn't touch you, did he?"

"No, nothing like that. But when I went to confront him, he was having an intense private conversation with Hamish. It sounded like he was blackmailing him. And the way he spoke, it was like he'd already forgotten what he'd done to poor Aggie. I didn't realize he could be so cold and calculating, did you?"

"The bloody bastard!" Lyndy stormed toward the manor.

Leading out to a flagstone patio from the drawing room, the French windows stood open, emitting the high-pitched, harmonic hum of bagpipes. With fists clenched, Lyndy strode through, Stella on his heels.

Knowing what he intended, he expected his wife to dissuade him, but whatever she said didn't cut through his outrage. He purposely avoided glancing at her, not wanting to be persuaded by the look of warning he knew he'd find.

How could Lyndy face his mother ever again with this knowledge? *Unless I do something about it.*

Upon seeing him, those in the drawing room, drinks in hand, froze as if in a tableau vivant accompanied by the shrill squeaking of bagpipes that suddenly fell silent.

"What's wrong? What's happened?" Virginia asked, setting her drink on the table.

"Sir Edwin, I demand a word." Lyndy approached the blackguard, who seemed to be having a tête-à-tête with Mrs. Agnew. "Alone."

The widow withdrew her arm, which had been draped over Sir Edwin's shoulder. The scoundrel's crooked smile faded. "My dear boy, whatever has gotten into you?"

"You assaulted a maid, and I'm here to call you out on it."

Gasps filled the silence.

"Now, now. A maid?" Sir Edwin scoffed. "I deny it, of course." He gathered the others in his gaze, letting it rest momentarily on Mrs. Agnew, who had moved a step away, before facing his accuser again. "Whyever would I?"

"That's what we want to know," Lyndy said.

"I have no need to force any woman to do anything she doesn't want to do. Nor could I, if I wanted to. Just ask my wife." He chuckled, eliciting a few knowing but nervous chuckles from the others.

"But the maid confided in me," Stella said, drawing shoulder to shoulder with Lyndy. "She named you."

"I'm sorry for the poor girl, but it's simply not true. I haven't even spoken to, let alone coerced, a single female servant since I arrived."

Lyndy, on the verge of believing him, fancying the maid, in her distress, mistook her attacker for Sir Edwin, unclenched his fists and wiggled his fingers. His knuckles were white.

"That's all right, then," Hamish declared. "Lyndy, have a wee dram."

Talk resumed when Hamish ordered the butler to pour Lyndy a whiskey and the bagpiper to continue playing softly outside. Stella was drawn away by Virginia and Alice, who wanted to know more about the maid, while the two golfers and Hamish engaged in a discussion about the unusually dry conditions of the Old Course.

Mrs. Agnew sidled up to Sir Edwin again, gripping his arm. Sir Edwin whispered something into her ear, causing the middle-aged woman to giggle like a schoolgirl. Lyndy took the offered drink and threw back the contents of the glass in one gulp. It burned all the way down.

"I'd give anything for another sherry," Mrs. Agnew said, pouting. "But I don't think Ginny would approve."

"She needn't know." Sir Edwin winked at the widow, who brightened with expectation and implied mischievousness. He strolled toward the cart, laden with cut-crystal decanters and glasses of varying sizes, humming.

It isn't right. This just isn't bloody well right.

Lyndy blocked his way. Sir Edwin tried sidestepping him, but Lyndy wouldn't have it. Thwarted, Sir Edwin crossed his arms against his chest.

"What's this now? Have more unfounded accusations to let loose, my boy?" Sir Edwin's mouth twitched upward in a questioning smirk. "Still wondering if your mother had reason to name you after me, are you? Or are we done here?" He glanced past Lyndy to the waiting widow.

"Lyndy." He heard Stella call his name too late.

"Not quite." With a quick jab, and all the force of his anger behind it, Lyndy punched Sir Edwin in the nose. "Now we're done."

One of the women shrieked. As Sir Edwin staggered back, blood gushed between his fingers as he tried to staunch the pain.

"Bloody hell, Lyndy! I said I didn't do it."

Lyndy shook out the throbbing in his knuckles as he shouldered past the others, shocked into silence. The bagpiper cut off his tune abruptly as Lyndy reemerged outside. Before he had time to wonder what his wife thought of his outburst, Stella was there, in step beside him, reaching for his uninjured hand.

"You also said you loved my mother, you bastard," Lyndy shouted over his shoulder.

CHAPTER 8

With the morning sun in her eyes, Stella rolled over in an empty bed, suppressing a pang of loneliness. Lyndy was already up and gone. She reached for the souvenir spoon she kept in the painted porcelain jewelry dish on the nightstand—the one Lyndy gave her for Christmas. Holding it always brought her comfort. Of course, the spoon wasn't there. And neither was the jewelry dish. They were in her bedchamber at Morrington Hall. For a moment, she'd forgotten where she was.

Memories of last evening flooded her mind. She covered her eyes, trying to envision the serene swells of closely clipped fairways and waving dune grasses of the links course instead of the blood spurting from Sir Edwin's nose. She tried to remember the exhilarating crack of a club on the ball, the cheers of the crowd when a player hit an exceptional shot instead of Aggie's fearful plea for Stella to leave well enough alone. It was no use.

Stella bounded out of bed, unwilling to wait for Ethel or her morning tray. She tracked down her riding clothes and boots in the wardrobe and was out the door before anyone saw her. What better way to clear her head than to take up Virginia's offer to ride Morag or Angus, two exquisite chestnut Arabians, anytime Stella wanted. After the incident with Sir Edwin, she and Lyndy had, in unspoken agreement, set out for the stables to acquaint themselves with the beauties. They spoke little of what happened or why, limiting their conversation to Morag's large, intelligent eyes or debating whether Angus's longer leaner muscling would make him the better of the two for racing. They'd wanted to saddle up then, but a sudden downpour prevented a ride. When they returned to the house, taking dinner on a tray and finally going to bed, they'd found comfort in each other's arms, but neither slept well. Awake half the night, Stella witnessed Lyndy's restlessness. Wanting to avoid having to ride with Sir Edwin, Lyndy had talked of accompanying Alasdair, whose start time at the Open Championship this morning was much earlier than Freddy's. That Lyndy followed through, as exhausted as he must be, was proof of how much he'd enjoyed the tournament and how little he wanted to be in Sir Edwin's company.

If only I could avoid him too.

In the early morning quiet, Stella's boot heels clicked along the stone path, stirring up chiffchaffs and song thrushes flitting around in the bushes. Leaves rustled in the chilly breeze. The sound of an industrious woodpecker echoed from high in a nearby tree. Stella slowed her pace, appreciating the peaceful simplicity.

So far, her trip to Scotland hadn't turned out as planned. She'd spent more time navigating friction and hostility than the fairways at the golf course. Perhaps they should've considered enjoying a *change of climate* elsewhere. Nothing said they had to try to conceive in Scotland. But then, she'd never would've met her Scottish kin. And that would've been her loss.

A red squirrel darted across the path in front of her. Stella stopped to watch as it scrambled up a pine tree.

But why did Sir Edwin have to be here?

He'd caused all the trouble, arriving unannounced, assaulting the maid, and then casting aspersions on Lyndy's mother.

Which was probably why Lyndy punched him.

As they'd left the drawing room, Stella had heard the mortified disparaging remarks whispered behind Lyndy's back. Was she any less to blame? Didn't she endorse his violence with her passivity? Stella suspected what he intended to do. His temper was his biggest fault. She could've tried harder to persuade him to restrain himself. But wasn't a part of her gratified that he was as disgusted by Sir Edwin's behavior as she was? Stella disapproved of violence. God knew she'd seen enough of it in the past year to last a lifetime, but she couldn't pretend she didn't understand it.

Stella rounded the corner, thick with overground shrubbery, but unhurriedly. The path to the stables led past the laundry building, and she wasn't in any rush to see it again. A few yards away, Aggie, in a crisp white apron, was parting the bushes just off the path and staring at whatever she'd found there. Stella had never seen her outside before. The maid looked lost and out of place. At the sound of Stella's approach, Aggie let go of the branches.

"Lady Lyndhurst! I . . ." she stammered, her eyes darting from Stella to the bushes and back again. For once, she didn't smell heavily of laundry soap.

"What is it, Aggie? What's happened?"

In response, Aggie stepped aside, fiddling with her apron strings. Inches away, shod feet and a few inches of black pant-leg stuck out from under the brush. Raindrops glistened on the new calfskin shoes, mud clumped on the heels, and a few blades of grass clung to the unscuffed soles.

Stella closed the distance between herself and the prostrate figure in seconds. She shoved back the shrubs, her riding jacket instantly beaded with raindrops from disturbing the leaves. Beneath them, the man lay motionless, not even the slightest rise of his chest. His nose was swollen, a line of dried blood streaking from it caking his silvery mustache, his forehead a mass of discolored skin. Above his well-trimmed beard, his battered left cheek resembled tomato aspic. His mouth gaped loose, revealing that three of his front teeth had chipped off.

"Oh, no!"

Stella's heel caught on a root as she reeled back. As the shrubbery sprung back into place, she staggered, grasping at air, at branches, and finally at the arm of the nearby Aggie to steady herself, anything to keep from falling near the hideously bludgeoned body.

"Is he—?" Aggie whispered.

"Dead?" There was no doubt. "Yes. Sir Edwin won't trouble you anymore."

CHAPTER 9

With the roiling of her stomach stilled, Stella let go of Aggie's arm, though her mind continued to spin with questions. How long had Sir Edwin been here? Who would want to kill him? What was she going to tell Freddy and Lyndy?

Are the police going to think Lyndy did this?

Stella tried to brush aside the unbidden thought. But like a spiderweb across a less trodden path that clings to one's face and hair, it wouldn't go away.

Yet there stood Aggie, shivering with shock. She had a motive. Sir Edwin had assaulted her, threatened her, squeezed her cheeks so hard he left his mark, and from the proximity of his body to the laundry building, appeared to have decided to come back to hurt her again. But Sir Edwin's white shirt, waistcoat, and tie were splotched and splattered with blood. How could Aggie have killed him without getting any on herself? Was she so cold-blooded that she'd change her clothes and apron and stand over the body again? That was ridiculous. And where was the murder weapon?

She took one last deep inhale, forcing her voice to sound

calm. "Do you know anything about . . . this, Aggie?" She resisted looking at Sir Edwin's feet.

Aggie shook her hands, palms out, as if warding off any hint of accusation. "Nay. I dinnae ken what happened. I found him like this on me way tae work." She dropped her arms to her sides and her gaze to Sir Edwin's legs. She took a step back and then another, her eyes wild, like a frightened rabbit on the verge of bolting.

"Don't move, Aggie. I'm going to look for the murder weapon."

With Aggie's slight nod, Stella risked turning her back on the maid to root through the nearby shrubbery, carefully avoiding exposing Sir Edwin's body. She wasn't sure if she could keep the contents of her stomach down if she saw what was left of his face again. She found a thick fallen tree branch big enough to possibly inflict that kind of damage to a man's head, but it didn't have any blood on it either.

While shooting Aggie the occasion glance, Stella fanned out, searching the area around her as she'd seen Inspector Brown, the detective from the Hampshire Constabulary back in the New Forest, do. She searched the path and the nearby lawn for any clue about what happened. But Stella feared going too far from Aggie, worried that the maid would take the opportunity to flee before Stella could determine whether she was involved or not.

"Did you see Sir Edwin this morning? Did he come back here to speak with you or to . . ." Stella couldn't bring herself to voice what Sir Edwin's intentions might've been, but she didn't need to. Aggie was shaking her head so violently that she must've been making herself dizzy.

"Nay. I havenae seen him since . . ." She paused, her breath dangerously short and shallow. "Since I talked tae ye, my lady." Stella wanted to believe her, but the maid's hesitation raised some doubt.

Stella had to notify the police. But how? Aggie could be a witness or worse. Stella couldn't risk leaving her on her own. But she couldn't leave Sir Edwin unattended for long either.

Stella glanced back toward the house. It was too far. If someone disturbed the body, she'd never know. She had to keep close enough to hear any disturbances. A horse's whinny reminded her of her original goal.

"You need to come with me." Aggie took a step away, and Stella grabbed the maid's hand. It was ice cold.

Adding a silent apology if she proved to be innocent, Stella tugged the reluctant maid along behind her, coming to a small squat cottage with a thatched roof hidden just around the corner. It was far closer even than the stables. Sweet woodsmoke trickled from the chimney.

"Who lives there?"

"That's Fergus's bothy." Aggie's tone shifted slightly to something lighter, almost wistful. She lessened her resistance. "Fergus is the McEwens' groundskeeper."

"Haud yer horses," a voice called from within as Stella banged on the green wooden door until it opened.

A burly man in his early twenties, unabashedly wearing an undershirt and grass-stained coveralls, stood on the threshold in his bare feet, toweling his tousled wet hair. He glanced at Stella but tossed the towel onto a chair when his piercing blue eyes rested on Aggie. He grappled to pull a plain white handkerchief from his pants pocket and offer it to her.

"Dear Lord, Aggie. What's happened?"

"Oh, Fergus!" Aggie's voice caught as she clutched the handkerchief to her cheek.

"Aggie may still be in shock. She stumbled on a dead body near the laundry building."

Stella watched the groundskeeper's reaction. She'd never met him or seen him and didn't have any reason to think he was Sir Edwin's killer other than the proximity of his cottage to the man's body. But she'd also learned not to assume anything when it came to murder. Sometimes it didn't make sense. Sometimes, you couldn't trust anyone. His response to her horrific news could be telling.

His face blanched despite his sun-darkened skin. *In genuine dismay.* But was it in sympathy for Aggie having found a body or the shock of her being the one to discover his crime? Fergus tore past Stella, nearly clipping her with his pointy elbow, to engulf Aggie in a crushing embrace.

"Ye poor lassie!" he cooed into her hair, kissing the top of her head.

Stella resented her suspicious mind. If she didn't suspect either was involved, she'd be more than grateful to leave them to each other's comfort. Hadn't Aggie been through enough? And how wonderful it was she had a beau. But Sir Edwin was dead, and Stella had experienced similar situations before. A timely careful investigation was vital.

And until the police could be told, Stella would have to conduct it.

"I'm sorry, Fergus, but I need you to go to the house and telephone the police."

"Are ye all right?" he asked the maid as if Stella hadn't spoken. When Aggie confirmed with a forced smile and a touch to his cheek that she was, he faced Stella. "Whit is it ye want me tae say?"

"Tell them they need to come immediately, that there's been a murder at Glenloch Hill."

"Sir Edwin's been murdered?" Stevenson's voice echoed from down the hall. As did the groundskeeper's reply.

"Aye. Aggie, the poor lass, found 'im near the laundry house."

Hamish slunk back over the threshold of his study, listening, the guest list gripped in his fist forgotten. His heart pounded in his ears.

"A proper lassie with a peculiar accent. I dinnae catch her name. She was dressed for riding," Fergus Lorrie, the groundskeeper, said, as if the latter would help pin down the woman's identity. The *proper lassie* must be Stella. But how had his American cousin gotten involved? Hamish had missed that bit. "She sent me up to ring the police."

The police!

Hamish listened for the servants' footsteps to recede. He didn't have to wait long. With such a dire message to deliver, even Stevenson would acknowledge the need for urgency. With the way clear, Hamish dashed into the hall and bounded up the staircase. Fighting the daily habit of turning left toward his bedchamber, he hurried in the opposite direction. Casting wary glances over his shoulder, he bumped into the Chippendale cabinet housing Virginia's seashell collection. The shells rattled against the glass shelves. Hamish steadied the cabinet in a nervous grip, silencing the clatter. He waited for someone to appear, asking questions, wondering what all the raucousness was about. When no one did, Hamish retrieved the crumpled list he'd dropped to the floor, shoved it into his trouser pocket, and continued more cautiously.

He couldn't recall the last time he'd frequented this wing of the house. Virginia and Mrs. Graham saw to the guest rooms. As he went from door to door, he read the cards, written in Virginia's florid hand, that had been slipped into each brass nameplate: Mrs. Jean Agnew, Lady Alice Searlwyn, Lord and Lady Lyndhurst, Mr. Frederick Kentfield, Mr. Alasdair McCormack, Sir Edwin Kentfield.

Hamish stopped at the last and entered without hesitation, quickly closing the door behind him. Having arrived unexpectedly, Virginia had put Edwin in the corner room at the end of the hall. It had once been a sewing room, but with so many frequent guests, they converted it into a bedchamber. It was a bit cramped with its furniture and fireplace but was decorated in sunny yellow, with plenty of large windows and a view of the lower lawn. On a clear day, one could see the distant sea. Today, Hamish could barely see the village in the valley beyond.

He approached the chest of drawers, yanking open drawer after drawer with no luck. The nightstand drawer yielded nothing. He rummaged through Edwin's clothes in the wardrobe, poking his hand into the man's jacket pockets and his waistcoat pockets, even tipping and examining inside each shoe. He'd found a train ticket, a few copper pennies, and a silver-plated watch fob. Nothing of any consequence.

"Damn. Where is it?"

He'd exhausted his search of the little room and had found nothing. Where could Edwin have kept it? Could he have lied? Had he ever had it?

Frustrated, Hamish kicked the nightstand, toppling over a framed picture of Edwin and a woman, ignoring the high-pitched crack as the glass broke. Could Edwin have hidden it there? Hamish feverishly slipped off the back of the frame. Nothing. Hamish reassembled the picture frame, slamming it back in its place before leaving in disgust.

Harry Finn, the suitcase banging against his leg, fretted every step between His Lordship's dressing room and Sir Edwin's bedchamber. He'd been polishing Lord Lyndhurst's shoes in the small room off the servants' hall when he'd heard the rumors. Sir Edwin murdered? He'd dropped what he was doing and taken the stairs two at a time up the narrow back staircase.

Finn had tried to return Sir Edwin's suitcase before and found the room locked. Now, with the police on their way, he wanted nothing more to do with it. What would they say if Sir Edwin's belongings were found among Lord Lyndhurst's things? Especially after what a footmen had told him at breakfast of Lord Lyndhurst's altercation with Sir Edwin the night before.

Was that why His Lordship had dressed so early this morning? To avoid seeing Sir Edwin? Or had he . . . No, Finn had known his master too long to suspect he had anything to do with Sir Edwin's death. Hadn't Lord Lyndhurst stood by Finn when he'd been suspected of murdering the vicar? Aiding the police to unearth the true culprit? No, His Lordship helped uncover murders; he didn't commit them.

Regardless, being found in possession of Sir Edwin's suitcase, with its letters and provocative picture postcard, wouldn't do. Finn had to return it straightaway. He'd leave the case in the hall if need be.

Unexpectedly, Mr. McEwen emerged from one of the guest bedchambers.

Despite his heart beating hard against his ribs and the disproportionate weight of the suitcase in his hand, the valet stood still against the wall, just steps from his targeted destination, his head bowed as he'd been taught from an early age. Mr. McEwen, grumbling and preoccupied, passed without acknowledging Finn's presence. That didn't mean he hadn't noticed him. *Or how I reek of shoe polish.* Finn prayed he hadn't.

With Mr. McEwen out of sight, Finn sighted the brass doorplate with Sir Edwin's name on it, tried the door, and thanked all that was good in this world that it was unlocked. He slipped inside, shoved the suitcase on top of the wardrobe, and left. Once again in the hall, Finn pulled a handkerchief from his vest pocket and wiped his face. He hadn't realized what a burden that suitcase and its contents had become.

How did His Lordship do it? Beset by secrets and lies and danger?

Eager to return to the humble but satisfying task of polishing His Lordship's shoes, Finn opened the green baize door at the end of the hall. Yet he paused, looking over his shoulder at where he'd been. He'd been so focused on getting into Sir Edwin's bedchamber before the police arrived, only now had it struck him.

What business drew Mr. McEwen there now as well?

CHAPTER 10

Docherty pulled the pipe from his mouth, leaned into the shrubbery to keep it at bay, and studied the bludgeoned head, with its one open eye staring blankly up at him. *Well, isn't this a bloody mess?* A murder a few miles from St. Andrews. With the world's eyes on the Open Championship, Chief Constable Gordon was not going to be happy.

Docherty had been enjoying the brisk early morning on the Old Course, overseeing his men getting settled in for the day's events. He hadn't expected any more trouble than a fool or two who'd wagered too much or drank too much or both. He certainly hadn't anticipated this.

Docherty stepped back, letting the bushes come together to hide the dead man's head and torso from view. When was the last time he'd investigated a murder? A year, maybe? He'd been at this game for quite a wee bit of time, but murders around here were few and far between. Especially one as spectacularly gruesome as this.

Docherty rubbed his considerable paunch, his stomach rumbling in protest. His breakfast of porridge and black pudding wasn't sitting well. Replacing his pipe between his teeth, he re-

garded the odd trio before him. The two lassies, both of a similar age, couldn't be more different. One, her face blotched with
red, wrung her maid's apron and sniffled. The other, a willow
of a woman with perfect porcelain skin, was dressed for riding,
top hat and all, and held questions in her unwavering green-
eyed gaze. The lad, too, was young but had the leathery weathered skin of one who'd already spent too much of his life in the
sun. Wearing only an undershirt, he'd forgotten to lace his
boots. *Must've been in a rush, that one.*

Docherty addressed the lad. "I was informed that the victim
is an Englishman, Sir Edwin Kentfield?" The maid whimpered
a bit at the name. "And was a guest of the McEwens?" Docherty continued with not a little sympathy. What was the poor
lassie doing here anyway?

The lad shrugged and looked to the posh woman, who replied
in an unfamiliar accent, "Yes, that's him, Inspector . . . ?"

Docherty couldn't ignore that the other two deferred to this
one. It would do him no harm to at least answer her question.
"Detective Inspector Ian Docherty, Fife County Constabulary
out of St. Andrews. And ye are?"

"Lady Lyndhurst. Like Sir Edwin, I'm staying at Glenloch
Hill."

Docherty stifled the urge to whistle in surprise. He couldn't
remember the last time he'd been in the presence of an aristocrat, let alone two, if he counted the dead man lying in the
bushes. Hamish and Virginia were certainly getting up in the
world.

"Now, what is a bonny lass like ye doing holding vigil beside
a dead man, eh, Lady Lyndhurst? Are ye kin?"

"No, though Sir Edwin was . . . never mind, it's too compli-
cated. I came across Aggie standing over Sir Edwin's body on
my way to the stables this morning. I thought it best to stand
watch until you came. That's why I sent Fergus up to the house
to call you. I didn't want anyone interfering with the body or
the area around it before you had a chance to inspect both."

Now, how was it that the young lass knew police procedures? Docherty, his curiosity winning out, asked.

"Unfortunately, this isn't the first murdered body I've come across." She wavered, as if deciding whether to elaborate, but stopped there.

What was he to make of that? Aristocratic women didn't stumble onto dead bodies. She was being more than a wee bit fanciful. But why?

Taking a long draw of his pipe, Docherty blew out the smoke and asked the maid, "And yer excuse?" She'd stared at her shoes from the moment he'd arrived. Now was no different. "Aggie, is it?"

She nodded. "Aye. I work in the laundry house." She pointed toward the small squat building a few dozen yards away. "And found him like this. Lady Lyndhurst insisted I stay."

Now, why would Lady Lyndhurst do that as well? He didn't understand this lass. And it was more than the class division between them. *She's peculiar, this one.*

Docherty squinted at the woman as he blew streams of smoke between his lips, the sweet taste of tobacco filling his mouth. Could either of them have done this? Docherty dismissed the idea with an airy wave through the smoke hovering about him. Of course not. The man was bludgeoned to death. No lass was capable.

"Well, ye can both go now," Docherty said, turning to the lad.

"But—" Lady Lyndhurst began. Docherty cut her off by asking the lad his name and role in all this. Or that was his intention. "Fergus is here because he lives in that cottage, and I needed someone to telephone you," she continued. "Like I said, I didn't feel it was right to leave Sir Edwin unattended, or I'd have done it myself. It's me and Aggie you need to talk to. By the way, how long do you think Sir Edwin's been dead?"

The question took Docherty aback. He wasn't used to answering such indelicate questions, especially from a lassie. But then again, she was nobility, and a guest of the McEwens. Should he placate her with what little he knew? Would she then go away and let him get on with it? Or should he refuse on professional grounds to keep what he knew to himself? Would she complain to the Chief Constable? Why did she want to know anyway? Docherty was saved from having to solve this dilemma by having to face another. Virginia McEwen, accompanied by Mrs. Agnew, the attractive middle-aged woman Docherty had met at dinner at Glenloch a couple of nights before, approached from the direction of the house. How did he prevent Virginia from getting too close and seeing the dead man's legs? Hamish would never forgive him if he didn't.

Abruptly brushing past the others, Docherty strode to meet Virginia and her companion.

"Is it true, Ian?" Virginia rushed toward him.

Virginia looked uncharacteristically drawn, deep creases about her mouth and eyes seemingly appearing overnight. It pained him to see. He hooked his arm around Virginia's shoulders and swiveled her about, facing her the other way. "Aye, I'm sorry, Virginia. Was he a friend?"

She withdrew from him as if his touch burned.

"No, no, no, no, no." She pressed her palms against her flushed cheeks, bouncing on the balls of her feet. "Not again. Not again." Panting like a fish gasping for air, Virginia pleaded with one hand on her heart, one outstretched to her friend. "Jeanie, tell me it hasn't happened again."

"Oh, Ginny," Mrs. Agnew said, taking Virginia's hand in hers.

Suddenly, Virginia went limp and collapsed. Mrs. Agnew's grasp kept Virginia from falling like a stone, but it was the quick work of the viscountess, dropping to her knees to catch Virginia, that softened the blow.

"What did she mean, *not again*? Has someone else been murdered recently?" Lady Lyndhurst addressed both Docherty and Mrs. Agnew.

Again, with her moans as she regained consciousness, Virginia saved Docherty from answering and revealing his ignorance. He had no idea what Virginia meant. Docherty chewed on the tip of his pipestem.

How was it that every question this viscountess asked made him feel like a raw recruit?

"I think it best that ye should help the ladies get Mrs. McEwen back to the house, don't ye, Aggie?" Docherty said as Mrs. Agnew and Lady Lyndhurst helped Virginia to her feet.

Virginia was able to stand under her own power, but her hand pressed against her chest was shaking. Docherty had never seen Virginia look so frail. Thank heavens she'd never spotted the dead man. The shock of it all might've done worse.

"But I haven't even told you about—"

"It's grand of ye to keep vigilance over the victim and to help Mrs. McEwen, lass," Docherty said, cutting off Lady Lyndhurst's protests, "but I need to get on with it. The medical examiner will be here soon." Docherty spied Hamish coming down the path. "Now off with ye ladies. I must speak to Mr. McEwen."

Lady Lyndhurst wasn't so easily dismissed. "But—" she'd begun when the laundry maid, following Virginia, stumbled.

"Ian! What happened?" Hamish said as Lady Lyndhurst offered the maid her support. "Are ye all right, hen?" Hamish cupped Virginia's cheek.

"I'm fine." She covered his hand with her own and held it there briefly before pointing vaguely toward the laundry house. "But it's Edwin, Hamish. He's dead."

"Over here, eh, Hamish? 'Tis a nasty business," Docherty said, calling him to the spot. "I've asked the ladies to go back to the house."

With Hamish's encouragement, the ladies moved away. But as Docherty began discussing the situation with Hamish, learning what he knew of the dead man, Lady Lyndhurst cast a parting glance back at them. Docherty recognized the piercing look in her eye.

That bonny lass isn't done with me yet.

"Are you all right, Virginia?" Stella glanced over her shoulder at Aggie, stumbling along behind them. She'd asked the same of the maid, but she'd withdrawn into herself and said nothing.

"I'm better now, thank you," Virginia said, though she didn't free herself from Stella or Jeanie Agnew's support, letting them draw her up the stone steps toward the house. "What you must think of me, Stella." She forced a mirthless chuckle. "I'm not usually this frail."

"You have nothing to apologize for." Stella remembered the first time she'd seen the dead body of a murdered man. She, too, had been intensely disturbed by it. Who wouldn't be?

"I haven't been quite myself of late," Virginia continued, as if Stella hadn't spoken, "and now this. Poor Edwin. It is shocking, isn't it?"

Stella reassured her again.

"It's more than shocking, Ginny," Jeanie added with a slight tremor in her voice. "It's downright dreadful. If ye hadn't done it first, I might've fainted away as well."

When they reached the top of the stairs, Stella gave in to her curiosity. She didn't want to burden Virginia but couldn't let it go.

"What did you mean when you said, *not again*?" Stella asked as gently as she was capable. "Was someone else you know murdered?"

Although she and Lyndy had encountered several dead bodies in the past year, Stella was all too aware how strange and unfortunate it was. She wouldn't wish it on anyone. One dead body was far more than enough.

"Did I say that?"

"Ye did," Jeanie Agnew confirmed.

"I must've been thinking of Richard."

Richard, who drowned. Richard, who Hamish and Sir Edwin were arguing about.

"But Richard's death wasn't suspicious, was it, Ginny?" Jeanie said.

Virginia pulled away, her cheeks flushing. "All I meant was that both brothers have now died under tragic circumstances." She hugged herself. "Why did Edwin ever have to come here?"

"Why indeed?" Jeanie Agnew agreed, eyeing her friend as if the answer was written on Virginia's brow. "And after all this time?"

"Did he ever explain why he showed up uninvited?" Stella asked. Sir Edwin had dodged the question repeatedly, yet the conversation between him and Hamish seemed to hold the clue. It all had to do with Richard.

"I have no idea," Virginia declared. "I knew him and Richard back in my school days. I hadn't seen Edwin in years."

Unsatisfied, Stella persisted. "When was the last time you did see him?"

"Last night, just after dinner," Virginia said without hesitation. "Wasn't it, Jeanie?"

Mrs. Agnew wasn't so forthcoming. The widow offered a one-sided shrug, then flicked away an invisible fly. "I think so. Aye. That sounds about right."

Jeanie Agnew was not a very good liar. Had the widow seen Sir Edwin later that evening or hadn't she? Stella wanted to press her on it but knew she probably wouldn't get the answers she wanted that way.

Stella changed tactics. "From the state of his shoes, Sir Edwin was killed last night. Did any of you hear or see anything out of the ordinary?" She made sure to include Aggie in the question.

Aggie had spoken so little since Stella found her bent over Sir Edwin's body. She was probably still in shock. Unfortunately, Stella knew what Aggie was feeling.

Unless she killed him. That was a feeling Stella couldn't conceive.

The maid, wringing the hem of her apron, shook her head. The other women weren't any more helpful.

"You sound like a policeman, Stella," Virginia remarked.

"I'm just curious," Stella admitted. "It's obvious Sir Edwin was murdered, and I can't help but wonder about it. Who would do such a thing?"

"Did ye kill him?" Mrs. Agnew demanded of Aggie as she held the French window open, allowing Virginia to enter the drawing room. The maid whimpered, burst into tears, and fled back the way they'd come. The widow, her hand still on the door handle, watched the maid until she'd disappeared beyond the trees. "If what Lord Lyndhurst said last night had any truth to it, that maid has the best reason of anyone to have wanted Sir Edwin dead. I would, too, if anyone ever raised a hand to me. But . . ."

"But what?" Stella said, hoping to finally get some answers.

"But Sir Edwin didn't seem the type. Honestly, I was astounded that he'd resort to such a thing. A rogue, he was, but violent? It doesn't sit right. If ye know what I mean."

Stella knew exactly what she meant. Nothing about this weekend had sat right.

"But who else would want to harm him?" Stella mused out loud.

"Besides yer husband, lassie, I can't think of another soul," Jean Agnew said without a trace of irony, before following Virginia into the dimness of the drawing room.

CHAPTER 1 1

Stella shivered in the cool of the squat stone stable. The dimly lit aisle, with dust motes swirling in the bleak light as she navigated it, was appropriate for her mood. With no dictate from Inspector Docherty to stay at Glenloch, Stella had turned on her heel the moment Jeanie Agnew insinuated Lyndy could've killed Sir Edwin.

I have to tell him.

Neither he nor Freddy knew about Sir Edwin's murder. Yet. Stella could picture Lyndy's righteous indignation when the police tried to question him or, worse, accuse him. He would only make things worse. She had to get to the Old Course before the police did.

With Morag saddled and alert with her ears up, Stella approached cautiously with a handful of plump strawberries, slightly mushy from being in her skirt pocket since she'd swiped them from the kitchen before setting out earlier. Morag's soft lips engulfed them eagerly. Shunning the groomsman's help, Stella hoisted herself onto the horse's back, patted her sleek shoulder, and urged the mare out of the stable door.

Stella never questioned whether Lyndy had anything to do with Sir Edwin's death. She knew as well as she knew her own name that Lyndy, despite his temper, was tender at heart. He was protective and passionate, not uncontrollably violent, hence his lashing out at Sir Edwin for his ill behavior toward an innocent woman. And yet others didn't know him as she did. If Mrs. Agnew thought Lyndy capable, so might Inspector Docherty. And if Docherty wasn't willing to entertain Stella's insights this morning, why would he listen to her when Lyndy's behavior appeared suspicious?

The air was cool but did nothing to ease the heat radiating from every pore. Stella's blouse clung to the sweat on her back. She welcomed the wind that kicked up and stung her cheeks as she urged the willing mare to gallop down the hill and across the open plain. They hadn't gotten far when a long line of woolly dirty-white sheep intersected the road on the opposite side of a stream. Bounding across the bridge, Morag clumped loudly on the boards. Stella had hoped to force a path through the herd, but the horse's noisy approach accomplished the opposite. Instead of being chased off, many of the sheep circled back the way they'd come, and a widening obstacle of milling sheep grew, blocking the way off the bridge. Stella yelled. She coaxed. She dropped from the saddle, flipped her reins across the guardrails to keep the horse from bolting, and entered the fray. She tried to shoo the sheep one way or another. None of it worked. Instead, she was encircled by the beasts, jostling, bumping, and bleating at her.

At least I haven't seen a police wagon yet. The police would have to travel this same road from Glenloch to the Old Course, wouldn't they? She still had time.

Movement in the distance caught Stella's attention. Bracing her stance against the occasional brush of nearby sheep, she raised her hand to shield her eyes from the sun. A carriage crossing the ridgeline of a small hill traveled from the stone city of St. Andrews toward an unseen destination in the direction of Glenloch Hill. Despite the vista from the house, smaller hills blocked the view of the distant landscape, hiding roads she didn't know about.

Defeated, Stella shoved her way to the bridge, retrieved the reins, and hoisted herself back into the saddle using the guard-rail like a ladder. She tried nudging Morag toward the end of the bridge, but the horse had no desire to mingle with the flock and wouldn't budge.

Minutes ticked by. Despite all Stella's efforts, the pressure squeezes, the cajoling clucks, and the light slapping of the reins on the mare's hindquarters, Morag refused to leave the safety of the bridge. Stella had never met such a stubborn horse.

Stella shouted at the flock or the horse or both, "Move!" She might as well have saved her breath.

A horse's whinny and a rattling of wheels piqued Morag's interest. As one, the mare and Stella glanced back at the approaching conveyance threatening to sandwich them in. It wasn't the police wagon but a simple farm cart stacked with hay bales. *There's still a chance to beat them.* A space, no bigger than the length of two sheep, cleared in the flock.

"Come on, Morag. We have to warn Lyndy."

Stella shifted her weight and clucked twice as she had a dozen times. Finally agreeing it was time to go, Morag trotted off the bridge and through the narrow opening as if the sheep weren't even there. Once clear of the flock and with her stomach in knots, Stella urged the mare to stretch her legs and run.

"Hell's bells, Inspector!" Dr. Farley said, scratching the bald circle on the back of his head. "Have ye ever seen such a beating?"

"Nay, ye know I haven't." Inspector Docherty lifted the handkerchief from his neck to see if he'd stopped bleeding. Seeing a single light pink blot on the unstained side of the white linen, he shoved it back into a pocket.

Both men had scratches as proof of their thorough survey of the area surrounding the victim before agreeing one of Docherty's lads could pull the body from under the bushes. Hamish stood a few feet back, scrubbing his mustache as if trying to rub out the hair.

"It's no' the ramblin' cart that fa's first ower the brae, eh?" Hamish muttered.

"Nay, yer right there. It's not always the person ye expect who dies," Docherty agreed. "But this one didn't die of natural causes either, did he?"

The medical examiner knelt beside the dead Englishman with enviable ease while Docherty peered over him, puffing on his pipe. The inspector didn't object to the blurring effect the haze had on the dead man's features, but more than once the doctor swatted away the smoke.

"When do ye put the time of death?" Docherty crouched closer, resting his hands on his thighs for support.

"From my preliminary findings, I'd say somewhere between ten and midnight."

"Big window of time there, Farley." That meant the body had laid out here all night. Docherty had thought as much, seeing as the spotty showers they'd gotten overnight had soaked the victim's trousers. "How do ye expect me to establish likely suspects' whereabouts during such a large stretch of time?"

The medical examiner, who Docherty had known and worked with on every murder case he'd investigated in the past ten years, pushed his spectacles up the bridge of his nose and shrugged. "That's yer burden, Inspector. From ten to midnight. Best I can do, I'm afraid."

"Can ye be more precise on what could've done this?" Docherty pointed to the man's bludgeoned face. He'd seen the results of pub brawls, uneven pugilistic matches, and the occasional wife-battering, but he'd never seen anyone beaten like this. "Could a lad do this with his fists?"

"Some of this might've been done by a hand, but look at the depth of the wound on the cheek, the distinct edges along the bruising on his forehead. Nay, I suspect yer victim was attacked with something more. Nothing too sharp or too pointy."

Docherty straightened, ignoring the crackling emanating from his spine as he stretched to relieve the strain and considered the possibilities: hammer, pipe, rock? Movement caught his eye. The lad he'd met this morning crossed the path down aways, pushing a wheelbarrow piled high with fresh manure. Docherty could smell it from here.

"Isn't that yer groundskeeper, Hamish?" Docherty asked.

Hamish spared a brief glance before returning to gawking at the body. "Aye."

"And isn't that the groundskeeper's bothy just around the corner?" Docherty clamped the wooden pipestem in his teeth while his hands sought the pocket in his jacket where he'd put his tobacco pouch and matches.

"It is. Ye dinnae think he had anything tae dae with this, dae ye, Ian?"

Docherty had no idea if Fergus did or didn't. He wasn't certain about anyone or anything, but he wasn't about to tell Hamish that. Besides, he didn't want to lose his train of thought. "Farley, could the murder weapon be a garden tool? Like a rake or a hoe or . . ."

The medical examiner sat back on his heels, tilting his head like the good-natured golden retriever Docherty had often seen the doctor walking around town. The pair even shared the same shaggy mane. "Nay, too sharp."

"A shovel, maybe?"

"I wouldn't think so. Even a shovel is unlikely. Considering how many blows the killer made, a shovel would be bound to leave a few sharp impressions from contact with its edges. I was thinking more along the lines of—"

"A cricket bat or croquet mallet?" Hamish said, paling.

"Aye. Either could be possible," the doctor said, standing with the dexterity of a man half his age, forcing Docherty to look up at him. The inspector hadn't realized how much enjoyment he'd gotten from being the taller of the two, albeit temporarily. "Or perhaps a golf club. I should be able to measure the size of the impacts to narrow it a bit."

"As ye ken full well, Ian, we have plenty of sporting equipment aboot the place. Anyone could've done this."

Docherty put a reassuring hand on Hamish's shoulder and indicated the dead body at their feet with his pipe. "I can assure ye, not anyone could've done this, mentally or physically. We're looking for an angry, disturbed, and perhaps impulsive man."

"It's not my place to question ye, Inspector," Farley said, brushing bits of grass, twigs, and dirt from his trousers, "but I'd keep an open mind if I were ye. Mr. McEwen is right. Given the right circumstances, like a well-placed first blow that incapacitated our victim, even a woman, given the downward force produced by a mallet or a club, could've done this."

Docherty's job just became twice as difficult.

"Cor, Farley!" Docherty said, tipping the contents of his pipe on the ground and banging on the side to get the last of the tobacco out. "Ye're supposed to be here to help."

Stella was too late. When she finally reached the links course and stabled Morag, play had been halted in both directions from the sprawling third green. Golfers and caddies, meant to be putting into the opposite hole or striking the ball down the parallel fairways, huddled whispering in place. Spectators, course officials, and a policeman among them, with his domed helmet rising above the sea of heads, surrounded Freddy in the middle of the green. Despite her efforts, the police had beaten her here after all.

Stella shouldered her way through the crowd of onlookers,

squeezing in beside Alice and Lyndy, who stood as close to Freddy and his caddie as they could get. Despite the chilly breeze off the water, sweat along her hairline cemented her hat to her forehead.

She stripped off her gloves, grabbed Lyndy's hand, reassured by the warmth of his skin, and whispered, "This is about Sir Edwin, isn't it?"

Eyes locked on Freddy, Lyndy affirmed her supposition with a prolonged blink and an inaudible sigh. Did he fear he could be a suspect? Was Lyndy worried about what the police might think? Had he spoken to them yet?

"Are you okay?"

Lyndy's face went blank, strangely slack even, with no outward indication of how he felt about the news, but he threaded his fingers through hers and tightened his grip. His hand had grown clammy. He shot a side glance at his sister. Alice wrung Freddy's cap in her fists, pressing it against her chest as she was wont to do with her magazines.

"I'm so sorry, Alice," Stella whispered.

"It is awful, isn't it?" Alice's eyes met Stella's with a flicker of fear and desperation. "Poor Freddy is beside himself."

"Who wouldn't be?" Even Stella had been inconsolable when her father died, and he hadn't had the redeeming qualities of Sir Edwin.

"This is absurd," Freddy shouted. All color had drained from his face, and he leaned on his golf club like an old man does a cane. "How can you ask me such a thing?"

The policeman fiddled with the top button of the long row of highly polished brass lining his uniform jacket, muttering in an undertone. His words were impossible to catch. Still clasping Lyndy's hand, Stella interlaced her free arm with Alice's and dragged the reluctant pair with her as she edged closer. They had to know what the policeman was saying.

"I dae apologize, Mr. Kentfield, but it's me job tae ask." He eyed the growing crowd, worrying the button until it looked to pop off. "Perhaps we can dae this somewhere more private?"

"No, I have nothing to hide," Freddy declared. "Last night I played billiards with my fiancée, Lady Alice Searlwyn."

Alice grew bold at the mention of her name, wiggled away from Stella, and hastened to Freddy's side. He deflated at the sight of her, his shoulders slumping under an invisible weight.

"They say Father's been murdered," Freddy explained, as if she didn't already know.

"I'm so, so sorry, Freddy." Still clutching Freddy's cap, she squared her shoulders to face the policeman. "I can confirm, Constable, that what Mr. Kentfield says is true. We were together until well past one."

"She won, you know." Freddy, retreating from his harsh reality, spoke to his shoes, a faint smile hinting at the fond memory.

"And this morning?" the constable persisted. "Where were ye then, Mr. Kentfield?"

"He had breakfast with me, my brother, Viscount Lyndhurst," Alice said, pointing to Lyndy with a jut of her chin, "Mr. McEwen, and Mr. McCormack." Alice indicated the golfer as he made his way toward them.

"It's true," Alasdair confirmed. "Young Kentfield was with me and Lord Lyndhurst from breakfast on."

"I didn't really have a chance, did I?" Freddy rambled, still hearkening back to last night's billiard game. "Who knew Alice was secretly a pool shark?" He chuckled at his jest. No one else found it funny.

The policeman shifted tactics. "Whit aboot ye, Mr. Birdwell? Can ye account for yer whereabouts?"

"Me?" Billy stammered, dropping the putter he'd been holding and leaving it at his feet in the closely sheared grass. "I went to bed early and had a tray in my room for breakfast."

"Can anyone confirm that?"

"The footman who brought up my tray."

"And the night before?"

"I was alone."

"Now, if there isn't anything else, Constable," Alasdair said, as if he'd tired of a neighbor's exhaustive description of the past week's weather, "ye've interrupted play long enough, don't ye think?"

"Yes." Freddy's head bobbed in vague agreement. "I was about to hit my second shot on the third hole."

What were they talking about? Freddy was in shock and needed rest, maybe even a visit from a doctor.

And Lyndy needs to get away from that policeman. Stella could tell that the constable had yet to broach the subject of Lyndy's fight with Sir Edwin, and Stella wanted to keep it that way.

"Freddy, you aren't still thinking of playing, are you?" Alice asked.

"Of course he isn't," Lyndy insisted, echoing Stella's thoughts. "He's had a shock. We're all going back to Glenloch."

"What are you saying?" Color now flooded Freddy's face as he lifted his club and swung it in a circle like a pointer settling on a compass. He stopped it at Lyndy. "You want me to quit? I'm already playing two under."

Stella recognized the pendulum between despair and anger that Freddy was riding. Grief was an unpredictable burden.

"But your father . . ." Alice pleaded.

"What did my father care about . . . golf? No, he admitted he didn't. Truly, when did he care about anyone but himself?"

In his grief, Freddy had forgotten how much Sir Edwin loved and supported him. Sir Edwin may not have attended Freddy's golf tournaments, but who encouraged and provided for him while he chased his dream? Certainly not Freddy's mother. And hadn't Sir Edwin commandeered an invitation to Morrington Hall at Christmas, again, despite Lady Isabella's objections, all for Freddy's sake? In time, Stella hoped he'd remember.

"No, I'm sorry, Alice," he said, "I didn't come all this way to forfeit."

Onlookers parted to make room as Freddy backed away into them. Hands of encouragement, sympathy, and commiseration patted him on the back as the crowd engulfed Freddy.

"Ye'll pardon me, Mr. Kentfield," the policeman called after him. "I'm not finished."

"I'd say ye were," Alasdair said.

Billy Birdwell smirked before lumbering off to catch up with his golfer. Alasdair turned his back to survey the resumption of play on the green. Summarily dismissed, the constable shrugged.

Stella held her breath. With the constable conceding he wasn't getting any more out of the others, would he now set his sights on Lyndy? But the constable tipped his hat to no one in particular and retreated from the course. He'd said nothing to Lyndy. Too caught up in her relief as she and Lyndy followed the others to the edge of the fairway, Stella didn't catch what Alasdair had said next.

"The laddie's playing well, though, I grant him," Alasdair was saying when Stella finally tore her eyes from the policeman disappearing down the fairway. Alasdair raised his arm and snapped his fingers to draw his caddie's attention. "He'll be tough to beat."

"Tough to beat?" Stella said. "You're not talking about Freddy, are you?"

"Aye. I am."

"But didn't you see how volatile he is? He's not normally like that. He shouldn't be playing golf."

"I don't know. It may be the very thing he needs to get through this. Besides, I've known men to shoot their best scores with broken fingers and fever chills, not to mention wee muscle spasms. I won my last tournament days after I lost my father. There's nothing to say Freddy won't—"

"*Fore!*" The warning cry cut off Alasdair's boast, and the crowd instinctively ducked their heads to avoid the dangerously wild shot careering toward them.

With increasing intensity, the golf ball whizzed past like a giant bumblebee returning late to the hive. It dropped to the ground, a few feet from Alasdair, bouncing several times before coming to a halt in the trampled grass.

"Terribly sorry!" Freddy shouted from midway up the fairway.

"You were saying, McCormack?" Lyndy said before Stella had the chance.

Alasdair chuckled with scarcely a hint of humor. "Perhaps it would be best if the lad forfeited."

"Yes," Stella said, "perhaps it would be."

CHAPTER 12

Resisting the urge to remove his shoes and massage his aching feet, Docherty crossed his ankles as he stretched out on one of a line of soft cushioned chaise longues set out on the flagstone patio. Smoke from Docherty's pipe blurred the sloping gardens and the approach of his two officers, the only ones he could reasonably pull from their duties. The rest of his men were tied up at the Old Course. The pair had crisscrossed his view multiple times as they searched the estate's extensive grounds. They'd combed the laundry house, the groundskeeper's bothy, the stables, and the gardens and had come up wanting. They trudged up the hill toward him in defeat.

Would Docherty's time have been better spent helping the men search? He waved away the smoke and squinted at Hamish, worrying his mustache and studying the vista from the chaise beside him. While Dr. Farley oversaw the removal of the body and his men conducted their search, Docherty had opted to stay with Hamish, blethering about the Open Championship, the weather, the launching of the world's largest ship from Clydebank last week, the house party, anything to draw out his friend, to elicit anything that might be useful. Yet Hamish had told him but little. Docherty did learn that Sir Edwin arrived, uninvited, two days earlier, that the Englishman and Virginia had been old friends but hadn't spoken in years, and that Sir Edwin was the father of Frederick Kentfield, the golfer, whom Docherty then dispatched a much-needed constable to inform. But when Docherty asked what excuse the victim had given for arriving unannounced, or why anyone would want to murder him, Hamish had scratched at his mustache, insisting he knew no more. When a topic arose that led to Docherty asking where or what Hamish was doing last evening, his friend evaded answering by changing the subject or falling silent and pensive. As he was now.

Docherty puffed furiously on his pipe in frustration. Inadvertently inhaling too much smoke, he started coughing.

"Inspector!" one of his men shouted, waving his arm. The two officers lingered near the movable summerhouse on the lawn's edge. Had they finally found something? Docherty had started to despair.

Clearing his throat one last time, he hoisted himself up, stiff from sitting so long, and lumbered to where the officers had planted themselves. Hamish was tight on his heels.

"Have ye lads found something?"

"Aye," Cuskar said, kneeling beside the summerhouse and pointing to dark red spots in the grass. He brushed aside waves of ginger hair he allowed to grow too long. "I think it's blood."

"What else would it be, your mum's raspberry jam? Of course it's blood, lad. Why didn't ye find this sooner?"

Thomson's large Adam's apple bobbed as he swallowed hard. Cuskar, lacking the sense to be sheepish, lifted and dropped his broad shoulders in an exaggerated shrug.

"We searched here earlier, but the shed was in the shade, wasn't it? But here Thomson was, mucking aboot with the wheel, and moved the shed around. That's when we saw it."

By accident? Docherty was reminded again why these two were all there was left to help him. But they'd proved useful after all.

"Ye two are a couple of bloody eejits, but at least ye found the spot where the victim was killed. So stop trampling all over it!"

Thomson scuttled back like a frightened squirrel. Cuskar, his mouth curled down in affront, stood his ground like the hairy coo he called to mind.

"But Edwin was found further along the path among the bushes," Hamish said.

"He was obviously moved," Docherty said, surveying the grass.

Docherty brushed past the immovable Cuskar and traced the possible path the killer might've taken from the summerhouse to where the body was found. *There and there!* Now that he was looking, Docherty detected subtle noncontinuous marks that might've been made by the heel of a man being dragged. The soft rain they'd gotten might've obscured some of the spots, the killer might've smudged others, but Docherty saw enough to confirm his theory.

"But why?" Hamish asked, having followed Docherty every step of the way.

"Aye, good question. But at last, we're making progress. Now that we've searched the grounds, do I have yer permission to search the house, Hamish?"

"Nay." Hamish shook his head vehemently. "Nay, that's just not possible, Ian. Virginia has been terribly upset by this whole thing. She's having a lie down. I cannae have policemen scouring the house. It'll make matters worse."

Docherty hadn't expected to be denied. He'd asked simply as a courtesy. Biting down on his pipe, he said through clenched teeth, "Hamish, I'm trying to find out who killed the Englishman."

"And I'm trying tae protect my family from further suffering. Nay, I'm sorry, I cannae allow it."

Docherty had known Hamish McEwen since the textile magnate had purchased Glenloch Hill. They golfed at the links in St. Andrews together when they could, played cards with the wives once a week, and attended the annual horse races on the North Inch in Perth. He understood how protective Hamish could be of Virginia, but this was a murder investigation. Docherty said as much.

"Are ye accusing me or my family or even my guests of murder?" Hamish's voice rose in pitch with each word.

How did Hamish think Sir Edwin died? Even Englishmen can't beat themselves to death. But Hamish's objection offered Docherty a way in.

"Nay, but we can't discount the servants, now can we?"

"Forgive me, Ian. I was thinking more of an intruder, but yer right. I wouldnae have thought it possible, but we cannae rule out the servants."

"Not at least until I've spoken to them." *Or searched their rooms.* But voicing his intention would jeopardize the delicate truce he and Hamish had come to.

"Very well. As long as ye can keep it downstairs, yer more than welcome tae speak tae any member of the staff ye need tae."

Docherty clutched his pipe in his teeth and rocked back on his heels, triumphant. He'd find more answers once in the house, upstairs or down. He was sure of it.

"That's grand, Hamish," Docherty said, already making a mental list of the servants he'd focus on.

"Only belowstairs, mind."

"Of course. Of course," Docherty agreed with the benevolence of a first-time father buying a round of drinks. "We'll catch the killer without Virginia ever knowing we were there."

Docherty placed a friendly hand on Hamish's shoulder, but his friend flinched.

"Aye. See that ye dae."

*   *   *

Mrs. Graham pulled at her earlobe as she checked the ledger against the stack of fresh bed linen in the open cupboard. The numbers didn't add up. Now was not the time for a shortage of bedsheets. Her ear burning, she dropped her hand and relaxed at the approach of heavy footfalls and the accompanying creaking of wicker behind her.

"Ah, there they are." The housekeeper sighed as Aggie trudged down the hall, a basket of the missing linen held out before her.

"I'm sorry I'm late with this morning's linens, Mrs. Graham."

Mrs. Graham had never seen Aggie so pale. Typically, lugging linens from the laundry house to the manor and up two flights of stairs was enough to keep the maid's face flush with a healthy glow. Was there little wonder Aggie suffered? If the rumors belowstairs were true, not only had the wee lassie been set upon by the English gentleman but she'd found the man's dead body too. It was too cruel and terrible to contemplate.

Yet Mrs. Graham took heart. The scales had a way of balancing out. Not that anyone deserved to die, especially as horrifically as that fellow, but at least now Aggie could forget what happened and move on. Justice, as harsh as it was, had been served.

She waved Aggie impatiently toward her. "I was beginning tae wonder."

Aggie dropped the basket at the foot of the cupboard, shoved her arms down to her elbows, and produced a stack of folded, clean white linen that hid her face from view.

"Dinnae ye go worrying over it, though. Ye had quite the unsettling couple of days."

Mrs. Graham spoke as she snatched three bedsheets from the maid's arms, relishing their fresh, sun-dried scent and adding them to the stacks in the cupboard. When she'd worked down the tall pile to reveal Aggie's doleful expression, the housekeeper's concerns flooded her thoughts and, no doubt, her face again. She grasped for her earlobe.

"It's not yer half day, I ken, but with the linens now well supplied, perhaps I could dae without ye for a couple of hours this afternoon? Time off might dae ye a world of guid."

"I'm going tae take more than a couple of hours, Mrs. Graham."

With well-worn practice, the housekeeper restrained her flash of annoyance to a pointed, "Oh, are ye now?" and continued to pile the sheets.

"The truth is, I plan tae give me notice."

"What?" Mrs. Graham tossed the last of the bedsheets in a heap on top of the nearest stack and shuffled back a step or two from the cupboard. "Why? Aren't ye happy here, lass?"

"Aye, but . . ."

"Then why dae ye need to leave, now that yer attacker's on his way tae the morgue?"

Aggie picked up the empty wicker basket, resting it on her hip. "Will ye ask the mistress if she'll accept me notice? I dinnae want tae leave without a reference."

Mrs. Graham did nothing to hide her hurt and displeasure now. They had a house full of people to care for. What was the lassie thinking of, abandoning her position at such a time? Without the courtesy of an explanation?

And after all I've done for her.

"If ye insist on leaving, ye'll be telling the mistress why, not me. And then it's up tae her if she'll let ye go."

Mrs. Graham assumed the prospect of facing Mrs. McEwen would deter the lass from her daft idea, but Aggie's grip on the basket spoke of her resolution. Her knuckles were white.

"Aye, if that's whit it takes. I'd be much obliged if ye'll arrange it. The sooner, the better, if it's not too much tae ask."

"If that's what ye want, lassie." Closing the cupboard doors suddenly took a great deal of effort. Mrs. Graham had never felt so defeated. "It's a shame. Ye're a guid worker, ye are, lass. We'll be sorely put out by yer going."

Aggie sniffed, tugging the corner of her eye with a knuckle.

If the housekeeper didn't know better, she'd think Aggie was keeping tears at bay.

"Aye, me too, Mrs. Graham. Me too."

Aggie's hastened retreat, made awkward by the wicker basket she carried, induced Mrs. Graham to pull at her earlobe again. "And I'm sore put out ye feel ye cannae trust me with the truth," she mumbled, knowing full well Aggie hadn't told her everything.

"What am I going to tell Mother?" Lyndy said.

They stood near the back of the fourth hole, where Freddy and the golfers he was paired with waited to tee off on five. Despite everyone's urging, Freddy had refused to quit the game despite hitting two over par on the three previous holes. A pillar of stillness, Freddy ignored everyone, even Alice, and stared across the expanse before him. In stark contrast, Lyndy scuffed the ground with his heel until he'd uprooted the grass, creating a bare patch in the sandy soil. Stella laid a calming hand on his arm to stop his destructive stomping, but it did little to ease his restlessness.

Sir Edwin was dead. Murdered. But why? With minimal effort, Lyndy could think of several reasons to dislike the rogue. But murder? With all his unfortunate experience with it, Lyndy still couldn't fathom what it would take to push someone that far, to contemplate doing such evil. Even when Lyndy thought Sir Edwin deserved a thrashing, he'd stopped short of anything more punitive than a punch to the face. Could Stella's Scottish cousins be insidiously viler than her father after all? Elijah Kendrick may have been a brute, but he'd never killed anyone. Or had the laundry maid done it? According to Stella, Inspector Docherty had been dismissive of the women as suspects or sources of information.

After their comfortable mutually beneficial relationship with Inspector Brown back in Hampshire, having the policeman figuratively pat his insightful wife on the head and send her on her way didn't instill confidence that he could be trusted to be thorough. And if he wasn't thorough—or worse, lazy—and didn't find Sir Edwin's killer?

What will I tell Mother then?

"We tell her we're doing everything we can to bring Sir Edwin's killer to justice," Stella said.

Such an empty promise would bring Mother little comfort. It did nothing for him. What were they doing besides allowing Freddy to grieve in public, exposing Alice to the humiliation of openly sympathizing stares?

The hint of self-recrimination felt like an ill-fitting boot, rubbing him in all the wrong places. Lyndy sought distraction. Billy and two fellow caddies had separated themselves from the group to conspire beyond the small cluster of patrons gathered around the three-wheeled wicker seller's cart parked just off the green. Billy was furtively looking about him. Propelled by the need to do something, Lyndy left Stella's side and weaved his way through the cart's customers to place himself as close as possible to the whispering caddies.

". . . that Sir Edwin's dead," Billy was saying. A cheer from the crowd gathered around the not-too-distant green covered his next few words. Then, as Stella abandoned Alice to join him, Lyndy caught, "no change of plans."

"Quiet!"

Whatever more Billy was going to say was cut off by the course marshal's cry, and he and the other caddies broke apart to join their respective golfers as Freddy and his playing partners approached the fifth tee.

Lyndy met Stella as she reached the seller's cart. He temporarily stifled the questions splashed across her face by motioning to the old merchant, whose dour expression and scruffy whiskers recalled Lyndy's beloved grandfather, and ordering two ginger beers. Lyndy was stalling, needing time to think.

What the bloody hell could the caddie be planning? He handed a drink to Stella as a player brought his club down on the ball, rocketing it high into the air. Lyndy lost sight of it until a cluster of spectators scrambled out of its way near the seaward rough. The second chap teed off with a swing full of power and grace, landing his ball what must've been a good two hundred yards away in the middle of the fairway. Cheers erupted at the brilliant shot as Freddy took his place, arranged his ball, and swung with abandon without waiting for the crowd to quiet. His ball veered sharply to the right and disappeared into the deep well of a bunker. Cheers turned to groans. Freddy slammed his club into the bag slung from Billy's shoulder and stomped away toward his ball. As the crowd dispersed to follow the players down the fairway, Stella increasingly slowed her pace, as if she didn't fancy catching up to the others. Lyndy matched her step for step.

"Billy and those other caddies. What were they talking about?" She tasted her ginger beer and scrunched up her face at the bittersweet zest of the lemon.

Lyndy should've known Stella would notice the caddies' odd behavior. "They were discussing Sir Edwin's death. And plotting something."

Stella flung her arm across his chest to stop him from walking any further. "Why, what did he say?"

"Billy mentioned something about there being 'no change of plans.'"

"What plans was he talking about?"

"I don't know. I couldn't hear the rest." Lyndy grasped a patch of uncut grass and broke off a tall stem. He crumbled it in his hand, scattering its seeds on the ground. He threw down what was left. "I can't help but wonder if it has something to do with Sir Edwin's murder."

"It's possible. From his own admission, Billy was alone all last night and only seen by a footman briefly this morning. He could've killed Sir Edwin. But why? And whether he killed Sir Edwin or not, what plans could he have had that Sir Edwin's death affected? Billy and Sir Edwin didn't even know each other, did they?"

"Not that I know of. But either way, we should notify the police. He's now a possible suspect."

"But so are you."

"Me?"

With a rush, as if she couldn't stand the taste of the words in her mouth, Stella relayed what Jeanie Agnew had insinuated, what Stella feared the police might suspect: that because he'd thrown a punch, Lyndy was capable of murder.

"How dare they? How bloody dare they think that I would kill my own mother's former paramour? What kind of monster do they think I am?" He clenched his teeth until his jaw throbbed. "It's absurd! Even if they thought me capable, I couldn't have done it. I've been with you or someone else the whole time."

"I know that," Stella said, reaching out to comfort him. Her soft warm hand cupped his cheek. Her touch was the balm he needed to calm himself and appreciate the irony of his outburst. "But will the inspector believe me or just think I'm lying to protect you?"

Despite the indignation still burning in his aristocratic blood, her warning sounded like ice crackling on a frozen pond. She was right. They'd have to tread lightly.

"Bloody hell." Without a whiskey to do the job, Lyndy threw back the remaining half glass of ginger beer, hoping the spicy warmth would ease his nerves. He raked his shaking hands through his hair.

"Which is why we need to find out as much as possible," Stella said. "We can tell your mother we did everything we could, and we'll keep one step ahead in case the police set their sights on you."

This was the point in the past where Lyndy would argue for Stella to keep out of it, to let the police handle the murder investigation. But how could he argue with her now?

"You stay here; keep an eye on Billy," she said. "See if he does or says anything else suspicious. Try to talk to Alice and Freddy if you can. I'll go back to Glenloch and find out what the police have learned."

"I should go back to Glenloch. As a man, a viscount," Lyndy stopped to tug at the hem of his jacket, "the inspector might be more inclined to speak to me. If not, I'll force him to talk."

"Haven't you been listening?" Stella chided him like so many governesses Lyndy had thwarted in the past. He didn't fancy acknowledging that her—and their—exasperation was well-earned. "You have to stay as far away from the police as possible. We don't want them getting any ideas in their heads. And until we can trust the inspector in charge, we'll keep what we've learned between us."

"Very well." If it were anyone else, he'd balk at his sudden impotence, stuck spying on a diminutive caddie and avoiding the authorities whilst Stella faced unknown dangers at Glenloch. But Lyndy knew not to argue with his wife when she was right. "But for goodness' sake, my love, promise me you'll be careful."

"Of course. You know me." She planted a light kiss on his lips.

He did. And that's what he was afraid of.

CHAPTER 13

Inspector Docherty had never been downstairs at Glenloch Hill before. He was well acquainted with the drawing room, the dining room, and Hamish's smoking room, but as he ducked beneath the low tradesman's entrance, he took in everything: the long unadorned whitewashed hall, the lack of natural light, the humid air, the rich smell of baking bread emanating from the nearby kitchen, the echoing footfalls of unseen workers going about their business despite the tragedy.

Could any of these observations help him solve Sir Edwin's murder? Probably not. But any insight into the life of Glenloch's staff could lead to understanding what might've compelled one of them to beat the English baronet to death. And that could be very helpful.

The housekeeper, a handsome woman who could be Mrs. Docherty's younger sister, met him at the door and led him, her keys jangling at her side, to a small tidy room, the desk and ledgers attesting to it being her private study. As a result of the manor being built on a hill, this room was partially above-ground and lit with a south-facing window. The housekeeper had taken full advantage; ferns overflowed from every available shelf, rivaling Virginia's conservatory upstairs.

"Mr. McEwen said ye'd need a private room for yer interviews, Inspector. I dae hope this suffices?" the housekeeper said.

"Aye, grand. This will do nicely." Docherty breathed in the earthy scent of the potting soil as he fiddled with the pipe in his hip pocket. She wasn't his wife's sister, but the resemblance was enough to deter him from retrieving it to smoke. "Thank ye, Mrs. Graham. If ye'd be so kind as to be the first to answer some questions?"

Docherty had no suspicions of Mrs. Graham, but to justify access to the house he'd have to make a show of interviewing the staff. Otherwise, he could've interrogated his prime suspect in the lad's bothy. Besides, one never knew how a housekeeper or a footman might shed light on this bloody business.

But Mrs. Graham, though diligent in her responses, provided no illuminating insights, and Docherty soon sent her in search of a footman and a chambermaid he'd chosen at random from the list of staff he'd been provided. As he suspected, neither knew anything useful. Without impunity, he could now summon Fergus, the groundskeeper, Docherty's main suspect. Even if the lad didn't have ready access to the possible murder weapon, the proximity of his bothy to the location of the murder alone made him a likely candidate. What possible motivation the groundskeeper might have against the Englishman was all he had left to find out.

Grass clippings clinging to the lad's shoes littered Mrs. Graham's newly swept carpet as the lad entered the room. He slipped the tweed cap from his head and held it in both hands at his waist.

"Please take a seat, laddie."

"If it's all the same tae ye, I'll remain standing."

"Very well. Can ye tell me where ye were last night?"

"Aye, at St. Andrews Links."

"At night? I find that hard to believe."

"Old Tom Morris and Mr. McEwen are friendly, so I'm well-acquainted with the old golfer. When the assistant grounds-keeper slipped into Hell Bunker and twisted his ankle days before the Open Championship, the R and A and Old Tom were in a bit of a bind. I offered up me services for the duration, and given that I dae me chores at Glenloch Hill first, no one's the wiser."

He was an enterprising albeit sneaky lad; Docherty would give him that.

"What do ye do?" Not that it pertained to his investigation. Docherty was simply curious.

"I rake out the bunkers. I repair divots. I mow. I pick up litter. Whatever needs doing."

"And ye do this at night, all night, do ye?"

"Nay, just after play is done and first light, if needs be. Then we lads go into town for a pint and some late supper."

Did Docherty believe him? It was easy enough to ask Old Tom, the others working the course, and the publican to verify if Fergus was telling the truth. But if so, that would eliminate him as a suspect.

And then where will we be?

Docherty retrieved his empty pipe from his pocket and began chewing on the tip. There had to be a way to get more out of the lad. "And yer telling me ye didn't see Sir Edwin lying along the path that passes yer bothy when ye returned from the pub?"

"Nay. By the guid Lord, I wish I had, though."

Docherty didn't expect that. "And why would that be, laddie?"

"If I'd have found him first, Aggie wouldnae have, would she?"

Docherty squinted at the groundskeeper. Had a fondness for the wee maid, did he? The same one the Englishman was accused of maltreating. Maybe Docherty couldn't rule out the lad yet after all. Grasping the bowl, he wagged his pipestem like a scolding finger.

"Ye can go, but don't go far. I might have some more questions for ye."

After dismissing the groundskeeper, Docherty asked Mrs. Graham, who never seemed far from her study, if she'd be so kind as to have someone fetch Aggie, the laundry maid. The inspector told himself he wasn't getting desperate, interrogating a wee lassie who'd already been through too much. Yet she had been the one to discover the body, after all, and if she happened to reveal something he could use against the groundskeeper in the course of the conversation, all the better. When the maid arrived, Docherty rose slowly, allowing time to study the fingerlike bruises on her face. Had she had them this morning? Docherty couldn't remember.

Docherty dragged the wingback chair Mrs. Graham usually kept beneath the shelves of plants and patted the crushed velvet cushion. "Take a seat, Aggie." The maid hesitated, biting the skin from her bottom lip. "It's been a long day already, lassie. Ye could do with a bit of rest. I insist." Given the excuse she needed, the maid shuffled forward in compliance and dropped into the chair. Docherty took up in the housekeeper's chair opposite.

"Now tell me about those bruises."

The maid reached up as if to touch them but left her hands hovering over her cheeks. She formed fists, the muscles of her upper arms straining against her tight-fitting sleeves, and pressed a knuckle to the corner of each eye to stem the flow of tears glistening in her eyes. Docherty noted the lassie's strength for the first time. Years of scrubbing, hauling water and wet clothes, and raising heavy metal irons over and over had built up strength not generally seen in a woman. How could he have missed it? Docherty had been convinced Sir Edwin's beating had come at the hands of a man. He wasn't so sure anymore.

Docherty produced a handkerchief from his coat pocket and handed it across. "When did ye get them and how?"

"I dinnae ken," she muttered, leaving the handkerchief clenched and unused in her lap.

"Can ye tell me where ye were last night?"

"In the laundry house."

"Ye do laundry after yer supper?"

"Aye, it's when I soak the bedsheets and dae the accounts."

"Did ye see Sir Edwin? Did ye hear anything? When ye finished yer work and came back to the manor to sleep, how is it ye didn't see Sir Edwin laying there?"

She bit her lip, squeezing the life out of Docherty's handkerchief and shaking her head to each question. "He wasn't there then."

"And when was *then*?"

"I dinnae ken."

Was she being purposely obstructive, or was the shock of it all too much to rattle free the memory?

"It makes me wonder. It does. So, I'm going to have to ask ye, lassie. Did ye kill Sir Edwin Kentfield?"

Aggie's chin slumped against her chest and her shoulders began to shake. Tears dripped from her face to dampen the handkerchief clenched in her fists. "It's all me fault. I dinnae mean him any harm. I'm so, so sorry."

Docherty collapsed against the back of his chair, rocking it unsteadily backward, his pipe dangling from the corner of his mouth.

Dear Lord! A confession? For murder? From a wee lassie?

In all the years he'd been doing this, he was never so taken by surprise. But what was the problem? Was he a big dafty? He'd found his killer. He should be pleased and relieved. Then why did it feel a wee bit too easy?

* * *

Stella approached the compact gray-and-white Shetland pony hitched to the small police wagon in the drive. Despite or maybe because of her worries, she couldn't resist saying hello. Much like her beloved Thoroughbred, Tully, he was a friendly fellow, nudging Stella for treats and allowing her to pet his muscular shoulder. With each stroke, Stella relaxed a little more, the questions and the worries that had plagued her on the ride back from St. Andrews quieting.

Footsteps crunched on the drive, and the gelding whinnied in greeting, drawing Stella out of her calming trance.

"Aggie!"

The laundry maid, handcuffed and as pale as the linens she washed daily, was flanked by two policemen in uniform. She stared ahead and staggered like a sleepwalker. Inspector Docherty, tapping his pipe pensively against his lips, followed. Had they arrested the maid for killing Sir Edwin? Stella couldn't believe it.

"What's going on?"

"The lassie's confessed," the inspector said as the policemen helped the maid settle into the wagon.

"Wait!" Mrs. Graham, leaving all decorum aside, raced toward them, her skirt hitched up to her knees. A ladder in her stocking ran up her right shin. She skidded to a stop before the inspector. "Ye have tae let her go."

Inspector Docherty gripped the bowl of his pipe in his fist and pointed the chewed tip toward the wagon. "But she confessed to killing the Englishman."

"That lass wouldnae swat a wee midge, let alone bludgeon a man," the housekeeper insisted. "She willnae even rid the laundry house of the bats that roost in the rafters. Rather clean up after them than harm the wee beasties."

Stella hated bats. With a frisson of fear coursing through her, Stella pictured dozens, maybe hundreds of them flapping, fluttering, and swooping down on the unsuspecting, their high-pitched chittering deafening in the infested laundry house. Stella might not have been so eager to enter the building if she knew they were there.

"I didnae kill him, Mrs. Graham," Aggie protested. How small and pathetic she looked seated between the two burly policemen.

"Can't change yer story now, lassie." Docherty had produced a tobacco pouch from his jacket and filled his pipe. "As much as I admit, I wish ye could."

"Did she actually confess to killing him?" Stella asked. Mrs. Graham, as if seeing Stella for the first time, brightened at finding an ally.

Docherty squinted at Stella in confusion. "Aye, I said as much. What are ye trying to get at, lassie?"

"Were those her exact words?"

Docherty retrieved a matchbox from his jacket pocket and lit his pipe, each deliberate puff sending a flair of sweet aromatic smoke through his lips before saying, "No, yer right. She admitted it was her fault. That she didn't mean him any harm."

"And ye took it that she meant she killed him," Mrs. Graham said, finishing his thought. "The lass simply feels responsible because it all happened because of her, not because she did it."

Docherty squinted harder at the housekeeper, his bushy eyebrows nearly touching, and demanded, "What happened because of her?"

Mrs. Graham purposely avoided catching the maid's pleading glare. Even now, Aggie didn't want the police to know what happened. "Aggie accused Sir Edwin of accosting her."

"I don't understand, Mrs. Graham. That sounds like motive enough for her to want to seek revenge."

"Aye, Inspector, but as I said, Aggie is a gentle creature. Others, on the other hand . . ."

When she said it, Mrs. Graham looked apprehensively at Stella. Stella's stomach flipped. The housekeeper suspected Lyndy too.

Don't look at me, Stella wanted to shout.

But it was too late. The inspector caught the silent exchange. "Others, Mrs. Graham?"

"Lord Lyndhurst, for one."

Stella braced herself for what was coming. The housekeeper snuck a peek to see Stella's reaction. Stella, having learned from her mother-in-law, refused to give her one.

"He punched Sir Edwin in front of the master and all his guests."

Stella inwardly sighed. She'd hoped to avoid, or at least postpone, the police learning about Lyndy's outburst. All her chances of learning what they knew about Sir Edwin's death were gone. Now she'd have to find out the hard way.

"Is this true, Lady Lyndhurst?" Docherty said, the use of her title a warning flag. She'd have to tread carefully.

"My husband had just learned about Sir Edwin's attack on Aggie. Something similar happened to me last Christmas, and Lyndy, being the gentleman that he is, has no tolerance for such barbaric behavior toward women."

"So ye don't deny it?"

"Why would I? Lyndy confronted Sir Edwin as everyone waited to go into dinner. But everyone also saw that Lyndy backed down when Sir Edwin denied it. Then, Sir Edwin had the gall to question the Countess of Atherly's virtue, insinuating Lyndy was not his father's son. So, yes, my husband punched him. Once. Regardless," Stella hastily added as Docherty seemed poised to ask something else, "my husband didn't kill Sir Edwin."

"Says a wife defending her husband. I admire your loyalty, lassie, but . . ."

"He couldn't have. He was with me all night, Inspector."

"But Aggie couldnae have either," Mrs. Graham insisted. "It's just not in her nature."

"Is this true, lass?" Docherty called toward the wagon. "Did ye confess to feeling guilty, not murder?"

"Aye. I didnae kill Sir Edwin, but all the same, he's dead because of me."

Docherty sighed and motioned for a policemen to unlock her handcuffs and help Aggie alight.

"I never thought a woman capable, and I was right. But a vindictive self-important English nob, on the other hand . . ."

"My husband is not . . . !"

"Ye lassies can go," Docherty said, cutting off Stella's defense of Lyndy. As Stella began to leave, her ears burning, her frustration fueling the race to figure out what to do next, he cleared his throat. "Not ye, Lady Lyndhurst." Again, he'd called her by her title.

Mrs. Graham urged Aggie to comply, but as she passed, Aggie whispered, "Ye should've left it alone like I asked."

Not knowing how to respond, Stella watched, dumbstruck, as Mrs. Graham whisked her away.

"Sounds like good advice," Docherty said, having overheard. "Now, ye and I need to have a wee bit of a chat about yer husband, lass." With his pipe clutched in his teeth, he jutted his chin toward the manor house.

How many times had Stella been told to leave well enough alone? Too many times to count. How many times had she regretted ignoring the advice? Never.

Until now.

CHAPTER 14

Lyndy silently added his sympathetic groans to those of the crowd as Freddy yet again missed a putt. He and Alice had followed his future brother-in-law from one hole to the next. Now, with the towering red sandstone Grand Hotel as backdrop, Freddy tapped his ball in at the eighteenth for two strokes over par for the hole. It had been a long day. Freddy had three-putted eleven and thirteen and found himself out of bounds twice. And yet each time Lyndy thought him beaten, Freddy would chip the ball into the hole from deep in a bunker or miraculously drop a twenty-five-foot putt. According to Alice, it was one of Freddy's worst performances, the highest score he'd shot since playing professionally. And yet he still shot low enough to be eligible to play in tomorrow's rounds. Freddy was that good.

"Young Kentfield certainly is tenacious. I can't imagine how well the laddie would've played had . . . well, ye know," McCormack said, leaning casually on his putter. Having completed his round earlier with the third-best score of the day, he'd joined Lyndy and his sister to watch Freddy finish.

"Hopefully he'll see sense by then," Alice said, "and not play."

Freddy thrust his putter into his bag on Billy's shoulder. The pair exchanged a few words Lyndy couldn't hear over the crowd's cheer as Freddy's playing partner dropped his long putt. Then they parted, Freddy trudging toward them, Billy over to a group of caddies gathering near the edge of the green. Billy spoke into the ear of one caddie and then another and then another, each caddie nodding in agreement.

What were they talking about? Sir Edwin's murder?

"What's he up to then?" McCormack quietly said as if reading Lyndy's mind. Then, in full voice, welcomed Freddy. "Well done, lad."

"I duffed the chip on eight and then again on twelve. I don't think I had a single up and down."

Alice wasted no time in lacing her arm through his. "But you finished. Sir Edwin would be proud."

"You got through it," Lyndy said.

"Ye'll play better tomorrow," McCormack said encouragingly. "Ye had quite the blow this morning."

"Tomorrow?" Alice said.

"Blow?" Lyndy said. "I'd argue it was a bit more than that. His father was murdered."

A bemused smile flitted across McCormack's lips. "A father who doesn't even bother to watch his promising son play. Is it much of a loss? What's yer caddie up to, lad?" Alasdair asked, purposefully cutting off any contradiction.

Lyndy tugged on the cuff of his jacket sleeve, noticed a green smudge, and scowled. Alice's gasp was audible, but Freddy rubbed the back of his neck, as if trying to remember what the question was. Had McCormack's affront even registered?

"Billy needed to compare notes. Or some such thing. Why?"

"Been with ye long, has he?" McCormack's keen gaze never left the caddies.

"Gave me my first niblick. Why?"

"What's all this about, McCormack?" Tension ached between Lyndy's shoulder blades. He'd been standing still too much. He itched to pace, to put some distance between Freddy's grief and McCormack's coy questioning, but if it had to do with Billy Birdwell, Lyndy needed to hear the answer.

"I didn't want to say earlier, but . . ."

"But what?" Freddy said, swatting at an invisible midge. Lyndy had been warned of the tiny swarming insects but had yet to be bitten.

"I saw yer caddie," McCormack emphasized the man's job description with a tinge of contempt, "sneaking out of Hamish's study while everyone was getting ready for dinner two nights ago."

"If you're suggesting Billy had anything to do with my father's death, you're daft." As the color rose in Freddy's cheeks, Alice tightened her hold. "Billy couldn't possibly . . ."

"Then who?" McCormack asked.

Freddy locked eyes with Lyndy. Lyndy, his grip on his jacket lapels, froze in midtug.

Bloody hell! *Does Freddy think I killed Sir Edwin?*

"Freddy!" The silent accusation hadn't slipped Alice's notice. She released her grip and stepped away, the blue ribbon on her hat flapping and fluttering in the steady breeze. "Lyndy didn't kill your father. How can you even think that?"

"I didn't say he did." Freddy held up his palms as if weighing Lyndy's fate with invisible scales. "But you can't deny you were furious with him, Lyndy. You did punch him."

Lyndy crossed his arms against his chest, raising his nose in haughty dismissal. "I bloody well did. So why would I need to again?"

"Of course you're right." Freddy's unconvincing capitulation stripped away Lyndy's bravado, twisting his gut with dread. Freddy was a terrible liar. "But it's as McCormack says. If not you, then who?"

*　*　*

Stella perched on the retaining wall at the top of the terraced garden. Her backside ached from sitting so long on the unyielding stone, but after being grilled by Docherty, she'd settled in to wait for Lyndy's return. With the countryside stretching for miles before her, she would spot him before anyone else. Stella sprung down the hill at the first sight of his carriage.

Lyndy alighted and bounded up the remaining steps between them. Without preamble, they both spoke at once.

"Docherty suspects you killed Sir Edwin."

"Freddy suspects I killed Sir Edwin."

"What? Freddy?" The betrayal tightened painfully in her throat. "How could he think that?"

"I punched his father. Perhaps in his grief, he can't think beyond that."

Lyndy's expansive shrug did more than express his incredulity; Stella watched his shoulders relax. She laced her fingers through his and led him back up the hill. Drawing in the earthy scent of Lyndy's cologne mingling with the sweet fragrant tree blossoms, Stella willed the tightening in her chest to loosen too. She wasn't as successful.

"The inspector asked to talk to you as soon as you returned. He's in the house now."

"So, you're saying that the police suspect me too? But why?"

"For the same reason as Freddy. You had a beef with Sir Edwin."

"As did the maid."

"But she didn't punch him. Besides, Docherty isn't even considering a woman could've done it." It was ridiculous. "The inspector is so frustrating. He ignored every question I asked. I'm as much in the dark as before. But Lyndy—" She paused beside a stiff feathery cycad. She'd never been interrogated like that before and hesitated to tell him. Look where his temper had gotten him so far. She reached out to touch the exotic frondlike leaf. Nothing like the feathery fronds of a fern, its sharp point poked her finger. "He questioned me about you, our relationship, your relationship with Sir Edwin, the McEwens, and Aggie of all people. He even wanted to know about your relationship with your mother."

"Bloody hell, that's going too far."

"Don't worry. I didn't tell him much. Only that you were with me the whole time, so whatever he wanted to know about you doesn't matter." Her legs trembled like the silk fabric of her dress in the evening breeze, and she urged Lyndy to sit on the nearest stone wall. When had her resentment at the inspector's intrusive questioning transformed into fear? "I've thwarted Docherty's attempts to officially accuse you for now, but . . ."

"But if we don't find out who actually did it, it's only a matter of time."

Stella grabbed Lyndy's hands, holding them tightly in her lap, silently imploring him to not look away. "So, we have to find out who did this. Whatever it takes." She meant it. "I'm not losing you."

To think she'd worried about not being able to have his children. That was nothing compared to the fear that shivered down her spine now. That problem they could solve.

But not if she lost him to the hangman.

Sensing her distress, Lyndy lifted her hands to his lips, warmth from his lingering kiss piercing the cold dread creeping through her. His mouth moved up her arm, compelling her to lean forward. He kissed her forehead, eyelids, and the tip of her nose before seeking her welcoming lips. Stella, her hands finding their way to his back, pressed herself against him, lips, cheek, chest, returning his affections with an insatiable craving to keep him this close forever, panicked that if she let him go, he'd disappear. When they finally pulled apart, breathless and shaky, Lyndy rested his forehead against hers.

"You will never lose me. Ever."

She wished she had Lyndy's confidence. Until Sir Edwin's murderer was caught, Stella wouldn't trust it was true.

Stella rechecked the hall before slipping into Sir Edwin's bedchamber. She hadn't gleaned much from the grilling she'd gotten from the inspector, but his frustration at not being allowed to search where and when he wanted had cropped up several times. Hamish had forbidden it. Why? With Docherty preoccupied by his questioning of Lyndy, she'd decided to find out. And Sir Edwin's room was the best place to start.

She clicked the lock, leaving the key in the door, and took a deep breath. The faint but rich floral scent of a French perfume lingered in the air. A woman had been in here recently. Virginia? Jeanie Agnew? A chambermaid with expensive tastes? Stella couldn't remember the housekeeper or Aggie smelling of anything but soap.

Stella drifted to the nightstand beside the bed where a framed photograph lay face down. Yet another surprise. It was of a much younger version of Sir Edwin with Lady Atherly, Lyndy's mother. Lady Atherly, almost unrecognizable in a frothy bustle-style dress layered with ruffles, pleats, and gathers, sat on the edge of a plush velvet armchair, Sir Edwin's hand on her shoulder as he stood like a guard behind her. The glass covering the photograph had a crack in it.

Dressed in their finery and their lips pinched so as not to blur the picture, the young couple's eyes radiated eager anticipation of their future together. A future that wasn't meant to be. Anyone who didn't know better would assume it was their wedding photograph. But they'd been forced apart, Lady Atherly compelled to marry the more suitable Earl of Atherly and Sir Edwin the Lady Isabella, who, thankfully, was now staying with one of her daughters in London. With no love lost between them, Sir Edwin had shamelessly flirted with other women, Stella included, right under Lady Isabella's nose. He'd seemed an incurable rapscallion. Even seeming to derive pleasure from goading Lyndy about the legitimacy of his birth. But this photograph, brought to Scotland and kept by his bedside, revealed where his genuine affection lay. For all his philandering, Sir Edwin never got over Lady Atherly. He'd admitted as much last Christmas, but here was proof.

And now he was dead.

How were they going to tell Lady Atherly? She'd made it clear that she was content in her marriage to Lord Atherly, but who doesn't hold a special place in their heart for their first love? If her actions at Christmas were any indication, Stella's mother-in-law would be heartbroken. Stella righted the frame, wondering again why it was face down, and pulled the slightly open nightstand drawer. The stub of a candle rolled to the front. Otherwise, the drawer was empty.

Stella continued through the room. More than just the nightstand drawer hadn't been fully shut. A servant would never be so sloppy. Had Sir Edwin, looking for something, been careless as he dressed for dinner last night? Or had someone else beat Stella to a search? After exhaustive scrutiny, Stella found nothing that might alleviate her predominating worries or provide answers to the numerous questions propelling her through the room. With only the suitcases on top of the wardrobe left, she was starting to get discouraged.

Stella pulled each from their lofty height, suspecting from their light weight that they were empty. She was right. Frustrated, she grabbed a chair to stack the suitcase back on the wardrobe. From that vantage point, she could see another case that wasn't visible from the floor. She grabbed it, but its unexpected heft threw her off-balance. She tipped the chair beneath her, and it toppled to its side, sending Stella and the suitcase crashing to the carpeted floor.

She pushed herself onto her knees, rubbing the spot on her backside that had taken the brunt of the fall. No real harm done; she'd fallen further and harder from the saddle. The suitcase, one corner deeply dented, had opened on impact, spreading its contents across the carpet. Envelopes, littering the floor like a street after a ticker-tape parade, lay among the crumpled articles of men's clothing. Not bothering to stand, Stella crawled, scooping them up one by one until the stack became too cumbersome to hold. She hoisted herself to her feet, settled on the edge of the bed, and spread out the letters on the counterpane. Each was addressed to Sir Edwin from his brother, Richard Kentfield. She thumbed through them, looking at the postmarks. The most recent was from around the time he was said to have died. She freed a letter from its envelope. She could barely read the contents. In the broad swirling scrawl, one of the few words she could easily make out was *cricket*.

Another was *Hamish*.

Sir Edwin and he had argued about Richard. Stella hadn't seen Hamish mad before that. Or since. What could it have been about? Had it anything to do with Sir Edwin's murder? Stella didn't want to think so. Hamish was affable and welcoming. He adored his wife. Hamish couldn't be a murderer, could he?

Absorbed with trying to decipher Richard Kentfield's handwriting, Stella jumped at the loud reverberating dinner gong. She folded the letter she was reading, scrambled to gather up those postmarked within weeks of Richard's death, and hid the slim stack in the waistband of her skirt. She stuffed the rest, including the clothes, back into the suitcase and slid it under the bed. Stella righted and moved the chair, leaving the room as she'd found it. She couldn't wait to tell Lyndy. Finally, here was something that might keep him safe, even if it meant pointing the finger at Cousin Hamish.

CHAPTER 15

"Now, Lord Lyndhurst," Docherty said, his teeth clenched on the stem of his unlit pipe, "tell me about this fight ye had with the victim."

The viscount, having taken Docherty's offer of a chair, sprung up and began pacing. Being as wee as it was, the house-keeper's study didn't offer the laddie much space before he was forced to turn around again and again. Like a caged animal. Docherty diverted his attention from the lad to the pale cracks in the worn leather ledger on the desk. Nothing and no one cowed Ian Docherty; he wouldn't have made inspector other-wise. But watching Lord Lyndhurst pace was making him dizzy.

"I'm certain you do not need me to tell you. You've spoken to my wife and McEwen, among others."

As the restless young noble pointed out, Docherty had had a full day, examining the body and the surrounding grounds, in-terviewing suspects and witnesses, composing carefully crafted telegrams to London's Metropolitan Police and the Hampshire Constabulary requesting information on Sir Edwin and Lord

Lyndhurst respectively, to Sir Edwin's solicitor and Lady Isabella Kentfield informing her of her husband's death. His teeth clamped harder on the pipe, adding another deep indent to the soft wood.

"So ye don't deny it?"

"Why would I?" The young lord's words echoed that of his wife. Had they rehearsed their answers? Or were they simply of one mind? Either way spelled trouble for the inspector.

"But can ye explain yourself?"

"Why should I?"

"Because the man ye punched was bludgeoned to death a few hours later."

"I resent your implication, Docherty," Lord Lyndhurst seethed, pausing in midstep to accentuate his displeasure. "Sir Edwin Kentfield was a close friend of my mother, the Countess of Atherly, and the father of my future brother-in-law. The man spent Christmas at our country estate, for God's sake."

"Then why punch him?"

"Because he was acting like an ass, that's why."

Lord Lyndhurst resumed his pacing. He reminded Docherty of a leopard he'd once seen at the old Glasgow Zoo. If the laddie had nothing to hide, no guilt weighing on his shoulders, why could he not settle in the armchair?

"Because of his behavior toward the laundry maid?"

"Behavior?" The viscount sneered as he dropped into the seat across from the inspector. "You say it as if Sir Edwin had cheated during a friendly game of whist. The man violently attacked a defenseless powerless girl. Not to mention defaming my mother's good name. If I'm to blame for being infuriated by such boorish unacceptable behavior, then so be it. But I didn't kill Sir Edwin. I made my point with a punch. I didn't need to bludgeon him to get my message across."

Docherty leaned back, taking the pipe from his mouth, the stem riddled with tooth marks, and took a sip of the tea Mrs.

Graham had thoughtfully provided. It was sugary and white, just as he liked it. He wasn't unsympathetic to Lord Lyndhurst's moral standards—his wife had explained how she'd been a victim of such harassment and how that had upset her husband—but Docherty couldn't discount the noble's passion. That righteous anger made him Docherty's best suspect yet.

"As you know full well, I didn't do this," Lord Lyndhurst said, as if it needed to be repeated. It made Docherty wonder. Was it righteous indignation or fear that propelled this man to protest again? "As my wife has told you, I was with her the entire evening and through the night."

"And as ye know," Docherty said, settling the empty teacup into the saucer with a clink, "she wouldn't be the first loving wife to lie to protect her husband from the gallows." The last word shot home. The lad flinched as if Docherty had slapped him across the face. "But let's hope it doesn't come to that."

And Docherty meant it. Charging an earl's heir for murder, even with ample justification, which Docherty didn't have yet, would not only be a lengthy ordeal he'd rather not endure, but it would silence the whispers of him replacing Gordon when the Chief Constable retired. Besides, there was something about the restless, arrogant lad Docherty admired. Was it the lord's wife's unrelenting loyalty? His unwavering sense of justice? Or Docherty's intuition that beneath the supercilious bluster, Lord Lyndhurst was a solid thoughtful lad. Docherty would have to learn more about the viscount to decide. But until then . . .

The dinner gong reverberated through the small room, causing the teacup to momentarily rattle on its plate. Lord Lyndhurst leaped to his feet as if involuntarily propelled by the summons to dress for dinner.

"If we're done here?"

"Ye're free to go, lad." With no sound reason beyond Docherty's failure to extract meaningful information from the lad,

Docherty couldn't compel Lord Lyndhurst to stay. But Docherty wasn't one to give up so easily. Docherty pointed his pipe at his most likely suspect. "Ye're free to go. For now."

Stella parted the drooping feathery branches that nearly touched the ground and ducked into the deeply shaded shelter beneath the towering hemlock tree, motioning for Lyndy to follow. She hadn't had a chance to tell him that she'd sneaked into Sir Edwin's room yet. Stella had wanted to tell him the minute they'd stepped out into the warm evening air after dinner but noticed Jeanie Agnew eavesdropping. She'd had to wait until they were far from the manor to relay the details. This secluded spot they'd found outside the walled rose garden was perfect.

"Lyndy, while you were with the inspector . . ."

Mistaking her intentions, Lyndy slid his arms around her and kissed her before she could continue. How could he be in the mood for romance at a time like this? The port on his breath, the strength of his embrace, warming more of her body than made contact, and the quickening of her heartbeat muddled her purpose, but nothing could weaken her determination.

Between kisses, Stella whispered against his eager lips, "I sneaked into Sir Edwin's room."

The effect of her words was like cold water splashed from a bucket. Lyndy winced.

"Wait. You did what?" With a moment to contemplate the implication, he leaned conspiratorially closer. "Did you find anything?"

"He had a photograph of your mother and him on his nightstand. Taken when they were very young."

"Why would Sir Edwin have brought a photograph of him and Mother to Scotland? And then imply I'm a bastard?"

"He was teasing you, not slandering your mother. He always said he was still in love with her."

Lyndy squished his face like he'd just eaten a lemon. Stella ignored him, though she found his offended sensibilities more endearing than she should.

"I also discovered letters from his brother, Richard. The one who died. They're almost illegible, but Hamish is definitely mentioned."

"Do you think Hamish is involved?" Lyndy stepped away, stripped a low-hanging branch of its needles, and crushed them in his palm. The sweet scent of grapefruit came to mind.

"I don't want to think so, but . . ." Stella still was unwilling to confront that possibility. Speaking of something else she'd rather not have to face. Dare she ask? "What did the inspector say?"

"What we gathered he would. Despite your assurances that I was with you, I fear he still suspects I had a hand in Sir Edwin's death. Stella?"

"Oh, no. I'd hoped that once he'd talked to you that would be the end of it."

Suddenly, the stifling dim light beneath the branches closed around her, and she burst from their hidey-hole. She gulped in the fresh air, scented by the nearby walled rose garden, and unlatched the small wrought-iron gate. Lyndy was beside her before she'd taken two steps down the stone path.

"Everything will be all right, my love. Docherty wouldn't dare arrest me. He has no just cause."

If only Stella could believe that. She didn't have centuries of aristocratic privilege to bolster her confidence. But then again, hadn't she always believed justice would prevail? And hadn't it, although so much of her experiences fell into the life's-not-fair category? Hadn't everything worked out in the end? Yet Docherty, like her father once had, threatened to turn her life upside down again. She'd once refused to be forced to marry Lyndy. Now, she refused to let him go.

And all she had to do was find Sir Edwin's true killer.

They strolled arm in arm in silence, Stella hoping the colorful oasis would soothe her worries, but she found no refuge there. Weeds sprouted between the cracks, buzzing bees hovered and flew from one profusely blossoming rosebush to the next, and the center fountain, an ornate marble tower of overflowing cascades, splashed cold droplets on her every time the breeze blew.

"I can't take this. Let's go for a ride." She tugged Lyndy's arm, leading him out of the garden, ignoring his protests that she wasn't dressed for a ride. "A skirt is a skirt."

Lyndy gave up. Whether he knew it was useless arguing with her or because he needed to be in the saddle as much as she did, Stella didn't know. And she didn't care. All that mattered was that he kept up with her rapid pace as she crossed the lawn to pick up the path to the stables.

Stella recalled Lyndy's outburst as they passed the summerhouse and paused. Lyndy kept walking. "Hold up a minute. Isn't this where you threw down your clubs last night?"

Lyndy came back to join her as she searched in and around the small building. "The groundskeeper must've picked them up."

"Of course he did."

"Why?"

"I don't know. Something's gnawing at me. Maybe we could ask Fergus about it before we head out?"

"What the devil is that?" Lyndy said over a loud repetitive banging emanating from the laundry house as they drew nearer.

The heavy thuds continued. Lyndy was the first to the door. They were welcomed by the odor of something akin to burning leaves or paper. Steam clouded the room, the vapor droplets streaking down the wall. Soon, Stella's whole body was damp from the heat. Obscured in the middle, Aggie, perspiration beading on her cheeks, wielded a heavy metal iron like a wrecking ball, slamming it down over and over against a cloth spread out on the narrow table before her. Its burned corner hung over the edge and flapped with each blow. It was stitched with the same family crest that was on the muddied cloth Stella had picked up the day Aggie was attacked.

"Ach, my lord, my lady!" Startled by their sudden appearance, Aggie dropped the iron and snatched up the cloth, shoving it into the deep pocket of her apron. The iron didn't land flat but clipped the rim of the table, toppled off, and smashed with a bang to the floor, barely missing the maid's foot. She deftly jumped back.

"Is everything all right, Aggie?" Stella asked. She hadn't been able to talk to Aggie since Sir Edwin's death.

"Ye startled me, is all."

"That handkerchief, or whatever you were ironing, is scorched," Lyndy chimed in. "You've quite ruined it."

Sheepishly, the maid fiddled with her apron strings, but the cloth never left her pocket. "I've been too clumsy lately. I must've left the iron on it for too long."

She wasn't fooling anyone. But how to get Aggie to confide in her?

"Lyndy, do you mind asking Fergus about your clubs without me?" Taking the hint, Lyndy readily agreed to leave the two women alone and strode from the building. "Now, Aggie, do you want to talk about it or should I let you get back to taking your anger out on that poor piece of fabric?"

Aggie reached in and produced the pathetic handkerchief, holding it out before her. Scorch marks in the shape of the iron crisscrossed it in a random pattern. The edge stitching on one side was singed and still smoking. At least the maid had chosen something easily replaceable and inexpensive. If she'd purposely ruined a dress or shirtwaist, the price would've come out of her earnings, and Stella wouldn't be the only one asking questions about it.

"Thank you, my lady, but there's nothing tae discuss." Aggie's expression tightened into one of blank determination.

"You can always come to me if you change your mind."
Stella had learned when not to press further. "I'll leave you to
your work."

Stella withdrew but observed the maid through the narrow
crack she left in the door. Stella's instincts paid off. Believing
herself alone, Aggie, in a fit of rage, crumbled up the ruined
handkerchief in her fist and hurled it to the floor.

Grateful to leave Stella to handle the jumpy maid, Lyndy
followed the path to the groundskeepers' cottage. The young
keeper, key in hand, was kicking aside a large rusty biscuit tin
holding open the door when Lyndy approached. The rocks
used to weigh it down rattled as it slid away, and the door
slammed shut.

"Fergus, isn't it?" Lyndy asked, proud of himself for remembering.

"Aye, it is, my lord. Whit can I dae for ye?" He turned the
key in the lock before slipping his cap off his head. He held it
before him like the wheel of a motorcar.

"You fetched me a set of golf clubs to use while I'm staying
at Glenloch. After playing with them last night, I set them by
the summerhouse, but they don't seem to be there anymore. I
assume you put them away?"

"Nay, wasn't me, Yer Lordship. Normally, I would've, but I
never did see any clubs lying about last night. Must've been
someone else put them away."

"And where would that be?"

"In the sporting room in the manor. 'Tis across from Mr.
McEwen's study. Old Tom Morris needs a hand in St. An-
drews, and I was tae be off, but I could look right quick before
I go if ye'd like?"

"No, no, it can wait until you get back." *Or Stella and I
could poke about. She'd love that.* "Don't let me keep you."

The groundskeeper slapped his cap back on and touched the
brim. "Kind of ye, my lord. If ye'll excuse me, I'll be off."

Lyndy followed the man's progress down the path toward the stables, swatting at something that had landed on his neck. The spot instantly began to itch.

Had anything gone right during this trip? Lyndy's trunk was still unaccounted for, the McEwens seemed a cagey bunch, Sir Edwin acted like a fool and got himself killed, and Lyndy was now the suspected culprit.

In light of all that, what were some missing golf clubs?

CHAPTER 16

"I wish I could leave now," the maid muttered, digging her heel into the scorched cloth.

Stella nudged the door with her shoulder and warily stepped back inside, hoping not to startle the maid. It didn't work. The maid jumped as if she'd seen a snake.

"Oh, my lady! I thought ye were gone."

"Aggie, what's going on? It's just a handkerchief." Stella retrieved the cloth from the floor and tossed it into an empty basket. "And why can't you leave? Your work looks finished."

"That's not what I—" Something rapped sharply against the window, frightening the maid into silence. Aggie curled her wrists protectively under her chin. "What was that?"

Stella flung open the window, a welcome draft of cool fresh air greeting her, and leaned over the sash. Beneath the window, the bushes cast lengthening shadows. It might've been a bird, confused by the reflection off the glass, flying into the window or a branch of a nearby shrub blown by the wind, but the ground was empty of dead birds, and the night was still, the gentle breeze not penetrating the woodland enough to rustle the branches. And yet, beyond the building, shrubs were still moving from whatever had disturbed them.

Someone was out there.

"Wait here, Aggie," Stella ordered as she hurried outside. When she rounded the corner, a skittish rabbit darted from its cover.

Stella watched, transfixed by the rabbit's bounding zigzag pattern of escape, until the frightened animal disappeared in the underbrush a dozen yards up the hill. The rabbit might've caused the bushes to wave around, but it couldn't have rapped at the window.

"Whatever was out there is gone," Stella said when she returned.

"I feel so daft. I'm not normally this jumpy." Aggie's shoulders sagged as she forced out an unconvincing chuckle. "Besides, it was probably Fergus, throwing a wee pebble tae tell me he was back. He wouldnae come in if he'd heard yer voice. Speaking of . . . Please dinnae tell anyone, my lady. It's not strictly forbidden, me and Fergus stepping out together, but it could cause us problems if word got out."

"I could speak to Mrs. McEwen on your behalf if you'd like."

"It's not the mistress I'm worried about."

"Then who?"

Aggie went over to the window and slammed it shut. Steam crept across the windowpanes, blocking out the view. Almost immediately, Stella missed the flow of fresh air.

Aggie lowered her voice. Stella had to strain to hear her. "Ye see, my lady, Fergus had just left when . . . I was set upon."

The maid's weighty pause was suggestive. She'd purposely not mentioned the perpetrator's name. Was she so scared she couldn't bring herself to voice it again?

"What difference does that make? Earlier, when no one knew who'd attacked you, I completely understood you trying to protect Fergus, fearing he might be accused, but now we all know it was Sir Edwin. Right?"

Aggie averted her gaze, licked her thumb, and rubbed at a faint spot on her apron.

"Right, Aggie?"

Aggie's response was to rub at the fabric until her thumb must've burned.

Stella sought a simple affirmation, but Aggie refused to give it. Why?

"Sir Edwin was the one who *set upon you*, wasn't he?" Aggie continued to fret away at the stain. "It wasn't really Fergus, was it? You're not trying to protect him, are you?"

Aggie's head snapped up as if a puppeteer was pulling her strings. "Nay, my lady. Fergus is as mild as milk. He'd never try anything like that."

A quick rap at the door, and Lyndy popped his head in. Aggie flinched, averting her gaze again. "Finished here? The groundskeeper suggests we might look in the sporting room for the clubs." He meant to sound indifferent, but there was a tightness, a clipped tension to his tone that Stella couldn't ignore.

"Aye, my lord. And thank ye for your concern, my lady." The maid bobbed in and out of a quick curtsy, a deferential way to ask her to please leave. Stella wasn't satisfied, but Lyndy beckoned haste, fidgeting with his gold cuff links.

"You're more than welcome, Aggie. Perhaps I'll check in on you again sometime."

Stella followed Lyndy, closing the door behind her, two questions banging away in her head like a barn door blown open by the wind. Aggie had stubbornly avoided confirming that Sir Edwin had harassed her. Could someone else have done it? And if the maid wasn't protecting Fergus, why lie?

Inspector Docherty held the back of his fist to his mouth and belched, his breath smelling of the fish soufflé in cream sauce he'd had for supper. He rubbed his gurgling paunch. Perhaps he shouldn't have had the wee second helping of onion custard. The inspector rapped the brass knocker once, twice, three times, and waited for Stevenson to answer.

The butler was slower than usual in opening the door and

profusely apologetic. "I do so apologize for making ye wait, Detective Inspector," he said, leisurely twisting the tips of his mustache. "I didn't know to expect you."

Docherty handed over his bowler. "This isn't a social call."

"Ah." Stevenson tapped a finger to the side of his nose. "Police matters again, eh? The master and mistress are entertaining guests in the billiards room. Shall I tell them yere here?"

"No need. But I would like a wee chat with Lord Lyndhurst again. If ye'd tell him I'm waiting?"

Docherty had received replies to most of his telegrams to England. The one from Sir Edwin's solicitor was the most illuminating. Did the young viscount know he was a beneficiary of the English baronet's will? Granted, it wasn't a vast amount, but Docherty had known men to be murdered for less.

"I believe His Lordship is taking the air in the garden with Her Ladyship," Stevenson said. "Shall I get someone to fetch him?"

Docherty felt another belch rising and turned his head just in time. "Aye. And because we have time, I could do with some peppermint tea while I wait."

"Very good, Inspector."

Stevenson ambled away, leading the policeman toward the library, knowing he preferred it to the drawing room. Not that Docherty didn't appreciate the fine volumes lining the walls or the large window that afforded a view of a raised stone fishpond surrounded by Virginia's cycads, but he preferred the library because here he could properly relax; Virginia prohibited pipe smoke in the drawing room.

Docherty settled into his favorite worn leather armchair, procuring his pipe and tobacco pouch from his jacket pocket. Stevenson paused in the doorway, showing no inclination to get on with his duties.

"Is there something else, Stevenson?"

"I don't know. It may not mean anything, Inspector."

"Let me be the judge, eh?"

"Aye."

Stevenson leaned against the doorjamb and stared out the window. Docherty followed his gaze but saw nothing unusual: the orange and pink blaze of the setting sun reflecting off the windows, the silhouettes of birds coming in to roost.

Finally, the butler said, "Last night, as I was locking up, I found a bag with a set of golf clubs near the wine cellar."

"The wine cellar. That is a wee bit odd, isn't it?"

"Very much. With all the guests and the excitement over the Open Championship, I would've assumed one of them must've left the wee bag lying about. But only my staff typically goes down there. What would any of the servants be needing with a bag of golf clubs? And why would they be leaving them about?"

Docherty had a mind to demand why Stevenson hadn't told him about this sooner, but his stomach rumbled uncomfortably again. The sooner he got his tea, the better.

"Did ye notice anything else unusual about them?"

"Nay."

"Where are the clubs now?"

"I've put them away. In the sporting room."

Docherty tapped the fresh tobacco he'd just packed into the pipe bowl back into the pouch and lugged himself out of the chair. Even when unlit, the aromatic flavor filled his nose with smoky sweetness.

Those clubs better have something to do with the Englishman's murder or Stevenson will be eating this tobacco.

"Time ye disturbed Mr. McEwen, Stevenson, and ask him to join me in the sporting room." Docherty would rather not argue with Hamish again, but he'd have to insist this time. He would examine those clubs and search the house whether Hamish agreed to it or not. "And get someone to fetch me that peppermint tea, eh?"

CHAPTER 17

Stella halted in the doorway. She wasn't sure what she'd expected of the *sporting room*, but this wasn't it. A cross between a library and a storage closet, all four walls of the small room were lined from floor to ceiling with lightly stained oak cabinets. Doorless, the paneled cubbyholes were open for all to see and access. Only the shotguns were behind glass. Every cabinet was packed with sporting equipment: archery bows, tennis and badminton rackets, cricket bats, croquet and polo mallets, stacks of balls of all shapes and sizes, and bags filled with golf clubs. Crowded yet organized, the space smelled of leather, polish, sweat, and soil, with an odd hint of peppermint.

A small unadorned oak table sat in the center. The detective inspector, his back to them, crouched over it, his palms flat on the table's polished surface, a gold-rimmed teacup hand painted with faded peach poppies by his hand. Hamish stood across from him, pinching his chin and frowning. Their attention was entirely on something set between them. It was a bag filled with golf clubs, the same set Lyndy had thrown onto the grass the night before by the summerhouse. One of the clubs had a distinct scratch across the brass plate that gave the wooden brassie its name.

Hamish caught her and Lyndy hovering in the door-way. Docherty, noticing Hamish's distraction, glanced over his shoulder.

"Ah, just the laddie I was looking for." Docherty selected an iron-headed club from the bag, some of its dotted grooves dark with soil, and faced them. Clutching the end, he pointed the hickory shaft toward Lyndy. Stella braced for the imminent accusation. "Did ye know, Lord Lyndhurst, that Sir Edwin Kentfield left ye a legacy in his will?"

Thrown off guard, Stella repeated the inspector's words in her head. They didn't make sense. What did Sir Edwin's will have to do with the golf clubs lying on the table like a cadaver on an undertaker's slab? Then it hit her. Not only did Inspector Docherty suspect those were Lyndy's clubs but the money gave Lyndy further motive for killing Sir Edwin. Stella tried in vain to keep the concern from her face. Lyndy, with many years of practice, on the other hand, gave nothing away of what he was thinking.

"I did not," Lyndy said.

"He left ye his horses, laddie. All of them. And I'm told a few are worth a wee bob or two. I also heard yer quite the punter too."

"We train and race horses, Inspector," Stella jumped in to say, still trying to make sense of Sir Edwin's generosity. He'd recently purchased three promising Thoroughbred colts. Inspired by Lyndy, he'd said. Sir Edwin even asked Stella to size them up before committing to the sale. She and Lyndy should be thrilled to add the trio to their stables. But at what cost? "We don't bet on them."

"Not much anyway," Lyndy quipped. "That was indeed kind of Sir Edwin. Was my mother, the Countess of Atherly, also mentioned?"

"She was, in fact."

"Then do you suspect she, too, had a hand in Sir Edwin's murder?"

Stella's heart dropped into her stomach. She should've known Lyndy would goad the policeman. She adored her husband, but didn't he realize his title, his family connections, and her money might not be enough to save him if Docherty arrested him for murder? Thank goodness Lyndy's remark landed softly. The inspector merely squinted over his unlit pipe.

"Been to the wine cellar here at Glenloch Hill, Lord Lyndhurst?"

"Why? Had Sir Edwin brought wine and left that to me in his will as well?"

Again, the inspector's questioning tactic had taken Stella by surprise. But it gave her something to do. Concentrating on puzzling out how the wine cellar fit in kept her mind and emotions in check. She couldn't keep Lyndy from being Lyndy—and wouldn't want to—and at least for now couldn't stop the inspector from suspecting him. But she could try to put the pieces together and build Lyndy's defense.

"Just answer the question, laddie."

"Ian, what's this aboot?" Hamish demanded. Neither the inspector nor Lyndy paid him any heed.

"It's Lord Lyndhurst, if you don't mind. And why would I go to the wine cellar? I trust McEwen to have an excellent staff who see to that sort of thing."

"Do ye recognize these clubs, Lord Lyndhurst?"

Stella had a sudden sour taste in her mouth. It was the question she'd been dreading.

But Lyndy shrugged noncommittally. "I'm new to the sport, Inspector. Isn't one set much like another?" For this, Lyndy addressed Hamish, appealing to his expertise. Lyndy knew full well those were the clubs he'd used, but he hadn't lied outright by denying it either.

"To the beginner, they might."

The inspector frowned. "But ye know the difference, Hamish. Can ye tell me, then, who was the last person to play with these?" Although the inspector addressed Hamish, he never took his eyes off Lyndy. Lyndy met his gaze with the arrogance and the entitlement of a man used to being shielded from any hint of persecution or disparagement.

From anyone apart from his mother, of course.

"I'm afraid anyone could've entered the room or borrowed the clubs. The door is seldom locked, and as ye ken full well, Ian, we have a golf course on the estate. With the golfers and a caddie staying in the house for the Open Championship, who kens who used them last."

"Why are the golf clubs so important, Inspector?" Stella asked, as if she didn't already know.

"For one, the wee Baffy club is missing from the set. And two, do ye know what this is?" He pointed to a dark smudge on the rim of the bag's shoulder strap.

"It's blood."

Docherty squished his brows together. "Aye, it's blood."

Stella had surprised him. He must've doubted her participation in investigating murders. Did he believe anything she said?

"You suspect Sir Edwin's killer touched that bag after murdering him?"

"Aye, I do, lass. I also suspect that the missing Baffy was used to bludgeon Sir Edwin. And if I'm going to put all my cards on the table, I'll go so far as to name who I suspect wielded the club."

Stella braced herself, waiting for Lyndy's name to drop from the inspector's lips like a death knell. Instead, a high-pitched shriek reverberating from the hall cut short his reply.

"She's dead! She's dead! She's dead!"

The woman's anguished, repeating cry beckoned. Stella,

Lyndy, Hamish, and Docherty, who brandished the golf club like a sword, dashed from the sporting room toward the screams.

"Dear Lord, not Virginia?" Hamish prayed as he sped past Stella, motivating her to pick up her skirt to catch up and wonder why he'd assume it was his wife.

The chambermaid, her mobcap askew, her hands covering her face, knelt near the open French doors on the far side of the drawing room. She rocked on grass-covered heels, inconsolable, repeating like a mantra, "She's dead. She's dead. She's dead."

Hamish stomped over to the maid and towered over her. "Who's dead? Is it my wife? Is it Mrs. McEwen? What's happened?"

The chambermaid cowered under his scrutiny, her forehead nearly touching the carpet. "She's dead," the poor woman moaned.

Stella recognized Hamish's fear but knew from experience it wouldn't help to bully the maid into talking. Besides, it could be anyone: Virginia, as Hamish suspected, or perhaps Jeanie Agnew, or . . . one of the servants, a close friend of the maid's even. It would explain her reaction. To learn what she could, Stella focused on soothing the poor maid. She couldn't afford to give in to the mounting worry that tragedy had struck her new family again.

"I'm so sorry. What's your name?" Stella cooed, urging Haish aside and kneeling slowly beside her. She placed a gentle hand on her shoulder. It was damp. The maid flinched but didn't look up.

"Orla, ma'am."

"Can you tell us who's dead, Orla?"

Footsteps pounded down the stairwell, and soon Freddy and Alice burst into the room. Stella's tense muscles softened at the sight of her sister-in-law. Lyndy's shoulders dropped visibly in relief. He, too, must've worried Alice was who the maid referred to.

"What's going on? We heard screams." Freddy's voice was raspier, more frantic than usual.

"Someone's died, but we don't know who, or how, or even where yet," Lyndy said.

The maid pointed outside, lifting her head and revealing red swollen eyes, streaks of tears on her pallid cheeks, a forehead beaded with sweat. "She's . . . doon there."

"Doon where?" Hamish demanded, his voice rising in panic. "Virginia and Jeanie went for a stroll, but I dinnae ken in which direction."

"And who's down there?" the inspector demanded, not much less gently than Hamish. The men were used to being obeyed.

"She's doon there." The maid collapsed forward, breaking into a hysterical sob that shook her whole body.

Stella worried for the woman's health. "Hamish, ring for your housekeeper. Someone needs to stay with Orla."

Hamish pressed the bell, which Stella could imagine hearing tinkling downstairs.

"We'll wait for the housekeeper," Alice said. "You go. See who it is and what's happened."

Without waiting to see who followed, Stella took the opportunity Alice gave her and hurried outside. Lyndy fell quickly into step as they searched the vista before them for any clue. But for the rustling, grunting, and snuffling of a hedgehog foraging under the nearby shrubbery, all was quiet and peaceful. Hamish and Docherty soon caught up, and the four of them headed down the hill. Stella feared the worst when the laundry house came in sight, but they found no evidence of a dead woman. Just in case, Docherty tried the door; it was locked. He peered through the windows, but the room was dark, and their reflection blurred all they could see.

"Aggie?" Stella called. There was no answer.

"Could the dead woman be in the stables, perhaps?" Hamish asked, his voice still shaking.

"Aye, or it could be someone was hiking through, hoping to

reach the wee monument on the hill," Docherty concluded. "It is a public footpath, isn't it?" Hamish confirmed it was. "Or she could be in or near the groundskeeper's bothy."

"Ye think Fergus is involved?"

"I don't know anything more than ye do, Hamish. So, ye and Lady Lyndhurst check the woodland trail. Lord Lyndhurst and I will check the bothy on the way to the stables."

Docherty still wants to keep tabs on Lyndy.

Stella and Lyndy's eyes met. In silent agreement, the couple split up. They'd placate the inspector; they'd learn more apart anyway. Stella went after Hamish, who'd cut around the back of the building to a hiking track that led into the woods behind. To Stella, it was a wild-goose chase. The chambermaid had said *down there* not *up the hill*. Docherty had sent Hamish this way, wanting to spare his friend from possibly finding Virginia by the groundskeeper's cottage or in the stables.

Stella rounded the corner and followed Hamish up the path into the shade of the woods but couldn't help looking back at the laundry house. She halted in midstride. The back door sat slightly ajar. Leaving Hamish to pursue the trail, Stella slipped off it, shoving and pushing aside the thick brush blocking her way to the laundry room door. Her skirts caught the branches more than once, but she didn't let that slow her.

The room she entered cautiously, listening, watching for any sign of danger, was dominated by the massive metal boiler, but unlike earlier, when she'd heard it chugging away and belching out clouds of steam, it sat dormant and quiet. Too quiet. Though the air was still sticky with moisture, the heat Stella expected had lessened. With the late evening sun momentarily escaping from behind a cloud, the boiler room wasn't as dark as it appeared from outside. And it was empty. No body lay sprawled on the floor.

The sunlight cut off again, and Stella tiptoed forward. Wiping her forehead with her sleeve, she called, "Aggie?"

No answer. Stella was alone. She was halfway across the room when the door creaked behind her. Stella grabbed a near-by washing board and whirled around with it held high over her head. Steps behind her, his hands held up in defense, was the love of her life, a twig stuck to his white waistcoat.

"Lyndy! I could've walloped you." Stella lowered the washing board, tossing it aside, and brushed the twig away. "What were you thinking?"

Lyndy grabbed her hand, keeping it close to his chest. "I could ask you the same thing, my love. I thought you were going with Hamish."

"And I thought Docherty wouldn't let you out of his sight."

"I managed to slip away, as I suspect you did." A sly half smile lit up his face. She wanted to kiss him. Then, his sudden pronounced frown clouded the moment.

"I saw the back door open and thought—"

"That it might be the laundry maid who's dead?" Lyndy finished for her. Stella nodded. Lyndy lifted her hand to his lips and sighed against it, his breath hotter than the laundry room. "Oh, my love, why must you always be right?"

"What?" Stella began to protest. "I'm not always . . ."

Lyndy gestured for her to turn around, and the words choked in her throat. He wasn't teasing, just truthful.

The setting sun momentarily streamed into the room. Shining through a heap of linens, draped and left to dry, the day's last rays of sun silhouetted a dangling body tangled among them. It was Aggie, the strings of her apron knotted around her neck.

CHAPTER 18

"Och, Lord Lyndhurst!" Docherty barreled into the laundry room after Lyndy had gone outside and shouted for the inspector to come. Stella wanted to stay with Aggie. "I thought ye gave me the slip. Two wrongs can dim the morrow, laddie. Ye'd be wise to remember that."

As Lyndy geared up to object, Stella rested her hand on his arm. This wasn't the time to argue. "It's Aggie, Inspector. She's in here."

Pulling a handkerchief from his vest pocket, the inspector rubbed his pipe as he followed Stella into the boiler room.

"The maid? Yer not saying . . ." The pipe hit the floor with a clunk, the inspector having dropped it the second he spotted Aggie hanging from the rafters. He snatched it up, shoved it safely back into his pocket, and coughed into his fist. "By God, I never get used to . . . lassie, ye shouldn't be here." He gestured toward the front door as Hamish burst through the one opened in the back.

"Did ye find her? It cannae be Virginia? Not in here."

"Nay, Hamish, 'tis the wee laundry maid. The one who ac-

cused Sir Edwin of imposing his ardor upon her. Lady Lyndhurst, please."

Stella didn't budge. "I won't leave her."

Docherty rolled his eyes but gave up. "Then for all that's
good and proper, get the lass down, will ye, gentlemen?"

"Is that wise?" Stella asked. "You haven't inspected the body,
the linens, the floor, or the rafters." He hadn't even seemed to
notice the note yet.

"There's no need, lassie. It's obvious what's happened here."
Docherty, rubbing his stomach, impatiently urged Lyndy and
Hamish to proceed. "Get on with it, will ye?"

"Aye." Hamish sighed in relief, though his posture was still
stiff. "And Virginia need not ken." Neither Stella nor Lyndy
agreed, but Hamish took their silence as such. "Will ye lend me
a hand, Lyndy?"

The two men cut Aggie's body from the excess linens holding her suspended and rested her gently onto the floor, wrapped
in a bedsheet as if in a shroud. Stella stared at the contours of
the maid's nose, cheeks, forehead, and chin, imagining what lay
beneath. A queasiness rose from the pit of her stomach. Not
from being in the presence of a dead body, she'd seen too many
now for that, but from pity and a sense of failure. Poor Aggie.
This didn't have to happen. Could Stella have done something
more to help? Did she do too much? Was it Stella's prying that
caused this, or was the maid doomed the moment her attacker
singled her out?

"You might want to read this."

Stella pointed to the small bench shoved against the wall devoid of anything but the plain brown vellum-covered laundry
log book. A page ripped from it lay on top. She'd found and
read the simple message scrawled across the empty preprinted
lines while waiting for the inspector to arrive.

Inspector Docherty squinted at her before approaching the
workbench. He read the ripped page.

"What does it say?" Hamish asked.

"That the wee lassie admits to killing Sir Edwin and couldnae live with the guilt."

Docherty folded the paper in half twice and slipped it into his breast pocket. He stepped over to the body and peered at her as if he could read more on her covered face than what she'd written before indicating the open doorway. They all dutifully proceeded him outside. After the humid stuffy laundry house, the cool air chilled Stella's skin. She inhaled it as if it could cleanse her insides of the gloom eking out of her pores.

"This ordeal is over, then?" Hamish said, his voice awash with relief.

"Aye, it seems so," Docherty agreed. "I'll call for Farley and some of my men to help cart the body away." The inspector shoved out his hand to Lyndy. "No hard feelings, laddie?"

Lyndy reluctantly shook the inspector's hand, remaining distinctly silent, offering no words to absolve the policeman of his false suspicions. Stella anticipated the relief that would wash over her like the cooling wind. It never came.

"Hamish? Inspector?" Alasdair called as he bounded down the path toward them. "Young Kentfield said a woman's been killed?"

"It's the laundry maid, Alasdair," Hamish said. "She's gone and hanged herself."

"Aye, right." Alasdair forced a laugh, then racked his fingers through his hair when no one contradicted Hamish. "I don't believe it."

Stella didn't either. Couldn't believe Aggie had killed Sir Edwin, at least. She'd seen the maid moments after discovering his body. Aggie had been genuinely shocked. And what was that earlier, when she wouldn't confirm Sir Edwin had attacked her, as if she'd lied about it being him? Aggie was angry, scorching that cloth, but was she capable of such a brutal murder? Stella would've bet their percentage of the purse money from Tupper's lastest win that Aggie wasn't. But was the maid capable of killing herself?

"I just spoke to her less than an hour ago or so," Stella said. "She wanted to leave Glenloch Hill, but she didn't seem suicidal."

"Ye never know what someone is capable of, lass," Inspector Docherty said. That much Stella agreed with, but . . . "Don't ye dwell on this unpleasant business for another moment."

"Aye," Hamish readily agreed. "Let's put all this behind us and enjoy the few days ye have left in Scotland."

"Besides, there's still two more rounds of the Open to be played," Alasdair added.

As the other men climbed the path that would bring them back to the manor and a telephone to alert the coroner, Lyndy offered Stella his arm.

"I don't fancy going to the links tomorrow, do you? Despite my recent enthusiasm, I'm not much in the mood to watch men wielding clubs at present." He chuckled mirthlessly.

"No, me neither." Stella forced a half-hearted smile. Why was she so glum? Lyndy was safe from suspicion, wasn't he? "It's such a relief, though, knowing the inspector no longer suspects you killed Sir Edwin."

"Yes, quite." Glancing up at the darkening sky, he tugged her a little closer. She cuddled against him as they strode toward the house, the familiarity of his cologne reassuring. "Shall we take that ride you wanted at first light, my love?"

"Yes. Let's." Lyndy knew her well. If anything could lift her spirits, it was being back in the saddle again. All she had to do was weather what promised to be a long sleepless night.

"You're not thinking of playing today, are you?"

Lyndy was selecting a slice of bacon from the breakfast trays on the sideboard when Freddy, dressed in golf trousers, entered the dining room with Alice. Dark shadows etched his eyes and he tottered like a man drunk on laudanum. Had he slept at all last night? Stella certainly hadn't, at least not until the early morning hours. Instead of riding at first light, Lyndy had let her sleep.

"That's what I said," Alice declared as Freddy held out her chair.

Lyndy couldn't remember the last time his sister's voice sounded so assertive. Stella was right. Being away from Mother was doing Alice good. She smoothed her skirt as she sat and encouraged Freddy to join her by patting the seat beside her.

"It's too much, what with his father and the maid. . ." Alice's voice trailed off, unable or unwilling to articulate yesterday's horror. With all the murders and dead bodies he and Stella had encountered, they'd never faced two in one day. "Besides, Freddy, you must admit you aren't playing your best."

Freddy nodded like the automaton Lyndy once saw at the Hippodrome in London, bobbing his head mechanically, without a thought to what he was doing. And then he shook himself, as if trying to wake from a dream.

"What do you want me to do, spend the day here wallowing in self-pity, indulging in grief? Alice, I know you think that's best," Freddy momentarily cradled her chin in his hand, "but trust me, playing golf will be a welcome distraction from it all."

"I totally agree," McCormack said, smearing marmalade on his toast. "Play as he did, though understandably so, he still qualified to start today. He has the right and privilege to continue if he wants." He chomped off the tip of the toast.

"What do you say, Lyndy?" Alice appealed as he set his breakfast plate on the charger and sat across from her. What could he say? Freddy and McCormack were right. If it had been him, he'd probably welcome the distraction too.

At Lyndy's shrug, Alice pushed back her chair and stood abruptly. "Stella would agree with me if she were here." She stomped to the sideboard and grabbed a plate. If it hadn't already been apparent, the careless clattering she caused as she returned the serving utensils to their trays spoke volumes about her displeasure.

McCormack winked and nodded toward Freddy when he rose silently to join Alice. McCormack seemed to find Alice's outburst and Freddy's acquiescence amusing. Lyndy saw two upset people who didn't know how to handle it. But McCormack's nearly whispered tone when he turned to Lyndy was far less lighthearted.

"Bad business last night, eh? I didn't get a chance to ask. Did ye find her?"

"My wife and I did. After a chambermaid discovered her, of course."

Lyndy didn't fancy talking about it. He bit off a piece of bacon, savoring the salty smoky meat, and focused on the plate before him, hoping the golfer would take the hint. The yolk of his egg had broken and seeped into his potato scone. He tried a bite of the egg-soaked scone. It was delicious.

"Yer poor wee wife."

"Yes." Lyndy turned away to look out the window. The sky was clear, but the trees within view swayed in the breeze. If it was blowing the trees up here, Lyndy could imagine its strength on the links course so close to the sea. "Conditions might be a bit windy on the course today."

McCormack, who had leaned in, sat back, wiping his lips with his napkin. "Aye. But do I care? It could be a dreich day. As long as I'm swinging a club, I'm happy."

"Ye not planning on winning, are ye, Alasdair?" Hamish teased, coming in later than usual. Unlike Freddy, Hamish looked more refreshed than he had since Lyndy met him.

"Aye, ye know I am, Hamish."

Alice and Freddy rejoined them at the table but picked at the paltry helpings on their plates in silence.

"How ye hauding up, Freddy?" Hamish asked. "Get any sleep at all?"

"I may never sleep again," Alice said after the tired shake of

Freddy's head. "I don't know how you and Stella do it, Lyndy. I didn't even see Sir Edwin or the maid and was haunted by it all night. Just consoling that poor chambermaid who found her was enough for me. I can't imagine how you feel, Freddy." She rested a hand on his arm. Freddy patted it.

"I'm fine, Alice. Or at least I will be."

"One never gets used to it," Lyndy said, "but over time, one learns to react less." Or so he hoped. Stella still took each death hard.

"I'm just relieved it's all over," Hamish said, filling his plate.

"It isn't for Freddy."

Freddy rewarded Alice's quiet grumble with a gentle chiding. She hid her reaction behind her teacup. Was Alice always so compliant? Lyndy noted Stella wouldn't have accepted such a rebuke, however kindly administered, so readily.

And bloody well right too.

"At least the culprit has confessed and ye can move on," Mc-Cormack said, unknowingly preempting Lyndy's sudden need to defend his sister.

"And he's a braw laddie, yer Freddy," Hamish said, slapping the newspapers tucked under his arm onto the table before settling into his chair. "He'll do fine."

"I suppose," Alice reluctantly agreed.

"I say we put it all behind us and focus on the day at hand, eh?" McCormack added.

Hamish heartily agreed. "Besides, it should be a bonny day with two full rounds of play. A bit windy, but I'm rather looking forward tae it. Put a bit of distance from yesterday's upset. By the way, those going tae St. Andrews will have tae leave," Hamish pulled out a gold scalloped pocket watch ornately etched with swirls and stars, "soon, I should think."

McCormack, in response, wiped his mouth again and threw his napkin next to his nearly empty plate. He'd left but a few bits of broken oatcake. Freddy followed suit, though he'd barely eaten a thing.

"Will you and Stella be ready tae leave at half past, Lyndy?" Hamish asked.

"We're not going this morning. I promised my wife we'd take out the horses."

"I ken what ye mean," Hamish chuckled. "Virginia so loves her horses."

"And whatever it takes to keep the lassies happy, eh?" McCormack teased.

Alice stole a glance at Freddy from beneath her lowered lids. He was too preoccupied with pushing back from the table without incident to notice. Clearly exhausted, how was Freddy possibly going to play golf?

"Ye'll find Morag, the mare, a bit stubborn," Hamish continued. "Needs a bit of coaxing, but Angus is a joy."

"What is he doing here?" McCormack frowned at Billy Birdwell, the caddie, hovering in the doorway. How long he'd been there Lyndy couldn't say. "Shouldn't he be on the course already?"

"I asked him to join me," Freddy said. "You can come in, Billy."

"No need. I'm ready if you are, Fred," Billy said, catching Hamish's eye.

It was brief, and if Lyndy hadn't been paying attention, he would've missed the silent exchange between the two men. Freddy, in his near stupor, certainly did. But glancing across at Alice, Lyndy suspected she might've seen it too.

"Come then, Fred." McCormack mockingly stressed the familiar address used by the caddie. "The links beckon."

With golfers' goodbyes said, Alice excused herself to change, leaving Hamish and Lyndy to finish their breakfast in silence, Hamish picking up *The Scotsman* and Lyndy wishing he'd brought his racing sheet to read. When the creak and rumble of a carriage drifted in from the drive, Hamish set aside his paper to watch out the window. With nothing better to do, Lyndy followed his gaze but spotted nothing more interesting than the swaying back end of the departing coach. Bored, Lyndy craned his neck to read the newspaper headlines. It was all bad news: a ship's sinking, an uprising, a devastating storm. When Lyndy sat back, Hamish continued to stare out the window, a satisfied smile slowly spreading across his face. Lyndy tugged the linen tablecloth taut, causing the glassware to wobble. Tonight, the newspapers would read, Two People Dead at Glenloch Hill.

What did Hamish McEwen have to smile about?

CHAPTER 19

"Ready?"

Not waiting for Lyndy's response, Stella spurred Morag into motion, the saddlebag containing picnic snacks bouncing in syncopated rhythm as she urged the mare into a canter. Stella didn't know where she was going, letting the mare lead the way into the valley in the opposite direction from St. Andrews. The breeze was gusty, humid, and cool. Who would've guessed it was June! Stella was glad she'd opted to wear her heavier tweed riding attire. They cut across fields, navigating flocks of sheep, and with every horse length they put between them and Glenloch Hill, the easier it was to relax.

Stella didn't need to look over her shoulder to know that Lyndy's muscular Arabian was covering the ground with ease, matching Morag stride for stride, but she wanted to see Lyndy and reassure herself that he was near.

Yesterday had been the most taxing day since her father died. It wasn't so much Sir Edwin's brutal murder. That was upsetting and abhorrent, yes, but she'd encountered death and murder many times and hadn't been particularly attached to

Lady Atherly's former lover. But the constant worry that Lyndy would be blamed for it was almost too much to bear. And yet when they'd discovered poor Aggie's confessional note, Stella didn't feel the relief she'd expected. Why? She'd spent half the night trying to unravel the root of her misgivings. Was it because she couldn't come to terms with Aggie's actions, the guilt she might've played a part in them, or her belief that the maid wasn't capable of murder?

Aggie certainly had a motive, assuming it was Sir Edwin who'd attacked her. But was it? But why would Aggie lie? To protect someone else, maybe? The only person Stella could think of was Fergus. But if so, why not simply confess to the crime? Why make the ultimate sacrifice for someone else? A year ago, Stella wouldn't have fathomed how anyone could do such a thing. But now? To protect the man she loved? That she understood.

Stella smiled at Lyndy, riding step by step beside her. He hadn't shaved this morning, and the stubble shadowed his dimpled chin, lending him a relaxed and rustic air. She'd believed the day she married him she couldn't love him more. And then, at Christmas, she'd thought so again. But these past days at Glenloch Hill, with him punching Sir Edwin and being suspected of his murder, Stella felt a fervent protectiveness she'd never experienced before. Not even of Tully, her beloved horse.

Lyndy was a grown man, obviously capable of defending himself physically. He didn't need her help. And yet . . .

A large stream, or burn as the locals call it, rose fast upon them. Together, they plunged their horses into it, spraying water onto their boots. Without warning, Angus slipped on the slick stream bottom and stumbled sideways, his legs sprawling for purchase. Lyndy flung himself out of the saddle, allowing the gelding to regain his balance, and landed with a resounding splash that sprinkled Stella's cheeks several feet away.

"Are you okay?"

Lyndy surged out of the water, soaking wet and gasping. "By God, that's cold."

Bits of something green and slimy clung to his pants and his jacket. He even had one trailing down his cheek. He absent-mindedly wiped it away.

"Not much fun, eh, old chap." Lyndy patted Angus, who stood stock-still but snorted in reply.

Lyndy ran his hands along the length of Angus's legs and, finding nothing noticeably wrong, retrieved the reins and led him the rest of the way across. Stella and Morag followed cautiously a few yards behind.

Stella slid from the saddle the moment Morag reached dry ground. "That was a close one. It's amazing neither of you got hurt."

"First lucky break in a while. We were due, wouldn't you say?"

They let the horses loose to graze and walked to the relative privacy of a copse of trees. Lyndy began stripping off his wet clothes.

"You didn't bring anything to change into. Do you want me to get a saddle blanket?"

"Maybe later."

"It's not that warm out." Stella still hadn't gotten used to the coolness of a British summer. "You'll freeze."

Lyndy laughed. "You might, but I'm used to this."

With nothing on but his riding breeches, he beckoned with open arms, and Stella snuggled into his embrace, his bare chest and arms damp against her, all her concerns momentarily held at bay. She plucked another bit of green from his hair.

"Besides, I can think of something certain to keep us both warm," he said, smirking.

"I'm sure you can."

He lowered his lips to hers, and Stella giggled against them. "Maybe now's the time to get that saddle blanket?"

*   *   *

Mrs. Graham could hear the muffled voice of the English lady's maid through the closed door. Eakins, whom her mistress oddly called by her Christian name, Ethel, had been busy mending a tear in one of Her Ladyship's skirts when the housekeeper passed the servants' hall on the way to her study. The scullery maid and hall boy, laying the table for the servants' morning tea, and the second housemaid, having paused in her sweeping of the floor, had been listening with rapt attention to one of Eakins's stories. From what Mrs. Graham gleaned in the few seconds she'd heard, Viscountess Lyndhurst was no ordinary noblewoman.

The housekeeper knew Her Ladyship was a horsewoman, hailing from America and a horse breeding farm that boasted supplying Thoroughbred racehorses to the King. But had she truly ridden against the men in a Boxing Day point-to-point race? Picturing the right and proper Mrs. McEwen, who also adored being in the saddle, Mrs. Graham couldn't imagine such a thing.

But then again, she couldn't believe wee Aggie was dead, branded a confessed murderer who'd taken her own life.

And she such a bonnie, God-fearing lass.

Mrs. Graham, trying to focus and failing, tallied the receipts from the butcher for the third time. A single tear dropped from the tip of her nose to blot the paper.

She'd been a wee bit put out, having the inspector commandeer her study yesterday to interrogate her staff and sullying her space with talk of murder. This little corner of Glenloch Hill had been her sanctuary since she'd become its housekeeper over a dozen years before. Where else could she have vented her frustration or shed tears away from the prying eyes and listening ears of the staff? No one—not the mistress, the maids, not even Mr. Stevenson—dared broach the threshold without her say-so.

Yet she couldn't keep Eakins's voice from seeping under the door. Nor could she quiet the memory of Aggie, some months ago, stomping in uninvited and complaining about the injustice of not being able to step out with Fergus as she'd like to. "Life wasn't fair," Mrs. Graham had told her.

"Ye can say that again, ye pure dafty," the housekeeper muttered, wiping her wet cheek with the back of her hand. How she wished she could return to fretting over such silly things as having her study invaded.

The housekeeper dropped the receipt and the pretext of getting anything done and got up to water her ferns, noticing the brass watering can could do with a bit of polish. Life wasn't fair, but Mrs. Graham held the power to deliver justice. But could she do it? She'd be risking her position, maybe even her life, to see Aggie get what she deserved.

Gasping for a cup of tea, Mrs. Graham abandoned the ferns, the accounts, and her study and ambled toward the servant's hall, steeling her features to hide her concern.

"Yer aff yer heid!" the scullery maid declared as the housekeeper's jingling keys announced her approach to the open doorway. Too caught up in her argument to notice, the maid vehemently continued. "Yer telling fairy stories, ye are. What kind of noble lady helps the police solve crimes?"

"It's true," Eakins shot back. "Inspector Brown of the Hampshire Constabulary is a regular visitor at Morrington Hall. And even on her honeymoon in York, my lady unearthed a murderer that the police couldn't catch."

"She's really seen that many dead bodies?" Jamie, a footman who'd arrived early for tea, asked.

"Let me see. First, there was the vicar."

The lady's maid proceeded to rattle off names, lifting a finger to count each one as she did. When she reached five, the housekeeper stuffed the handkerchief she'd been using up her sleeve and stepped in. The footman and chambermaid, afraid to have been caught slacking, immediately bent their heads and bustled about with their chores. The boisterous maid squeaked in surprise and dashed back to the scullery. Satisfied, Mrs. Graham addressed Eakins.

"That's enough blethering on aboot that, lassie. It doesnae dae anyone any guid, especially after . . ." With Aggie's specter hovering over them, she didn't elaborate. The scullery maid had already invoked the fairies. There was no need to be calling up ghosts. "Now, mind yer work and clear this away." She waved her hand as if to make the spools of thread on the table disappear. "We're aboot to have tea."

The lady's maid, properly chastised, gathered up Lady Lyndhurst's damaged skirt and her sewing kit and said nothing more. But Eakins, with all her talk, had given Mrs. Graham an idea, a hope. Perhaps she could do something for Aggie after all. If the lady's maid's boasts had any merit, Mrs. Graham had found the person she could unburden her awful secret to.

But when and how?

The housekeeper hid her doubt and gratitude behind a steely stare that chased the lady's maid from the room.

After their brisk morning ride, Stella tried savoring the comforting heat of her wool tweed skirt, a patchwork of tightly woven, crosshatched shades of woodland browns and greens. She'd had the tweed ordered from the Isle of Harris specifically for this trip. But although the skirt swished heavily around her legs like a blanket, thoughts of Lyndy being suspected of Sir Edwin's murder still brushed the edges of her mind, giving her chills that no fabric, no matter how thick, could warm.

Why couldn't she put it behind her?

"Didn't realize I was so peckish until now," Lyndy said as they headed for the side patio where the others were having luncheon outside. "Must be all that exertion during our . . . ride." He chuckled mischievously at his barely veiled innuendo.

"Lyndy!" Stella laughed nervously, shocked he'd say such a thing out loud.

She playfully swatted his arm while hoping no one was within earshot. But there was Mrs. Graham, the housekeeper, her posture as straight and still as a guard at Buckingham Palace, her eyes darting around like she was anticipating something. When their eyes met, the housekeeper spurred into motion toward her.

"Watch out!" Stella called, helpless to do anything more to keep the housekeeper from stepping into the path of a footman carrying a tray intended for the luncheon table. How could Mrs. Graham not have seen him coming?

The housekeeper, flailing her arms out in front of her in an attempt to keep her balance, careered into the footman, upturning his silver tray. The porcelain serving dish slipped off and clattered to the parquet floor, leaving a heap of inedible Scottish smoked salmon fillets scattered across the hall. Still unsteady and lurching about, Mrs. Graham stumbled straight into Stella. With Lyndy distracted by the distraught footman kneeling on the floor between them, Stella caught the woman's weight, the force compelling her backward. It was a wonder they didn't both tumble to the ground.

"Meet me at the Monument at half-past two, alone. Please."

The barely whispered entreaty gained volume in Stella's head as Mrs. Graham promptly regained her balance, overly apologetic for being lightheaded and "imposing upon Her Ladyship."

Had Stella heard right? Had Mrs. Graham just requested a secret assignation? Had the housekeeper's fumbling and bumbling been an elaborate charade orchestrated in order to have a private word with Stella? Or had the housekeeper taken the opportune time to convey her request? And why the monument on the hill's summit? What could Glenloch Hill's housekeeper possibly have to say that required meeting in such a remote spot?

Unless it had something to do with the recent deaths.

Her curiosity piqued, but conceding she wouldn't learn more now, Stella asked after the distraught chambermaid who found Aggie and graciously accepted more of the housekeeper's profuse apologies before she and Lyndy left Mrs. Graham bellowing for the footman to fetch more help to clean up the mess.

They stepped onto the patio to join Hamish, Virginia, and Jeanie Agnew at the table. She'd hesitated to eat outside in this chill, but the hedges sheltered the spot from the wind and the midday sun lit the crisp white linen tablecloth like a beacon. The faint scent of roses mingling with freshly baked loaves encouraged Stella further.

"Did you hear what the housekeeper—?" She leaned into Lyndy but stopped in midsentence.

"Dinnae worry yersel aboot it, hen. It's over," Hamish emphatically declared as if he didn't want to discuss it again.

"Is it?" Virginia said.

"Sorry we're late," Lyndy announced, straightening his tie. Had he seen the way Hamish flinched? Virginia's abruptly downcast eyes?

"Lord and Lady Lyndhurst," the widow said. "We were told ye were having a wee picnic along the burn." Only Mrs. Agnew had welcomed them with something other than surprise. She looked amused, like a cat contemplating its trapped prey.

"No, just a light snack."

Lyndy focused on the top rail of the chair he held out for Stella, but the slight smirk gave away what he was thinking. Or remembering, to be precise. Stella couldn't stop the blood from rushing to her cheeks. Mrs. Agnew chuckled knowingly.

"Just glad ye could make it," Hamish said, remaining in his seat. The McEwens didn't stand on ceremony. "Sit down. Sit down. We've only just started."

"Had a bit of a run-in with a few members of your staff,

though, McEwen." Lyndy took the empty seat beside Stella. He'd shown no indication that he'd heard the housekeeper's whispered message, and Stella hadn't finished telling him.

"I do hope everything's all right?" Virginia asked, looking more haggard than ever. The toll the past few days had taken on her was evident on her face.

Stella hadn't seen the mistress of the house since dinner the night before. Had Virginia gotten any sleep at all?

As if preempting Stella's questions or Lyndy's answer, Hamish patted Virginia's hand, clutching the edge of the table, and said, "I'm sure everything's okay."

Virginia kneaded the back of her neck until her pale skin turned red. "Stella?"

"Nothing terrible. It's just that the smoked salmon might not be on the menu anymore." Stella forced a lighthearted laugh she didn't feel. Virginia's uneasiness was contagious. But Stella's reassurances worked. Virginia relaxed her hands, appeased.

"That's grand," Jeanie Agnew said. "I don't have to pretend to fancy it, then." Her barrage of high-pitched giggles, aimed equally at everyone at the table, eased the tension.

"Oh, Jeanie. Why didn't you tell me you don't care for salmon?" Virginia chided.

"How can ye forget Ole Fish Tongue? I've never eaten salmon again after that."

Lyndy enthusiastically sampled the hot stew the butler set before him as the two women bent their heads, giggling like schoolgirls about a prank played involving a smoked salmon fillet and a school instructor's pet dog's tongue. Stella didn't find their past antics funny but appreciated Virginia's desperate need to laugh.

"So, McEwen, how was the golf this morning?" Lyndy asked.

"Lively but a bit wind-battered. We thought we'd get a wee rest and a bite before returning tae catch the final round's last few holes. Alasdair and Freddy opted tae dine in town. Lady Alice chose tae join them."

"And Freddy?" Stella asked, blowing on her spoonful of hot stew, her stomach growling at the scent of beef and oats. "How is he doing?"

"I fear the young laddie is trailing a bit."

"A bit?" Jeanie scoffed laughingly, slathering butter on a roll. "Freddy Kentfield shot the highest round in the field."

"Sadly, that's true," Hamish agreed, settling his teacup.

"But Alasdair is doing quite well," Jeanie added. "He's tied for third place."

Stella couldn't care less about anyone's golf score, but it told her what she wanted to know. Poor Freddy was taking his father's death hard.

The conversation shifted to the merits of the Old Course versus other link courses around the country, but Stella paid little attention. Her mind drifted from Freddy's golf score to his state of mind to thoughts of Sir Edwin's murder to questions about Aggie's death to what Hamish and Virginia were whispering about before she and Lyndy arrived at the table. What had Hamish meant? That the horror of the past few days was over? If so, why did Virginia question it? Was she like Stella? Bothered by the *facts* of the case, bothered like a scratch she couldn't reach?

When the table fell silent for a minute, Stella took advantage of the lull. "Did Aggie have any family?"

"Now, what does that have to do with Muirfield?" Jeanie Agnew said. "I thought we were talking about golf courses. Did yer laundress hail from Gullane, Ginny?"

Virginia's face fell. "No, her aunt and sisters live in Edinburgh."

Stella could imagine how that grief would be compounded by learning how and why Aggie died. She said as much.

"They'll be devastated, I'm sure," Virginia continued, now plucking at her eyelashes, one coming out between her fingers.

She blew it away. "And not just by the loss of Aggie. I have it from Mrs. Graham that the maid diligently sent most of her earnings back home."

What else did the housekeeper know? Lifting the chain of Lyndy's pocket watch tucked into his waistcoat, Stella grabbed it and flicked it open. It was one thirty.

"And what of that poor laddie she had her eye on?" Jeanie's compassionate sigh drew a frown from Virginia.

"What lad?"

"Aye, well . . ." Hamish said, in a tone meant to convey he wanted to move on to something else, "So, Stella, tell me a wee bit about this long-lost cousin of mine. I'd love tae ken more about Elijah."

"Daddy?"

The reference took Stella by surprise. Hamish refused to discuss the maid, who sent money home to her family and wanted nothing more than to be able to meet with her beau without fear of reprimand, who'd been demoralized and traumatized to the point of murder and suicide, but was willing for her to talk about Elijah Kendrick who, with the hindsight she'd gained from almost a year past his death, was nothing but an oppressive self-serving tyrant? Stella paused, pressing her nails into her palms as she tried to control her mounting frustration. How could she satiate Hamish's curiosity without expressing her aversion to his choice of subject matter?

Lyndy cleared his throat. "I think the less said, the better."

"Oh?" Jeanie Agnew leaned in, intrigued by Lyndy's deflection. "But isn't that in part why yer here? To enlighten Hamish about the Kendrick side of his family?"

Hamish agreed. "From what I ken, yer father built his racehorse breeding dynasty with his own hands. I, too, am a selfmade man. I can appreciate the difficulty of succeeding when all the odds are against ye. It warms my heart, it does, that kin of mine emigrated and thrived in America."

But at what cost? Stella wanted to shout. Elijah Kendrick

sold his daughter, like one of his racehorses, for the price of entry to Mrs. Astor's ballroom.

Hamish, wearing a self-congratulatory smile, as if he could take some of the credit by mere familial association, added, "Is it true that yer father once sold a Thoroughbred tae His Majesty when he was the Prince of Wales?"

"Really?" Mrs. Agnew exclaimed.

"Did you get to meet His Majesty when he visited America?" Virginia wanted to know.

The three of them waited in anticipation, expecting her to expound on the virtues of her father, his business acumen, and his supreme luck to have the current King of Great Britain as a former customer. But Stella couldn't stomach one more word of misplaced pride. Echoes of her father's ugly empty boasting bounced in her head like the scattered pearls of a broken necklace. Besides, she now saw a way to extricate herself from the table to meet Mrs. Graham.

"No, I didn't. Now, if you'll excuse me." She threw down her napkin, pushed back her chair, and strode away.

CHAPTER 20

Lyndy lingered, flipping the silver soup spoon between his fingers, torn between following Stella and sitting back down. He wanted answers. But when he'd risen from his chair, Stella had waved him off. Lyndy abhorred seeing her upset, especially about her deceased father, but he also knew his wife. He'd seen the faraway, preoccupied glint in her eye. She was up to something. And then there was the husband and wife, clearly on edge. Something wasn't right here either.

"Ach, I dinnae mean tae upset yer wife," Hamish said, gently squeezing Virginia's shoulder. She offered Lyndy a sad sympathetic smile. "Bad blood there, eh?"

"Stella will be the last to tell you, but Elijah Kendrick was not a gentleman by birth or behavior. Now, if you'll excuse me."

"But Lord Lyndhurst," Jeanie Agnew objected, batting her lashes at him. "Ye just got here."

The snip snip crack of someone trimming hedges made up Lyndy's mind. He'd give Stella the space she needed and, ignoring the widow's pout, stretch his legs a bit. If he learned something by chance, all the better. With a courteous nod,

Lyndy left the table and strode toward the sound to find the groundskeeper slashing the evergreens at a reckless pace. The scent of the freshly cut laurel reminded Lyndy of Battenberg cake.

"I say, Fergus, is it?"

"Aye." Boughs tumbled as the shears crashed together without stopping.

"I wonder. With your cottage so close, did you happen to see the laundry maid at all yesterday, before . . ."

Lyndy couldn't bring himself to finish the sentence. He didn't even know why he was asking. The maid had killed Sir Edwin and then herself. Full stop. Lyndy should take his own advice and leave it be. So, what propelled him to the base of this hedgerow to question a possible witness to the maid's temporary madness? Was it Stella's unease? Or did he, too, hold some doubts?

The scrape of iron on iron as the shears connected again and again grew in intensity as the groundskeeper, no longer watching what he was doing, hacked at the innocent hedge, marring its previous symmetry.

"By God, I wish I had. If only I hadnae been too busy. If only I'd realized how distraught Aggie truly was."

If only, if only, if only. The phrase had no place in Lyndy's vocabulary. He wasn't one to question his actions or why fate had dealt him a particular hand. He was more the type to face challenges as they came—some for the better, like Stella, and some for the worse, like the police's suspicion of him in this ugly business. *If only* never did anyone a bit of good.

"You can't blame yourself. What's done is done."

"Easy for ye tae say."

With a particularly violent slash, Fergus took a gouge out of the top. Leaves and stems fluttered everywhere, and before Lyndy knew it, he was looking down the stretch of the sharp shears from the wrong end. Fergus's face flushed, and his lips flared like a distressed horse baring his teeth.

"From where I stand, ye have everything and I have nothing."

From where Lyndy stood, Fergus was a man capable of violence. Unfortunately, Lyndy was all too familiar with the type. It was why the police had suspected him, after all. But Lyndy had never raised his hand to any man who was undeserving or hadn't proven himself a threat.

With only his fists for defense, Lyndy backed up until the groundskeeper returned to taking his hostilities out on the hedge. If all was as the police claimed it to be, there was nothing more to say. But if it arose that Aggie hadn't killed Sir Edwin, as Stella suspected, then the groundskeeper was an excellent suspect.

"You have my deepest sympathies."

And he meant it, remembering the rage, the thirst for retribution, the sense of impotence to protect Stella he'd felt when he'd learned a man had pressed his unwanted attentions on his wife. No, Lyndy and this groundskeeper were not so different. But at least Lyndy knew he hadn't killed Sir Edwin.

But this chap? Lyndy wasn't so sure.

Stella was breathing hard after the steep final quarter of the climb. Curiosity had propelled her up the path at a heart-pumping pace. Breaking through the last line of trees, she entered a grassy clearing at the hill's summit, dominated by a large stepped stone pedestal with a circular column and a beautifully carved unicorn jutting a dozen feet into the air. The panoramic view was breathtaking: miles and miles of lush green hills, valleys bursting with villages, and the North Sea hazy on the distant horizon. How right Hamish was to suggest a visit.

Unfortunately, Stella hadn't come for the view.

Dwarfed in the monument's shadow, Mrs. Graham craned her neck, contemplating the unicorn as if she expected it to leap off its perch and ride away. Without acknowledging Stella's approach, she declared wistfully, "It's said that this mercat cross once stood in the square of one of the local villages a hundred years ago."

"What's it doing here, then?" Still trying to catch her breath, Stella massaged a cramp in her side.

"Rumor has it a previous occupant of the house won it at cards." Stella expressed her disbelief. No one wins a town's monument from a turn of a card or a roll of the dice. "Some truths are harder tae believe than others," the housekeeper answered cryptically.

"That's true enough, but you didn't feign being lightheaded and secretly ask me up here to tell me that."

"Nay, I need tae tell ye some of those difficult truths and couldnae take the chance of being overheard or suspected of meeting with ye."

Mrs. Graham regarded Stella for the first time, sizing her up like a new scullery maid. Stella withstood the scrutiny in silence, hoping to get to the bottom of things quickly. She was near bursting with curiosity, wanting to know what was going on.

"I'm risking me position, maybe even me life, tae tell ye what I ken."

Stella's stomach flipped with dread and anticipation. "Why trust me?"

"I have tae tell someone. When I heard yer lady's maid speak of ye solving crimes and seeking justice, and with ye being an outsider, I hoped if I could trust anyone with me information, it would be ye. I pray I'm right."

"You can trust me." Stella appreciated the woman's confidence and, shoving aside any thought of the cost or consequences, urged the housekeeper to continue.

"Aggie planned tae leave Glenloch Hill."

"I suspected as much from what Aggie told me."

"She also intended tae run away with Fergus, the groundskeeper. They've been courting without permission for some time."

Stella didn't know about Aggie's plans to leave with Fergus but did know of their attachment. "I knew some of this too."

Mrs. Graham eyed Stella with admiration. "I'm impressed, my lady. From what I ken, Mrs. McEwen was the only other person in the house who kenned of any of this. At least, that is if Aggie spoke tae the mistress like she'd planned tae."

So, Virginia knew about Aggie's plans. Or did she? Stella would soon find out. But was that it? She'd hoped the house-keeper, with her theatrics and clandestine meeting, might've been able to shed some light on either Sir Edwin's death or Aggie's suicide. Stella had hoped Mrs. Graham could tell her something she didn't already know.

"Is there anything else you want to confide?"

Mrs. Graham gazed out over the vista and the darkening clouds lining the horizon and let out a loud resigned sigh. "Aye."

Stella steeled herself for the next revelation.

"I ken a secret about Aggie that I vowed tae take tae me grave. Now that she's in hers, I'm willing tae break me promise tae clear her name before it's too late."

Too late? Stella asked the housekeeper what she meant.

"Aggie was a God-fearing Christian and I cannae stand idly by and watch her buried in an unconsecrated grave."

The words resonated more than the housekeeper could ever know. During their honeymoon in York, Stella and Lyndy had encountered two people who'd gone to terrible lengths to en-sure a dead man was buried in the hallowed ground of a churchyard. The heart-wrenching circumstances had cast a pall on what should've been a celebration of her and Lyndy's rela-tionship.

But that was nothing compared to the recent accusations threatening to take Lyndy away. Stella brushed nonexistent dirt from her tweed skirt to ward off a sudden apprehension, the rough hairy texture oddly soothing.

"I'm sorry, Mrs. Graham, but you and I both know that

someone who commits suicide can't be buried in consecrated ground."

"But dinnae ye see, lassie," Mrs. Graham, in her distress, forgot the social barriers between them and grasped Stella's shoulders as if she intended to shake some sense into her. Stella hugged herself tightly in defense. "Aggie didnae kill herself."

"How do you know this?"

Mrs. Graham stepped back and mimicked Stella by crossing her arms across her chest. From a distance, they must've looked like two adversaries facing each other down. Instead, they were two women fighting to keep the ugly world at bay for a few more minutes.

"Did ye ken that it's required of all laundry maids tae be able tae read and write?"

"I didn't, but what does that have to do with anything?"

"Because Aggie couldnae dae either. She was me best mate's eldest bairn. Before Freya died delivering her youngest, I promised tae look out for the wee lass. Aggie came tae me illiterate but strong and eager, and Glenloch Hill was desperate for a capable laundry maid. We designed a system so Aggie could keep track of the laundry with no one being the wiser. I always meant tae teach her but never found the time."

"So, Aggie never learned to read and write?"

"Nay. Never."

Stella's mouth went dry. "Then she couldn't have written the suicide note. Someone else must have."

"Aye. Exactly."

CHAPTER 21

"May I?" Stella had returned from the hilltop to find Lyndy gone and the McEwens and Jeanie on the lower lawn.

Virginia, a blue cashmere blanket draped across her lap, gestured for Stella to take the wicker lounge chair beside her. Between the chairs sat a small table laden with a silver tea service.

"Help yourself," Virginia said, watching Jeanie and Hamish play tennis over the rim of her teacup. The pair laughed and goaded each other as one or the other made a good shot.

Stella declined the hot tea. With the hike and the housekeeper's revelation, her mouth and throat were dry. What she needed was a tall glass of cold water. Stella said as much, and Virginia sent the footman, standing unobtrusively along the tall hedges surrounding the lower lawn, to fetch a pitcher and glass.

"I'm sorry for leaving so abruptly."

Virginia dismissed the apology. "Lyndy explained everything. I'm sorry to learn your father wasn't a kind man."

Hearing it from a stranger was odd. Stella fought her desire to defend Daddy as she'd done many times, but Virginia was right. Elijah Kendrick had been a lot of things, but kind wasn't one of them.

"Weren't you going to watch the final round of golf?"

"I'm not up to it, but Hamish and Jeanie still are. They just wanted to get in a quick game before they went. Hamish can only take so much standing and watching. He much prefers to participate and play. I'm here for the fresh air."

They sat in silence, listening to the rhythmic plonk of the tennis ball being hit back and forth, back and forth, as Stella considered and rejected subtle ways to learn what she wanted to know.

After several minutes of frustration, Stella gave up deliberating and blurted, "Did Aggie give you her notice?"

Virginia's throaty laughter faded as quickly as it had erupted. "Sir Edwin said you were curious to a fault."

"He wouldn't have been the first," Stella admitted.

Virginia set down her empty teacup, her free hand clutching the cameo broach pinned to the lacy bodice of her dress. "I'm sorry, Stella. That came out wrong. You took me by surprise, is all. And to answer your question, yes, Aggie did approach me about her desire to leave our service."

"How did she seem?"

"Upset, determined, a bit frightened. To be honest, I was more confounded than suspicious. I remember discussing it with the others right after the maid gave notice and how . . ." Virginia paused, as if trying to find the right word, "dreadful the whole incident was, and how none of us could fathom why she felt the need to leave. Her attacker was dead. She was safe. She'd never have to face him or worry about him doing anything to her again. So why leave now?"

Her words grew weighted and heavy, as if she was trying to fathom the maid's reasoning, imagining how she would feel in Aggie's shoes. Stella knew because she'd done the same thing. Any woman would.

"Of course I granted her wish, with the understanding she'd stay until a replacement was found. I never did consider that she'd killed Sir Edwin, but it explains a lot, doesn't it? Jolly good shot there, Jeanie," Virginia shouted and clapped as if she hadn't just been discussing murder. But her hands were shaking as she hid them under the blanket in her lap. "Why do you ask?"

"Because something just doesn't feel right."

"A murder and a suicide? Of course it doesn't feel right."

How could Stella explain her suspicions to Virginia when they weren't clear in her own head? "Did Aggie say anything about Fergus, the groundskeeper?"

Virginia laid back her head and closed her eyes. "Oh, Stella, I don't know anything more."

Stella didn't believe her. And knowing what she did about Aggie, Stella couldn't let it go, even if Virginia looked exhausted. "Hamish didn't know the Kentfields, did he? It was you who knew them from school. The Kentfields and Alasdair McCormack, right?"

Virginia's eyes popped open. Her breath grew suddenly more shallow and rapid, her cheeks flushed as if with fever. She shifted in her seat, unable to find a comfortable position. "Yes. Why?"

Virginia's clipped tone sounded defensive. Had Stella touched on a sore subject?

"Because I overheard Hamish and Sir Edwin arguing over the last time Hamish saw Richard Kentfield."

"Hamish and Edwin? Arguing? About Richard? I can't think why. Besides," her words became stilted, as if she'd dredged up an old memory, a rote lesson from her school days memorized and rehearsed, "that's all over. It's all in the past. Dwelling on it won't change anything. As Hamish likes to say *Look afront tae where you'll live*. Look to the future because that's where you'll spend the rest of your days."

What was she referring to? What was in the past? Richard's death or whatever connected Hamish to the Kentfield brothers?

"I'm just trying to understand how everyone is connected. You stayed in contact with Alasdair but hadn't seen Sir Edwin in years. Why would he come to Glenloch Hill after all this time? How does Hamish even know Sir Edwin and Richard?

And why would Richard mention Hamish in his letters to Sir Edwin?

Virginia curled her arms against her chest like a frightened child and began biting her nails and rubbing her neck. "Please, Stella, I don't know."

"Oof!"

Trying to smash the tennis ball over the net that stretched the width of the grassy court, Hamish had miscalculated how close he was. Before he could slow his forward momentum, he'd hit the net midtorso, flopping over it like a mail sack across a saddle. He dropped his racquet and, staggering back, fell onto his backside. The ball bounced high, well out of Jeanie's reach.

"That's game." Hamish laughed hoarsely.

Virginia flung off the blanket, her inhalations too quick, too shallow, as she swung her feet around and stood. "I'm sorry," she muttered.

Stella, having risen from her seat as well, lunged barely in time to catch the fainting woman. Virginia's weight propelled Stella, tumbling back against the table, rattling the tea set. Stella clipped the tray with her elbow, toppling the teapot and creamer, which splashed black tea and milk across the polished silver and dripped into the grass.

With all her strength, Stella nudged Virginia's body to the side, relieving the pressure against her chest. "Are you okay?"

"I'm so terribly sorry," she whimpered in embarrassment.

Her shoulder dug into Stella as Virginia struggled to rise. Stella pushed her from behind to help. Shouting for assurances, Hamish used his racquet to push himself from the ground, but Jeanie was first at Virginia's side, grabbing her friend's outstretched hands and swiftly pulling her off Stella's lap.

"I'm so sorry," she repeated between shallow gasps as Hamish joined them. Despite her apparent frailty, she ran to him like a widow seeing her drowned sailor return from the sea's depths. "Oh, Hamish, but you gave me such a fright."

"Me? Hen, ye nearly collapsed."

What was going on? Had Virginia's palpable nervous distress and exhaustion caused her to overreact and faint? Or was it all an act? Stella hated how suspicious her nature had become but didn't believe in coincidences. Virginia had purposely avoided Stella's inquiries about the connection between Sir Edwin and his brother and Hamish. What didn't she want Stella to know? Or was the truth so horrible to face that she had collapsed? Again.

"Please go back to your game," Virginia was saying. "I hate that I interrupted your fun."

"Nay, nay. I'll take ye back tae the house."

"No." She waved off her husband and stretched out on her lounge chair again. "Please, it would make me feel better if you finished your game."

"Are ye sure yer all right, Ginny?" Jeanie asked, frowning at her friend.

"She's not," Hamish insisted. "She needs tae lie down."

"Don't make a fuss, Hamish. I *am* lying down. Just let me rest here a bit, and then when you go to the Open, I promise to have a proper nap."

Hamish and Jeanie resumed their game, reluctantly at first and then enthusiastically again. The footman, who'd returned with Stella's water, whisked away the soiled tea tray, promising to return with a fresh pot while Virginia returned to biting her nails. Stella emptied her glass, the refreshing water cooling her throat.

"That's game, set, and match!" Jeanie declared triumphantly across the lawn, the look of pride and pleasure in direct contrast to her friend's wretchedness.

Stella set down her glass, careful not to rattle it on the metal tray. She didn't know if Virginia could take even the slightest of sudden noises.

"You're not okay, are you, Virginia?" Stella was starting to regret her persistent questioning.

Virginia sighed, curling tightly into her blanket as if the soft thin fabric could protect her or make her invisible. "No, Stella. Two people are dead and . . . Well, would you be?"

"I've been thinking about what you said." Stella urged Morag through the open gate before pulling alongside Lyndy and his horse again. "That whoever wrote the note might've wanted everyone to know Aggie killed Sir Edwin. That perhaps someone saw her do it."

When Lyndy returned after his talk with Fergus, Stella had suggested a private stroll about the estate grounds. She'd told him everything, from Virginia's near collapse while under Stella's interrogation to Mrs. Graham's revelations. In return, Lyndy described Fergus's capacity to seek revenge against Sir Edwin for Aggie's mistreatment. With conflicting suspicious information, they'd decided to order the horses saddled and ride into St. Andrews to tell Inspector Docherty what they'd learned.

"And?" Lyndy said.

"I think you have it backward. I don't think Aggie murdered Sir Edwin, and whoever did, tried to pin it on the maid. Either they were opportunistic, seeing that she killed herself and couldn't deny it, or . . ."

"Whoever killed Sir Edwin also killed the maid? But why?"

Stella shrugged, though Lyndy didn't see her. At that moment, Angus, his gelding, had stopped to graze the tall grass growing along the stone wall that lined the meadow they were crossing, and Lyndy's concentration was on keeping his horse heading toward St. Andrews. They rode the rest of the journey in contemplative silence.

But when they arrived, the inspector wasn't there. According to the desk sergeant, he was attending the last few holes of the golf tournament. They found him on the seventeenth green, where Alasdair's and his playing partner's ball lay along the edge of the road leading to the train station. It wasn't called the Road Hole for nothing. Jeanie Agnew and Hamish hovered at the far end of the crowd, close to Alasdair as he made his attempt. They must've left Glenloch Hill soon after Stella and Lyndy. Freddy and Alice were nowhere in sight.

"May we have a word?" Stella whispered into the inspector's ear as all eyes were on Alasdair.

"Shhh! Just a wee moment, please. I want to see if he makes it."

Stella thought the shot impossible. The ball was on a road, after all. But Alasdair pitched it high into the air, and the ball landed a few inches from the hole. The crowd held its collective breath as it slowly rolled, finally dropping in.

"I say, he is quite fantastic," Lyndy said, his voice raised above the cheers.

"Aye," Inspector Docherty agreed. "With that shot, Mr. McCormack just tied for second, with the eighteenth left to play." As the crowd and players gravitated toward the next tee, he added, "Now, what was it ye wanted to talk to me about?"

"Not here." Stella led the way toward the sound of the surf. She crested a hillock and the North Sea spread out before her, seagulls dashing and dipping among the waves. She appreciatively inhaled the fresh salty air.

"What's all this, then?" the inspector fumed. "Do ye want me to miss the last pairing?"

"We've learned something you need to know about Sir Edwin's murder," Lyndy said.

"I thought I'd closed that case."

"But this new information questions your conclusion," Stella said.

Docherty squinted at her. "And what new information would that be, lassie?"

"The laundry maid who confessed to killing Sir Edwin in her note couldn't read or write."

"And ye know this, how?"

Stella couldn't tell him. Mrs. Graham had taken too many risks already. "On good authority."

"And ye trust this good authority implicitly, do ye?"

Stella never thought to question Mrs. Graham. What motive did she have to lie about such a thing? If the housekeeper were Sir Edwin's killer, she'd have left well enough alone, and if she wasn't, by lying she was putting her life and livelihood at risk by exposing the killer's mistake.

"I do."

Docherty produced his ever-present pipe from the inner pocket of his waistcoat. "But ye know what that means?" he said, pointing the pipestem at Lyndy and then at Stella. The metal band around the bowl caught the light and the eye of a seagull who swooped in to grab it. Docherty shooed it away.

"It calls into question your conclusions," Lyndy said. "There's a possibility that the maid didn't kill Sir Edwin."

"She may not have even committed suicide," Stella added.

"Aye, but nay." The inspector shook his head slowly, frowned, and shoved his pipe between his teeth. "It means ye two should've left well enough alone."

"And why is that?" Stella asked. Shouldn't they be doing all they could to find the truth?

The policeman rummaged around in his pocket and pulled out his tobacco pouch. But instead of plunging the pipe into the loose tobacco leaves, he pointed it at Lyndy. "Because until the maid confessed, ye, laddie, were the best suspect I had."

CHAPTER 22

Cheers and applause resounded after the defending champion, James Braid, putted the last few feet to win the title again. Stella clapped, but her heart wasn't in it, the inspector's words echoing in her ears above the din of the crowd. While the caddies shook hands, Alasdair grudgingly congratulated the winner. Braid acknowledged Alasdair's defeat with a conciliatory pat on the back.

"McCormack will be disappointed," Freddy said, standing beside Stella.

They all stood beside the eighteenth green: Stella, Lyndy, Alice, and Freddy on one side, Hamish and Jeanie on the other. Freddy's caddie, Billy, had been nearby, whispering with a golfer Stella didn't recognize but abruptly walked away when Old Tom Morris joined them.

"What was that about?" Lyndy asked Freddy. "Your caddie has been acting odd throughout the tournament." Alice nodded in agreement.

"I don't know," Freddy said, sounding as surprised as he looked exhausted. He'd finished his round a half hour earlier, barely making it into the top thirty. From his showing on the first day, Stella knew Freddy was capable of winning the tournament. But then his father was murdered.

"The wee laddie must have an aversion tae me," Old Tom Morris quipped, rubbing his hand down the length of his considerable white beard, explaining how he'd had that effect on the caddie from the beginning. Every time Old Tom passed by or approached, Billy Birdwell would stop what he was doing and skedaddle. "I dae have tae wonder why."

Stella wondered too. After Docherty's threat that Lyndy was again his prime suspect, reiterating that Lyndy had a motive in the Thoroughbreds Sir Edwin had left him and showed no qualms about physically assaulting him, Stella had been on edge and on the lookout for someone else she could point the policeman toward. Billy Birdwell's slinking about wasn't much, but it was something. It also made her think of Fergus, the groundskeeper, and what Lyndy had told her about their encounter. He hadn't initially acted suspicious, but he'd not helped himself by blowing his temper with the sharp hedge clippers. Stella asked Freddy or Alice if they'd noticed anything suspicious or threatening about the groundskeeper. They hadn't.

"If yer talking aboot Hamish McEwen's groundskeeper, I ken him well," Old Tom said. "How's he hauding up after his poor lassie died?"

"Not well," Lyndy said. "He's angry and blames himself. Do you think he has cause?"

"To be angry? Aye. He was in love with the wee lass. But tae blame himself? Given the circumstances, he's simply been doing what he thought was right."

"What circumstances?" Stella asked.

Before Old Tom could answer, Alasdair and the others joined them in a round of equal parts congratulations and commiserations. Out of sorts, Alasdair ignored their comments, slipping off his cap and swatting it against his leg as if his loss had sullied it.

"Better luck next year, McCormack," Old Tom said.

"Luck has nothing to do with it," Alasdair griped. "If I weren't so distracted. Does yer caddie ever shut his gob, Kentfield?"

"I say," Freddy sputtered.

"Really, Alasdair," Jeanie chided like a good-natured nanny, rubbing a speck of something from his chin. "You're acting like a child."

Alasdair gave her a stiff smile and removed her hand. "If ye'll excuse me, I must make my loss official." He sulked away.

Stella was happy to see him go. And not just for his ill mood. She wanted to hear what Old Tom was going to say before the others interrupted. "What was Fergus up to, Mr. Morris? You never got to say."

"Well, given that the pair planned tae wed at Hogmanay, he's been working in me shop after hours tae earn extra wages."

"I didnae ken that Fergus was working with ye, Tom," Hamish said.

"Been a couple of months now. He's been right handy during the Open."

"If they've been secretly courting against yers and Ginny's wishes all this time," Jeanie mused, an approving smile on her lips, "then that explains why the maid used the unfortunate incident with Sir Edwin to beg out of service. Even after he was dead."

"I think it was more than an unfortunate incident," Stella said, annoyed that what she'd witnessed, what the maid had gone through, had been reduced to that. "And it was a valid reason for wanting to leave Glenloch, Fergus or no Fergus."

"I suppose," the widow conceded. "Virginia wouldn't have let her go so easily otherwise, would she, Hamish? Such hardworking, loyal maids are so hard to find. Too many girls these days aren't even entering service, but instead are opting to—"

She broke off when Lyndy, unconcerned with such domestic affairs as finding suitable staff, asked, "Was Fergus with you, then, Morris, when Sir Edwin was murdered?"

Freddy flinched as if a bandage had been ripped off.

Old Tom nodded. "Aye, he was there most of the night, repairing clubs."

Like a winter gale through an open window, Old Tom Morris's declaration snuffed out any flickering hope that Fergus was Sir Edwin's killer. With another potential suspect exonerated, Stella was in the dark again.

"Hamish, there's someone I'd like ye to meet," Old Tom said. Catching the eye of a nobleman overly dressed in a black top hat and dinner jacket, the revered elderly golfer added, "Now, if ye'll excuse us."

"Why are you bringing all this up again, Stella?" Freddy complained before the two men and Jeanie were barely out of earshot. "I thought we already knew the maid killed my father."

"Freddy," Stella began, reaching out tentatively toward Freddy, wanting to comfort the blow of what she was about to say.

Fearing what the gesture meant, Alice gripped the crook of Freddy's arm. "What is it?" Alice asked.

"We have reason to believe that the maid might not have been responsible," Lyndy said.

"Then who was?" Freddy repeatedly ran his finger across the scar on his eyebrow, scratching up a fleck of dried skin. "You?"

"Freddy!" Alice gasped. "How can you say that?"

Freddy shrugged her off and took a few steps back before stomping away, Alice on his heels, pleading with him to return. She clutched her skirt in her fist and caught up to him, grasping his elbow. He hadn't gotten far.

"I'm sorry, Alice." Freddy held up his arms, palms out, his focus leveled on Stella and Lyndy a few yards away.

Without releasing her grip on him, Alice looked over her shoulder to follow his gaze.

Stella sought Lyndy's hand and saw a flicker of concern crinkle in the corner of his eye, the question reflecting back at her. The question that had eluded them so far. The question that they needed to answer. The question Freddy voiced in frustration for all to hear.

"But who else can it be?"

With his protruding belly pressing the edge of the examination table where the dead woman lay covered from ankle to chin, Docherty clenched the unlit pipe in his teeth, the residual sweet scent of tobacco close to his nose counterbalancing the stench of death and formaldehyde a wee bit. Between thumb and forefinger, Dr. Farley held open one of her eyes. Docherty squinted into it, trying not to imagine the maid glaring up at him with an unspoken accusation. The brilliant summer sun bounced off the white-tiled walls, but even that wasn't enough to illuminate what he was looking for.

"I don't see anything."

"Here." Dr. Farley shoved a hand lens at him. "Ye aren't looking carefully enough."

Docherty leaned closer and peered through the thick magnifying glass. As the medical examiner described, tiny red dots marred the victim's eye. "What did ye call it?"

"Petechial hemorrhage. It's uncommon in suicidal hangings."

"But not unheard of."

"Nay, but I also found bleeding into the neck muscles and fractures of the thyroid cartilage, neither of which I suspected tae find with a suicidal hanging."

"The lass left a suicide note, Farley. Even ye said the scratch marks around her neck came from her nails when she changed her mind and tried to loosen the knot."

"And ye said it was a suicide. I had a look under her fingernails. No cloth fibers, but a wee bit of skin. She might've scratched herself trying tae unloosen the knot, but now it seems more likely she fought her assailant as he was choking her."

Docherty refused to believe it. How had he gotten it so wrong?

"The bruising on her neck?"

"Dinnae ye see it, man?"

Farley lowered the thin, overly bleached linen sheet just far enough to reveal the victim's neck. She had fingerlike bruises on her cheeks that Docherty, having seen them in life, assumed had come from Sir Edwin's attack on her. Seeing those paired with that on her neck, he couldn't believe he hadn't recognized the similarities.

"And why didnae ye never mention what she hanged herself with? If ye'd told me bedsheets, I would've been more suspect from the beginning."

"Why?"

"Bedsheets dinnae leave bruise marks, but manual strangulation does." The doctor bristled with anger, his arm shaking, his knuckles white as he stabbed a finger at the inspector. "Ye really botched this one, Docherty. Ye wanted tae tie up the Englishman's murder in a tidy bow by blaming this here poor lassie. Ye should've kept yer conclusions tae yerself until I had a proper look at her."

Docherty flinched. Farley had never had the cheek to speak to him like that. But the inspector had never deserved it before. He distanced himself from the table, pulled out his tobacco pouch, reassured by its weight and the smooth softness of its leather, and cleared his throat.

"So it's yer professional opinion, Dr. Farley, that this lassie didn't commit suicide?" Docherty knew the answer, but had to hear it out loud.

"Ach, what have I been saying tae ye, ye daft bugger? Nay, this wee woman didnae commit suicide. She was murdered."

Docherty stepped back further as Farley respectfully covered the maid's face.

"Out with ye, now," Farley barked, waving Docherty from his examining room. "With two people dead, I'd say ye've got some making up tae dae. And dinnae let them well-heeled friends of yers stop ye from doing yer job."

Farley was right. He'd let his friendship with Hamish and Virginia and his desire to solve Sir Edwin Kentfield's murder quickly so as not to spoil the golf tournament get the better of him. He'd let this poor lass down, not to mention Sir Edwin Kentfield. And time was running out. Docherty had two unsolved murders on his hands, and if he didn't act fast, he could likely be looking at more.

CHAPTER 23

"I've already told ye, Ian. Virginia's having a lie down and I cannae have her disturbed."

"And she won't be." Docherty upended his pipe bowl and tapped it. A few dried bits, vestiges of his last smoke, fluttered out. "My men will be as quiet as a pub come Sunday morning."

Armed with the information that Aggie was murdered, Docherty stood in the drive at Glenloch Hill, his carriage horse snorting and swishing her tail at a fly behind him. Typically an easygoing man, he'd dreaded this confrontation. The inspector and Hamish McEwen had been friends for years, but Docherty couldn't take no for an answer this time. He filled his pipe and headed toward the front door. Having arrived moments earlier from the links, Hamish tossed the reins of his horse to the groom and stepped in Docherty's way.

"Think twice on a thing." Hamish motioned for Stevenson, who came to stand behind him. Now, two men blocked Docherty's path to the door. "Ye dinnae ken whit ye're asking."

"I do, Hamish."

Docherty moved forward, and the two men walked backward to match. When Docherty stepped to the right or dodged to the left, the pair mirrored his movement step for step like twin goalies on a football pitch. He resorted to barreling straight for the door until Stevenson's heel unexpectedly met the threshold, and the butler toppled backward into the open doorway. Docherty stopped short.

"This is absurd. The maid was murdered. Sir Edwin Kentfield was murdered. Both victims were found on this property. Let me through."

Hamish glanced over his shoulder but returned his glare at Docherty when he saw his butler steady again. The stubborn butler mopped his high forehead with a handkerchief but stood his ground. Hamish took a high-kneed exaggerated step back and pointed at the offending threshold.

"Both were found outside the house. I've no issue with yer men crawling and creeping into every inch of the groundskeeper's bothy, the stables, the laundry house, the summerhouse, the gardens, or the grounds. But if ye cross that, ye're risking oor friendship, Ian."

"Ach, it doesn't have to be like that, Hamish. Ye know, I'm just doing my job. Besides, I've already been in the house."

"Belowstairs, aye. But now ye want to rummage through the drawing room, library, and bedchambers, for God's sake. Is nothing sacred?"

"I've given ye all the leeway I can. Now step aside or I'll have my men restrain you."

"Ye wouldnae!" He held his arms tightly against his sides, his nostrils flaring with indignation. "Are ye also going tae drag Virginia from her bed so ye can look under the mattress?"

"Ye know it won't come to that."

"Where does it end, Ian? Ye once said ye'd no need tae search the house, only talk tae the servants. And then ye demanded tae search the sporting room. And now ye want unlimited access tae oor home? How can I trust yer word? I thought we were friends, yet all ye dae is flaunt yer position and intrude on my privacy."

Docherty drew slowly from his pipe, tasting the sweet aroma in his throat. "I'm sorry, Hamish. We are friends, but I'm also a detective inspector sworn to uphold the law." Docherty sighed. How had it come to this? He'd never known Hamish to be so obstinate. "Please, Hamish. Move out of my way, or I'll have to arrest ye for obstruction."

Hamish glared at him for a moment longer before slowly, purposely stepping aside. Docherty put his pipe in his mouth and clenched it between his teeth.

"Thank you for seeing reason, Hamish. We'll be as fast as we can."

"But not with that, ye dinnae. Or did ye already forget Virginia doesnae like ye smoking in the house?" Hamish pointed to the pipe as if it was a loaded pistol. Docherty took it from his mouth.

"I am sorry, Hamish."

After Docherty passed into the hall, Hamish hovered so close, like a bird dog on a scent, that if Docherty hesitated, Hamish would've bashed into the back of him.

"If she gets worse, Ian, it'll be yer fault," he muttered.

Virginia had been looking frail of late, and rumors were spreading that she'd not stepped foot off Glenloch Hill for days, but Docherty had never had cause to wonder why before. She'd always been a courteous and affable hostess, laughing at his jokes, beating him at croquet and snooker, feeding him until he'd thought his buttons would pop. She'd been nothing if not accommodating and friendly. But then again, so had Hamish.

Until now.

"I promise ye. If it can be at all avoided, we won't bother Virginia." But that was where his promise stopped.

As he barked instructions to his men to fan out and search the manor house, Docherty resisted the urge to study Hamish's face, acknowledging he'd see seething disappointment and not the explanation for what he prayed he'd never have cause to expose—what it was his friend was trying to hide.

Having promised to search the service areas, the servants' rooms, and the more communal spaces of the house first, leaving the bedchambers—and any disturbance of Virginia—until last, Docherty witnessed Hamish's visible relief. He continued to dog Docherty, but his demeanor softened as room after room produced nothing of note. He even voiced regret for his overreaction. Docherty appreciated his friend's apology and his return to his usual congenial self but remained dubious as to what had caused the violent objection in the first place. And as Hamish's mood lightened, Docherty grew more glum. How would he solve these crimes if he found nothing to help him?

"Is that every room either downstairs or on the ground floor?" Docherty asked Stevenson as he and his men gathered in the hall.

Beside him, a bouquet of pink roses picked from the trellises that climbed the exterior walls sat wilting in a vase, a cloud of tiny flies swarming around the decaying petals. Next to it lay the salver empty of calling cards. No one wants to visit a home where murder runs rampant.

"Aye, I believe so." Docherty's frown reflected Hamish's at the butler's reply. They'd have no choice but to search upstairs now. "Though there is a storage area under the stairs that I believe hasn't been searched yet."

"Take me to it." Docherty insisted.

Stevenson trudged down the hall, through the green baize door, and down a flight of back stairs. Docherty noted that the storage room was on the way to the wine cellar.

"Why didn't ye show this to us before?" Docherty protested, rubbing his aching knee. He hadn't anticipated having to do calisthenics in the line of duty.

Stevenson shrugged.

After opening the door, the butler dutifully stepped aside. Docherty ducked his head to peer in. With its sloping ceiling, the space was almost the size of a small attic bedchamber. Docherty ordered Arbuckle, one of his more capable uniform policemen, to enter, then followed, the musty smell of rotting wood engulfing him as he squinted to see in the darkness. He wasn't a tall man and was able to stand upright. Arbuckle, more long-legged than most, was nearly bent in half. Hamish, ever the watchdog, squeezed in behind. Waiting dutifully in the hall, Stevenson handed Hamish a lit candle to see by. Against all four walls lay neat stacks of travel trunks, hatboxes, and suitcases as high as they would go. The scurrying scraping sound of an animal's nails on the bare plank floor accompanied Arbuckle's attempt to lift the highest case from the top of the stack. He immediately dropped it to the floor.

"Ach! Careful!" Hamish chided.

"Who do these belong to?" Several trunks were labeled with baggage stickers and nameplates, but Docherty wouldn't readily admit the light was too dim for him to read by.

"Our guests, of course." Hamish pointed to a stack of trunks and cases on the far wall. "Those are oors."

Docherty instructed his officer to search the nearby trunks while he swatted away cobwebs to tackle the McEwens' luggage. With the spiders' silk still clinging to his fingers, he lifted the lids in a quick perfunctory way, trying to convey to Hamish that he didn't expect to find anything. And, happily, he didn't.

"Inspector." Arbuckle knelt beside a trunk with no identifying tags or stickers. "I found this one with the lid cracked open."

"Then what are ye waiting for?"

His man paused. Lifting the lid slowly, he peeled back each piece of tissue paper with pinched fingers, one by one, skittish no doubt of finding another of the furry pests among them. Despite the somber circumstances, Docherty couldn't hold back a chuckle. He'd seen Arbuckle wrestle a drunk weighing more than twenty stones to the ground. Like the mighty elephant, who knew a mouse would be Arbuckle's undoing?

Luckily, he didn't find one.

As his officer was forced to rummage deeper, it became apparent the trunk was fully packed.

"Do you know who this belongs to?" Docherty asked. "Why would so much of this man's wardrobe be stored here?"

"We did have a wee bit of a mix-up with the luggage a few days ago," was all Hamish would admit. "But I thought it had all been straightened out. Stevenson?"

The butler poked his head through the doorway and cleared his throat. "I was aware that Lord Lyndhurst was still missing a trunk."

"Then why wasn't this brought tae his room?" Hamish demanded before Docherty had the chance.

"I believed, sir, that His Lordship's trunk simply never arrived. I had no idea it was here all along."

"But ye didnae look?" Hamish rolled his eyes. "Whit were ye thinking, Stevenson?"

The butler cleared his throat again. "It has been unusually chaotic of late. I do apologize."

"Well, dinnae just stand there looking apologetic. Dinnae pile *would* for the morn. Get this wee trunk to His Lordship's room now!"

Stevenson called for help.

"And I'll want whoever was responsible for putting the trunk in here instead of where it belongs in my study within the hour," Hamish added, his arms crossing his chest. "He and I will be having words."

Loitering nearby, perhaps out of curiosity or guilt, two footmen promptly arrived. As they ducked into the storage space, forcing Hamish to make room by stepping back into the hall, Arbuckle held up his hand.

"Haud off a wee bit, will ye?" He reached into the bottom of the trunk, his arm disappearing past the elbow, and carefully lifted something out. "Dear Lord."

Arbuckle raised his fist, gripping the shaft of a golf club with one trouser leg wrapped around it, the other leg dangling lifeless to the side. The club's wooden head, reflecting the flickering candlelight, looked shiny and polished. But the etched metal ridges on the club face were darker than usual. Could it be dirt or mud or . . . ?

Docherty shooed everyone out and into the brightly lit hall. Arbuckle held out the club for inspection. Docherty didn't need Dr. Farley's hand lens to know what he was looking at this time.

"Lord Lyndhurst's trunk, you say?"

Speechless, the butler nodded. Docherty hadn't believed the young lord capable of such brutality despite his display of temper, but now there was this.

"Is that—?" Hamish asked.

"The club that killed Sir Edwin? Aye, I believe it is."

CHAPTER 24

Stella slipped off Morag and handed the groom the reins without taking her eyes off Inspector Docherty. The inspector stood in the drive, clutching his pipe and sending bursts of smoke into the air. Beside him was a younger uniformed policeman at least a foot taller. They turned at the sound of the horses neighing. The young policeman handed a golf club, its handle wrapped with a handkerchief, to the inspector.

Stella exchanged a concerned glance with Lyndy as he handed Angus's reins to the groom's outstretched hand. Another groom had taken charge of the carriage horses as Alasdair, Alice, and Freddy alighted.

"What's all this, eh?" Alasdair was the first to speak. "Ye look too dour to be our congratulatory committee."

Inspector Docherty ignored the golfer and approached Lyndy. Stella, her heart beating so hard it hurt, grabbed Lyndy's hand. His palms were sweaty.

"Is this the golf club ye used to kill Sir Edwin, laddie?"

"I say!" Lyndy objected.

Alice emitted a strangled cry while Freddy's sharp inhale was audible several feet away.

"You're wrong, Inspector." Stella released Lyndy's hand and placed herself between him and the police, her arms outstretched as if she were a barrier no one could circumnavigate. "As I told you before, Lord Lyndhurst was with me when Sir Edwin was killed. He didn't do it."

"But can ye deny that this club was in yer possession the night of the murder?" He addressed Lyndy over Stella's shoulder as if she wasn't there.

Lyndy gently lowered Stella's arms and urged her aside. She wanted to protect him and resist, to demand to know what he thought he was doing, but the determination in his face spoke volumes. This was his battle to fight.

Lyndy tugged the lapels of his jacket. "I don't deny it was in my bag, nor that I had occasion to use it on Hamish's course that day. But the last time I saw that club, it was with the others in the bag I abandoned on the lawn near the summerhouse."

"Moments before you punched Sir Edwin in the face in front of multiple witnesses."

Stella could've screamed at the inspector's self-righteous calm. But she said nothing because he was right.

"I don't deny that either, obviously, but I will say, in no uncertain terms," Lyndy paused and, speaking through clenched teeth, added slowly and deliberately, "I did not kill Sir Edwin and resent any suggestion otherwise."

"Then why did we find this particular club hidden at the bottom of yer travel trunk?"

The revelation was like a blow to the stomach. Whoever this killer was had tried to incriminate Lyndy. It made finding out who it was all the more urgent.

"It was in Lord Lyndhurst's trunk?" Alasdair said, as if a veil had been ripped off, revealing an ugly truth.

"My trunk has been missing for days," Lyndy said.

"Aye, it was in a storage cupboard," Docherty said. "But ye knew that, didn't ye, lad?"

"No, I'd no idea or the trunk would be in my bedchamber now and not stored away. It's been a bloody nuisance. I've been wearing the same blasted dinner jacket since we arrived." To emphasize his point, Lyndy tugged at his sleeve as if he were wearing the offending jacket instead of his tweed one.

With her mind several steps ahead, racing through a list of everyone working or staying at the house, Stella asked, "Who had access to the closet? Who knew the trunk was there?"

As usual, Docherty ignored her. "Then we will find yer fingerprints on the club, won't we, Lord Lyndhurst?"

Docherty's sudden use of Lyndy's title irritated Stella like fingernails on a chalkboard. Whatever happened to the congenial irreverent *laddie*? And why wouldn't he listen to her?

"Fingerprints? What wee jibberish is this?" Alasdair scoffed.

"Aye, we use quite the modern technology here, Mr. McCormack. If Lord Lyndhurst handled this club, we'll know."

"Then you'll find them," Lyndy said. "But what does that prove? I've already admitted to using the club."

"And you've already established that those clubs could've been picked up or used by just about anyone," Stella reminded him, if he would only listen.

"So?"

It took Stella a moment to realize he was answering her. "So, what if you find someone else's fingerprints on it?"

"His Lordship's fingerprints on the club will be irrefutable proof that he had the means to kill Sir Edwin." He didn't answer Stella's question. "That and the fact that ye profit from the baronet's death and committed a previous assault on the victim makes you, Lord Lyndhurst, the only one with the means and motive to kill him."

"But not the opportunity," Stella insisted. How many times did she have to tell the inspector Lyndy was with her?

"Dear God," Freddy moaned. "He did kill him."

Alice looked at her fiancé, grief-stricken. She was too shy to voice her sense of betrayal. Stella couldn't mourn the rift that gaped suddenly between the two. She was too caught up in her own misery.

Puffing away on his pipe, Inspector Docherty ignored them all. "Lord Lyndhurst, I'm arresting ye on suspicion of the murder of Sir Edwin Kentfield."

"Bloody hell!" was all Lyndy said as the uniformed officer clapped handcuffs around his wrists and, with pressure on his back, guided him toward the waiting patrol wagon. "Bloody hell!"

"No!" Stella shouted, for the first time understanding Lyndy's desire to bash someone with her fists. "I've already told you he couldn't have done it. He was with me." She lunged for Lyndy to prevent them from taking him, but Alasdair grabbed her around the waist, holding her back. She tried to squirm out of his restraint, but his grip was firm. "Lyndy!"

"Bloody hell!" Lyndy repeated like a scratched phonograph record as the officer shoved him into the wagon.

"Yer not helping yer cause with yer tirade, my lady," Alasdair whispered as she continued to struggle against him, trying to pry his fingers off her. "Ye need to calm down and think straight."

"Let me go," she said, seething and preparing to stomp on his foot if he didn't comply.

The golfer released his grip and raised his hands in supplication. "I only meant to help."

"You can't take him, Inspector. He didn't kill anyone!" Stella watched her love and her life rumble away in a wagon, and her fears transmuted into anger at her helplessness.

Alice appeared at her side, tears welling in her eyes, and looped her arm through Stella's for mutual comfort. "What are we going to do now, Stella?"

"What's going on?" Jeanie Agnew appeared in the doorway, dressed in a silk embroidered robe and slippers, the lace of her chemise conspicuous at her neckline. She cinched the belt tighter and sauntered outside, her hand shading her eyes from the sun's sudden appearance through a gap in the clouds. The dinner gong reverberated in the hall behind her.

"Seems Lord Lyndhurst killed Sir Edwin after all," Alasdair said, mournfully shaking his head.

"What? Really?" Jeanie said.

"No, he didn't!" Stella declared. "Lyndy didn't kill anyone."

"The police just arrested him, Stella," Freddy said, as if she needed reminding. "Why else would they do that?"

"They're horribly mistaken."

Alasdair frowned at Stella in sympathy. "What do ye all say to a wee dram? I'm sure Young Kentfield could use one."

Almost sick, Stella freed herself of Alice's tight clinging hold, picked up her skirts in her fists—better that than to use them to punch someone—and ran after the groom leading Morag and Angus to the stables.

"Where are ye going, my lady?" Jeanie called.

"To get my husband freed from jail," Stella shouted over her shoulder.

"Don't be daft, lassie," Alasdair shouted. "Contact a good solicitor; don't go chasing after him. That won't do either of ye any good."

Stella plunged down the path, past the summerhouse, into the woodland, and past the laundry building, her hat's brim flapping as she ran. She yanked out the pins, tearing a hole in the straw, and flung the hat into the bushes.

"Stella!"

Stella almost collided with Hamish as he rounded the corner. A few seconds sooner, before she'd dropped the hatpin, and she might've accidentally skewered him.

"Whoa. Whit's the rush?"

Bent on her goal, she didn't stop or slow her pace.

Hamish reached out as if to grasp her shoulders to prevent her from dashing past. Stella dodged around him, out of arm's reach, and from the wide-eyed look on his face, surprised him into inaction long enough for her to slip past.

"Haud on a wee minute, lass!"

What did everyone expect her to do? Sit on her hands, wait

on a solicitor, drink, dine, and play cards as if Lyndy hadn't just been hauled away like an old cow to slaughter? As if the man she loved wasn't accused of murder? Did they think she should put up her feet and let them hang Lyndy for something he didn't do?

Hang on, Lyndy!

With the stables up ahead, she put all her strength into reaching it. Spotting the groom about to remove Morag's bridle, she waved and shouted for him to stop. The mare, hoping for a treat, nickered in acknowledgment. Without a word, Stella grabbed the reins from the startled groom, launched herself into the saddle, and, with a quick tap of her heels, implored Morag to run.

"Was that quite necessary?"

Lyndy jerked his hand back the moment the constable, a man with pocked skin and onion breath, finished rolling his little finger onto the paper. On the desk lay an imprint of the pads of each of Lyndy's fingers. He studied his inked fingertips, reminded of the times he'd helped Miss Judd, the lovely faithful old servant, pick bilberries near the vicarage. He fancied he wouldn't be rewarded with a mouthwatering pie today.

"Ye ken it is," the constable sneered, revealing two chipped teeth and the likelihood Lyndy wasn't the first to want to punch the smug satisfaction out of him. "We need tae compare yer fingerprints tae those we pulled from the club tae prove yer the cold-blooded killer who's beaten a man to death."

"I didn't kill anyone."

How many times had he said it? It wouldn't sway anyone, his denials. Only when they'd discovered the real culprit would he be believed. But he'd continue to say it, even if simply to make himself feel better.

"Ye keep telling yerself that. But as me gran used tae say, *Nae whip cuts sae sharp as the lash o' conscience.*"

Lyndy had done plenty in his life to warrant the lash of a

guilty conscience, but this wasn't one of them. "I didn't kill anyone."

The constable snatched the steel handcuffs he'd dangled from a nail and snapped one around Lyndy's wrist, the rims of the cold metal biting into his skin again. The constable secured the other cuff to a rung on Lyndy's chair. He tugged to test the strength of the cuff's locks. He did little but rattle the chair.

"That should keep ye."

Lyndy had never been in so little control before. Not even when he'd been forced into a marriage, not of his choosing but required by duty. At least then, Lyndy had felt he had a say as to how he'd treat his new wife, how much time he'd spend with her, how much, and in what ways he'd make his mother pay for requiring it of him. Fate had brought Stella as that bride, and she was everything he'd ever wanted in a lifetime companion. He knew now he didn't deserve her.

Neither do I deserve this.

How often had his temper landed him in a spot of trouble? How often had his title, family, and privilege gotten him out of the tight spot he'd found himself in? Too many to count. And here he was again. He'd be willing to take the blame and pay any penalty for thrashing Sir Edwin. He still didn't regret it. The punch was justified for what his fellow aristocrat had said and done. But accusing Lyndy of murder? That was different. With their suspect in custody, the police would stop searching for the real culprit. Nothing and no one could save him this time.

Except Stella.

"When can I speak with my wife?"

"In due time. That is, if the bonny lass hasnae already run for the Highlands."

Lyndy bristled at the familiar reference to Stella on the brute's tongue. Before he said something he'd regret, Lyndy turned his attention to the procedure playing out before him as the silent Constable Arbuckle studied the fingerprints.

"Well? How long is this going to take?"

The tedium and his nerves were getting the best of him. He already felt like a caged animal. Lyndy tugged at his shirt's sleeve with his one free hand, remembering a split second too late about the ink that now stained the white fabric.

"I dinnae think ye're in a position tae ask too many questions, laddie." The cocky constable poked Lyndy in the back of the neck with the dull end of a pencil. Lyndy snatched at it but restrained, he didn't have a chance. The man danced out of the way, laughing. "Besides, yer not going anywhere, no matter how long it takes."

"Cuskar," Docherty admonished the constable upon entering the room. He rubbed his stomach and belched. Relief flooded his face. "Ye will afford Lord Lyndhurst the utmost courtesy."

"Me apologies, my lord." Unrepentant, Cuskar offered Lyndy an exaggerated mocking bow.

"What have ye found, Arbuckle?" Docherty peered over the silent Arbuckle's shoulder. "He handled the club shaft all right."

"Tell us something we don't know," Lyndy said.

"Please, my lord," Docherty said. "Keep yer comments to a minimum while we sort this out." Lyndy shifted uncomfortably in the wooden chair but held his peace. "But did ye find any other fingerprints, Arbuckle?"

The constable frowned. "And plenty." He pointed to a smear on the club. "This here is but one partial print that doesnae match oor suspect." He spoke about Lyndy as if he were not in the room. Lyndy opened his mouth to object, to remind the man not to speak of him that way, but a look from Docherty stilled the reprimand on his tongue. "I found quite a few others that dinnae match either."

"So, Hamish was right. Anyone could've handled it," Docherty mused to no one.

Lyndy straightened up in his chair, hopeful this would be the end of it. "Then you have no choice but to release me."

"There's mair tae ploughing than whistling, I'm afraid."

Whatever did that mean? Lyndy pressed on. "But if anyone could've had access and anyone could've handled the club, then anyone could've killed Sir Edwin."

"Aye, that's true, but ye, my lord, are still the sole *anyone* with reason to kill the victim." When Lyndy started to object, the inspector pointed his empty pipe at him. "And don't say the maid or her lad. The lass is dead, and the groundskeeper, no matter how much he'd bayed for the Englishman's blood, had an alibi."

But the maid, although she'd been murdered, still could've been guilty of killing Sir Edwin. Nothing said there couldn't be two killers. Lyndy said as much.

"Are ye offering yerself up for the maid's murder as well?" Docherty pressed his hand kindly into Lyndy's shoulder when he blanched at the suggestion. "I didn't think so. Assuming we stick to just the Englishman, ye are still my best suspect. So ye'll understand why I'm not inclined to release ye until I have someone better. Put Lord Lyndhurst in the cell, Cuskar."

The constable, smiling like a hyena, his tongue running over his chipped teeth, unlocked the cuff attached to the chair, yanked Lyndy's arm and hauled him to his feet. "It'll be me pleasure."

"I say!" Lyndy tried to free himself of the man's grip, but it was no use. The constable was as strong as a wild stallion.

"Say all ye like, my lord," Cuskar goaded, chuckling at his witticism as Lyndy futilely struggled against him. "It willnae dae ye a wee bit of guid."

CHAPTER 25

The wind whipped the tears from Stella's eyes but did little to clear her blurry vision. She'd followed the road into St. Andrews she'd taken with Lyndy earlier in the day, but clouded by fear and anger, nothing looked familiar once she got there. Which road led to the police station? She couldn't remember. She led Morag down one broad street and then a narrow one until she was deep in the heart of the town, every sandstone building looking like the next. Despite not knowing where she was going, she couldn't stop. How could she? She had to keep moving. She had to find Lyndy. She had to get him out of jail.

A young woman with a tattered wool shawl with enormous baskets strapped to her back trudged down the middle of a quiet street, eyeing Stella suspiciously. Two old men in tweed caps reeking of fish admired the chestnut Arabian from their stoop as Stella wandered past. Carts and carriages passed, a greengrocer restocked produce outside his shop, and the chime of a church bell rang.

As if life went on as usual.

Suddenly, Morag was off-balance, the rhythmic *clip-clop* of her hoofs off-kilter. Stella pulled up the mare like a jockey in the middle of a race and slid out of the saddle. Sure enough, something was wrong. Poor Morag had thrown a shoe, losing part of her hoof as well. Stella swiveled about, searching for signs of a farrier or stable that could help. It was a broad street she found herself on, and after brushing the tears from her eyes with her sleeve, Stella spotted a stable several blocks away and led Morag toward it. Stella's nerves were on fire, her feet itching to run, but she couldn't risk hurting Morag with anything but a careful slow walk.

The groom offered to stable the mare, but he periodically threw Stella dubious glances as he wrote her and the horse's names in his record book. Following the man's gaze, she noticed her mud-splattered skirts and, putting her hands to her head, remembered discarding her hat. She didn't need a looking glass to know her hair was a windblown mess. Her eyes weren't probably much better.

"Are ye all right, lassie?"

"Not really." Stella smoothed her frazzled hair, what little good it would do. "Could you tell me where the police station is?"

The groom blinked at her accent, and she had to repeat herself. "'Tis but a wee walk."

To Stella's relief, the directions he gave her were simple and she was there in a matter of minutes.

"I'm Lady Lyndhurst and I've come to see my husband." She'd never used her position, money, or new title to demand anything of anyone before, but she'd never felt so desperate.

The constable, a burly man with leering eyes, flipped through one ledger among many on the long mahogany counter and picked his teeth with the sharpened end of a pencil. "I'm afraid that's not possible. My lady." He took in Stella's disarray and chuckled as if he'd told a joke. "He's being processed."

Like a slab of slaughtered meat.

Stella's race into town had been fueled by anger, but now

dread drained her of all energy. She smoothed her hands over the lace bodice of her pink linen dress, brushing away horse hair and soot, willing herself not to give in to despair.

"Then I'd like to speak to Inspector Docherty, please." She'd learned early in life that civility went much farther than demands. She hoped it would prove more successful now too. "If that's possible, Constable . . . ?"

"Cuskar. And it may be." Appeased, the constable took one more lingering look before leaving the desk.

Docherty found her fiddling with the large decorative buttons on her cuffs. "Lady Lyndhurst? Have ye come here all alone, lassie?" As if the impropriety of it was Stella's biggest concern.

"Is he all right? Is Lyndy okay?"

"Judging by his contempt for my officers, His Lordship is quite himself."

Stella sagged against the desk in relief. Docherty indicated the plain wooden bench lining the wall. A stack of unread newspapers sat gathering dust at the far end. Stella refused to sit. She'd finally gotten Docherty's attention.

"You can't seriously think Lyndy killed Sir Edwin?"

Docherty leaned his elbow on the counter, supporting his head in his hand as if he were too tired to stand. "I don't like it either, lass. But seeing as we found the murder weapon among yer husband's belongings and with his fingerprints on it, I had no choice but to arrest him."

"No choice? What does that even mean?"

"Ye must understand. I'm a detective inspector. I'm responsible for the welfare of the citizens of Fife. And what do I have," he counted on his fingers, "not one but two murders, just a few wee miles from where the most prestigious golf tournament in the United Kingdom, if not the world, was being played and—"

Stella's anger returned. "And you need an arrest to make everyone feel comfortable in their beds."

"In a way, aye."

"And you've decided my husband is to be that someone."

"He is the best suspect I have."

"But as I've said repeatedly, I can vouch for his whereabouts on both occasions. He couldn't have done it."

Docherty shrugged. "And ye could be a loyal and bonny wife lying to protect her murdering husband."

Behind her, Stella heard the door slam. Startled, she flinched before swiveling around to see the Countess of Atherly in a spotless cream traveling suit and matching hat, its lavender feathers sticking up perfectly straight, stabbing the point of her closed umbrella toward the inspector, Alice peering from behind her shoulder.

"The Viscountess Lyndhurst does not lie," Stella's mother-in-law declared in her most scathing tone, the one that made even grown men tremble. "And my son, Viscount Lyndhurst, killed no one."

"Oh, Lyndy!" Lady Atherly sighed, dropping back her head in dismay, her umbrella forgotten.

Standing out in the street, her bare head getting damper by the minute, Stella drew closer to offer her mother-in-law comfort, but pulled away at the last moment. Lady Atherly, her eyes held on the sky in supplication, didn't seem to notice.

Inside the police station, Lady Atherly had raised her nose in the air, declaring rank had its privileges and demanding Lyndy be released immediately. Her unquestioned status in the world hadn't prepared her to be politely but insistently escorted from the building. She was too used to getting her way. Stella had stifled her frustration, knowing Lyndy's mother was only doing what she thought best while watching her chance of seeing Lyndy, let alone argue the case for his release, dissipate with every one of Lady Atherly's indignant sighs and subtle jabs.

Raindrops splashed on Lady Atherly's upturned face. Now they all stood on the street, exhausted and defeated and wet.

"I'm so sorry about Sir Edwin," Stella said.

Lady Atherly's expression revealed nothing but fatigue as she nodded in acknowledgment and signaled to the McEwens' carriage driver waiting nearby. "Thank you. It was quite a shock. To you, too, I suppose. You were the one who found him?"

"After a maid alerted me, yes."

"And after all our efforts to keep that insufferably dear man from the gallows," she said, bitterly referencing last Christmas, when Sir Edwin was suspected of murder. Lady Atherly had reached out to Stella to help and she'd freed him of all suspicion. The two women had been on relatively good terms ever since. "At least his reputation is intact."

Stella tensed. However Lady Atherly had learned of her first love's death, she appeared unaware of the accusations made against him. Stella didn't have the heart to say anything yet.

"How did you learn about Sir Edwin's death?"

Lady Atherly, the fight gone entirely out of her, indicated her daughter with a glance. "Alice wired me, of course."

Alice, who studied her shoes, the cold increasingly steady rain dripping from the brim of her hat, had said nothing since she'd arrived. She shivered. "I thought Mummy should know."

Stella wanted to hug her. Hadn't she and Lyndy been dreading having to tell his mother? And here Alice had quietly done it for them. Instead, Stella gently tugged the closed umbrella from Lady Atherly's grasp, opened it, and held it over everyone's heads.

"And you were right too, Alice. She deserved to know. But why travel all the way up here, Frances?" as Lady Atherly now insisted Stella call her. "It wasn't because of Lyndy. He was arrested before you arrived."

"With Lord Atherly in America, I had no reason not to."

Was Lady Atherly admitting she was lonely?

With Lord Atherly having left for his fossil dig in Wyoming

and Stella, Lyndy, and Alice in Scotland, Lady Atherly was the only family member left at Morrington Hall.

Or was she here determined to meddle?

"After traveling all day, you must be—?"

"I've been en route for two days," Lady Atherly said, cutting Stella off and holding up a hand to forestall her questions. With the express train, it shouldn't have taken that long. "Don't ask. Suffice it to say it was enough for me to arrive too late to prevent the police from unceremoniously hauling Lyndy off. But the moment I heard, I borrowed your cousin's carriage. In hopes of securing Lyndy's release, of course. I must say, considering the circumstances, Mr. McEwen was most accommodating, but I digress. I erroneously believed that the police could be made to see sense. I should've known you have already tried to reason with them."

Lady Atherly's rush of words was a testament to how nervous she was for Lyndy. For her, this almost constituted rambling. Again Stella had to resist the urge to comfort her somehow.

"If reason or the truth had anything to do with it, Lyndy would be with us now. I've argued with them until I was blue in the face."

"Of course you have." Lady Atherly briefly laid a hand on Stella's arm, doing what Stella had a moment ago resisted. Lady Atherly's flashes of kindness these past six months still surprised her. "Need I ask whether you and my son had taken advantage of the *change of climate* before all this happened?"

And there it was.

Stella had wondered how long it would take her mother-in-law to bring it up. It never ceased to amaze her how Lady Atherly recoiled from any number of innocuous questions but had no trouble inquiring into Stella's most intimate affairs. Even most Americans would hesitate to discuss the state of Stella's womb. But as her mother-in-law had repeated countless times, *the future of Morrington Hall depended upon it. Nothing more, nothing less.* Always a pragmatic one, the Countess of Atherly.

"No, you don't need to ask."

Since she'd arrived in Scotland, Stella hadn't had much time to think of it, and when she did, she'd successfully pushed any concern away. At first, she and Lyndy had basked in their freedom, enjoying each other as any newly married people might, not giving the consequences much thought. But then, with the murder of Sir Edwin, the death of the laundry maid, and Lyndy's subsequent arrest, Stella was more consumed with losing him to the gallows than trying to become pregnant. Little else mattered if she couldn't find a way to free him.

Satisfied, Lady Atherly patted Stella's arm. "Then we can hope coming here had at least one advantage."

The McEwens' coachman parked the carriage alongside them, and Lady Atherly and Alice climbed in. When Stella remained on the curb, Lady Atherly beckoned impatiently and, in a tone Stella recognized all too well, exclaimed, "Get in! Get in! You'll catch your death from cold, and then what use will you be to my son?"

With strands of hair plastered to her wet cheeks and the damp clinging to her dress, Stella wished she could cooperate. At least she still had the umbrella.

"I'll be fine, Frances. I rode one of the McEwens' horses into town. She's at the stable getting a shoe replaced. I should wait. Besides, the ride back will do me good."

"Then at least allow us to give you a ride to the stables." It was only a five-minute walk, but Stella gave in. She gave the coachman the general directions and climbed in beside Alice, who gave her a brief but brave smile. The carriage lurched forward, and Stella, unseeing, gazed out the rain-splattered window, counting the feet, the yards, the ever-growing distance between her and Lyndy. She shivered, hating the thought of leaving him there.

"Now, I know we only have a few minutes," Lady Atherly began, slapping her lap to focus everyone's attention, "but I want to be fully apprised of everything that's happened and of what you intend to do to get my son released."

CHAPTER 26

Finn dared not move a muscle or he'd betray how distraught he was.

With Lord Lyndhurst in jail, Finn had been beside himself trying to figure out what to do. He'd already brushed and polished his master's shoes, laid out his clothes for dinner, and selected His Lordship's studs and cuff links before word reached him that Lord Lyndhurst's travel trunk had been found and His Lordship arrested. Finn had not been allowed to unpack the luggage—police orders—and he'd already packed an overnight case; His Lordship couldn't be expected to wear the same attire he'd had on all day, now could he? Even if he was in jail. First Lady Lyndhurst and then Lady Atherly, who'd arrived at Glenloch Hill unexpectedly moments later, had left for St. Andrews without it. The best Finn could hope for was to be permitted to bring it to His Lordship himself.

That's not entirely true, Finn silently corrected himself.

The best he could hope for was for His Lordship to be released and cleared of all wrongdoing. And the more Finn had pondered on it, whittling away the time refolding silk pajamas and rolling recently washed stockings, the more convinced he'd become that he knew something that could bring that about.

He'd returned to Sir Edwin's room to retrieve the French postcard, thinking it must be important. The room was unlocked and the suitcase moved, but the picture postcard was nowhere to be found. Its absence burned a hole in his trouser pocket as he stood watch by the window in Lord and Lady Lyndhurst's bedchamber, overlooking the drive. He'd know the moment Lady Lyndhurst returned. She'd helped the police solve multiple crimes, and she of all people would want His Lordship exonerated. Wasn't she then the best one to tell?

The moment the carriage rumbled up the drive, Finn grabbed the packed valise and bounded down the main stairwell. But only the countess and Lady Alice disembarked. Where was Her Ladyship? Entrenched outside the front door, Finn waited and waited. Before long, Stevenson admonished him for loitering about. Finn made a show of rounding to the back entrance but crept back to the corner of the manor house. He had to catch Lady Lyndhurst the moment she arrived or he'd come undone.

Finn hesitated when Lady Lyndhurst finally arrived, alone and on foot, bedraggled and wet from the recent rain. He'd seen her hatless and disheveled before but never so much so. And the distress on her delicate features was heartbreaking. Should he leave her to her ruminations? Would she begrudge him a moment at what might seem an inopportune time? Finn decided he had to take the chance.

"Your Ladyship. Might I have a word?"

"Of course, Finn." She offered him a strained weary smile. "But first, I want to assure you that Lord Lyndhurst didn't do anything wrong. He's completely innocent."

"I have no doubt, my lady. That's what I must speak to you about."

Lady Lyndhurst's eyes betrayed her surprise. She led him a

few feet into the recess between the drive and the servants' entrance and lowered her voice. "Do you know something, Finn?"

Finn, the knot in his stomach loosening, relayed everything, from seeing Mr. McEwen come out of Sir Edwin's room to finding an *indelicate photograph* such as one might see in the stalls on the streets of Paris. He couldn't help but blush as he described the picture postcard he'd found in Sir Edwin's case, but he refused to let his embarrassment get in the way of helping clear Lord Lyndhurst's name. Lady Lyndhurst listened patiently, almost eagerly, without interruption or a hint of reproach.

"It isn't my place, my lady, to speculate what Mr. McEwen's business was in Sir Edwin's room or why Sir Edwin would have such a postcard in his possession."

"But you think it's important or you wouldn't be telling me this. Please go on. Tell me everything."

Finn's head swam with relief. He'd been right. Lady Lyndhurst would know what to do. "You see, my lady, when I went back to get the postcard, it was gone."

"But you said Mr. McEwen left Sir Edwin's room before you returned the case with the photograph in it."

"Yes, Your Ladyship."

"So that would mean someone else besides Mr. McEwen entered Sir Edwin's room after he'd been murdered." Lady Lyndhurst flattened the rounded tip of her nose with her finger, gazing at the ivy climbing the wall beyond Finn's shoulder. In this protected recess the ivy leaves were dry. "Unless Hamish came back?"

"At first I was thinking more along the lines of a servant. I can imagine a footman or hall boy finding the, um . . ." Finn cleared his throat, "postcard much to their liking, if you get my meaning."

"But what servant would know it was there?"

"My eventual conclusion, my lady."

"How would anyone but you and Sir Edwin know it was there, for that matter? Unless either you or Sir Edwin told someone else about it?"

Finn swallowed hard and shook his head violently. "Not me, my lady. This is the first I've breathed a word of it."

"I know, Finn. I'm just thinking out loud." She tucked a strand of hair behind her ear, a darker shade than her usual light brown having been dampened by the rain. "You've said nothing, so either Sir Edwin told someone, and it was important enough to that person to take it, or someone found it by accident when they were searching his room for something else after his death."

"But why would anyone do either of those things?"

Lady Lyndhurst bounced on the balls on her feet and seemed poised to hug him, but instead, she clapped her hands to her chest as if in fervent prayer. "Find that answer and maybe we'll find Sir Edwin's real killer."

Stella arranged to meet Finn outside Sir Edwin's bedroom after dinner, but she, Alice, and Lady Atherly had arrived from St. Andrews too late to join the others. Virginia, urging Lady Atherly to stay at Glenloch Hill *until the matter of the murder is settled*, had arranged for the women to have a late supper. Stella would've skipped the whole meal, but Virginia and Lady Atherly joined forces against her, insisting. The pair hit it off the moment they met. Temporarily hampered, Stella had sipped the rewarmed oxtail soup, took three bites of the cold poached salmon, and ate several asparagus spears before making excuses and scampering off to meet Finn.

"Show me where the postcard used to be," she said.

Owning it wasn't out of Sir Edwin's character to have such a provocative photograph, Stella held out hope that it might prove helpful. But that depended on whether she could figure out why Sir Edwin had brought it to Scotland, who took it from his room, and why. Stella had her work cut out for her. She didn't even know where the French postcard was.

"Under here."

Finn crouched beside the bed, slid the suitcase Stella had searched earlier out from under it, and flipped the case's latch. As he did so, the catch on the bedchamber door clicked. Finn kicked the suitcase back under the bed and leaped to his feet like a circus acrobat, and as he did, Stella swirled around in surprise.

"Good heavens!" Lady Atherly stood in the doorway, one hand on her heart, the other still clutching the doorknob. "How dare you two frighten me like that."

"My apologies, my lady," Finn said.

"Us?" Stella shot back. "You nearly scared me silly. What are you doing sneaking in here like that?"

"I was not sneaking," Lady Atherly declared as she shut the door behind her, her tone putting an end to further discussion. "I simply wanted to see the last place Edwin laid his head."

Besides on the cold damp ground beneath prickly overgrown shrubbery. Stella's stomach quivered at the memory.

"What, may I ask, are you two doing here?"

How to tell your mother-in-law about a risqué nude photograph that belonged to her former sweetheart? Stella hesitated. Lady Atherly folded her arms across her chest, waiting for an answer.

"Something that might help Lyndy."

That changed Lady Atherly's demeanor. "What have you found?"

"It's what we haven't found."

Lady Atherly's gaze swept the small room as if she might discover what had eluded Stella in plain sight. Spotting the framed photograph, she approached the nightstand and took up the youthful portrait of her and Sir Edwin.

"That hopeless, hopeless man. I did so love that dress. I got it in Paris. I thought it might be my wedding dress. Was I ever that young and foolish?" Lady Atherly chuckled, then lifted her gaze to regard Stella with a momentary wistfulness. And then it was gone. "What is it you haven't found?"

Lady Atherly's attention remained glued to the photograph of her younger self as Stella explained about the picture post-card that had gone missing. When Stella finished, Lady Atherly returned the frame to its former place.

"Well, I certainly don't know of any Parisian postcard. We had, as you are aware, Stella, only recently renewed our acquaintance. But I can assure you, even at our most intimate, Sir Edwin would never have exposed me to anything so indecent. Perhaps Isabella knows something of it?" A glint in her eye reminded Stella of Lyndy when he was about to get up to no good. "Shall I send her a telegram inquiring? She's staying at a daughter's house in London, is she not?"

Lady Atherly and Sir Edwin's widow were not on the best of terms, and Lady Atherly knew such a telegram would embarrass Lady Isabella in front of her daughter. It's true, at Christmastime Lady Isabella had driven everyone crazy with her judgmental tones and her incessant praise of her daughters, but the woman had just learned of her husband's death. Stella gently reminded Lady Atherly of the fact.

"As if she doesn't welcome her new status as a widow," Lady Atherly said heartlessly. "She and Sir Edwin were never a good match and have been estranged these last seven months. I don't think they've exchanged ten words between them in all that time."

Curious to learn how Lady Atherly would know this, Stella was about to ask when voices coming up the stairs stilled her tongue. Jeanie Agnew's high-pitched staccato giggling was unmistakable.

"Maybe we shouldn't be found in here," Stella suggested.

Lady Atherly readily agreed and impatiently shooed Finn

forward to open the door. Safely away from Sir Edwin's bedroom, they came upon Virginia and Jeanie Agnew making their way toward them. Jeanie's laughter had died, but whatever she'd found amusing lingered on her lips. Occasionally tripping over her own stocking feet, her pair of strikingly red dress shoes dangling from one hand, she waved and called out in greeting as if they were blocks down the street and not a few yards away in the hall.

"Who's the laddie, my lady?" Jeanie eyed Finn like an offering in a Parisian bakery case.

Lady Atherly crinkled her eyebrows into a chevron of displeasure. "That's my son's valet."

Jeanie covered her mouth and giggled again, making a slow tottering advance toward Finn. "Not taken, then, eh?"

"Leave him be, Jeanie." Virginia caught her friend under the arm as she staggered into the wall, tilting a dark but realistic painting of two horses working in a shipyard. Stella had admired it earlier. Jeanie attempted unsuccessfully to right it. "Are you settling in all right then, Lady Atherly?"

"I am, Mrs. McEwen. Thank you. You are most kind to let me stay, considering the current accusations against my son."

"I wouldn't dream of you staying anywhere else. Your daughter, Alice, is a darling, and I can imagine what a comfort your being here gives Stella."

Lady Atherly a comfort? Stella had to stifle the impulse to laugh at the irony.

"Too bad ye missed out on all the excitement, my lady," Jeanie added, slurring her words slightly. "And here I thought it would be a few boring days spent watching golf. As everyone knows, I prefer participating in my sport than being sidelined as a spectator." She winked at Finn.

"Yes, well . . ." Lady Atherly didn't know what to say to that. "I think someone's had a bit too much to drink."

"Let's be honest," Jeanie said. "It's me. Though frankly, I

didn't admit to anything I wouldn't have said sober. It has been more exciting than usual. Isn't that right, Ginny?"

"I think I need to get this one off to bed," Virginia said. "Good night, then."

"Good night, Mrs. McEwen. Mrs. Agnew."

"Good night, Virginia. Jeanie," Stella said.

"Good night, fair lads and ladies!" Jeanie called out, reaching for Finn as she passed.

Virginia tugged away her friend's arm, half-supporting, half-dragging her down the hall.

"Who would've thought?" Finn whispered. He was boring a hole into the backs of their retreating hostess and her friend.

"I'm so sorry, Finn," Stella said. "You shouldn't have had to put up with that."

"It's not that, my lady. She's a bit older, I'll grant you, but I recognize her as the woman in the French postcard."

Slack-jawed, Stella watched Jeanie Agnew flip her silk shawl over her shoulder and let loose her staccato giggles.

"Jeanie Agnew is the woman in the picture?"

She was a giggling, heavy-drinking flirt, but posing in the nude for money? Stella couldn't imagine it.

"No, my lady," Finn corrected her, "it's the other one. It's Mrs. McEwen."

CHAPTER 27

Stella spent a fitful night, the room stifling and hot, and woke with a start at the melodic squeals of bagpipes wafting through the crack she'd left open in the window. Groggy and bone-weary, she reached for Lyndy. He wasn't there.

Then she remembered. She sat up, wide-eyed, to face a world where Lyndy had spent the night in jail instead of in bed beside her. It hit her as if she'd been thrown from a galloping horse on a hard-packed racetrack, as if he'd been wrongly accused all over again. The knots in her chest tightened and her nails dug into her fleshy palm. She'd cried last night until her head hurt. She was done feeling sorry for herself.

Stella threw off the bedsheets, twisted into a clump on top of her, and forced herself out of bed. There must be something she could do to free Lyndy.

"Virginia," she reminded herself out loud. Stella would confront her about Finn's revelation last night.

Without waiting for Ethel or her breakfast tray, Stella slipped into a white shirtwaist, the one with Swiss eyelet embroidery that didn't have a million buttons down the back, and a simple pleated high-waisted lilac skirt and went in search of the mistress of the house. She knocked on all the bedrooms, startling a pair of chambermaids making up a bed in the third one she tried. Flustered and suspicious, neither was very helpful. With the other bedrooms empty or locked, Stella charged into the dining room to ask Hamish. It was empty, not a crumb, a napkin, or an out-of-place chair to hint that breakfast had been served.

Where was everyone? What time was it? Didn't the bagpipes play at breakfast?

Stella found the grandfather clock in the hall. It read twenty-two minutes past ten. Stella had overslept. Why hadn't Ethel woken her? Why hadn't she brought her a tray? A warm breeze wafted past, and as a distant door opened, voices and laughter reached the hall. Stella followed and found that the French doors in the drawing room had been left open to allow for the breeze. Stella stepped into the brilliant warm sunshine, shielding her eyes from the glare. Out on the lawn, beyond the curving drive, Hamish, Jeanie, Freddy, and Alasdair played croquet while Alice and Lady Atherly nestled into white wicker armchairs and looked on.

Jeanie whacked her ball into another and sent it hurtling away from the wickets. It rolled until it hit a small fallen branch. Alasdair grumbled something incomprehensible and Jeanie peppered him with her giggles.

"How can ye not have some aftereffects from last night, Jeanie?" Hamish asked. The widow rested a hand on his arm and twittered louder.

Stella's ears burned with irritation. How could they be playing and laughing and enjoying themselves? And hadn't Alasdair and Freddy had enough of striking a ball around the grass? Then she checked herself. It wasn't their fault she was anxious for Lyndy, that Lyndy had been arrested.

Unless one of them was the murderer.

Lady Atherly sat beneath the shade of a lace parasol stuck in the ground behind her chair and waved Stella over. Alice smiled wanly, a stack of magazines in her lap.

"Look what Mummy brought."

Alice held up the newest issue of *The Ladies' World*. She didn't wait for Stella's response to return to flipping through the pages. Out of the corner of her eye, Stella caught Freddy's frown.

Was it because with her mother around, Alice had retreated into her fantasies again and he lamented it, or because Freddy disapproved of his fiancée speaking with someone he thought was a murderer's wife?

Maybe a little of both.

"I do hope that lady's maid of yours didn't disturb you after all," Lady Atherly huffed.

"No, someone was playing bagpipes. Why? Did you tell Ethel to let me sleep in?"

"I thought it best. I'm certain Mrs. McEwen will happily arrange for her kitchen to prepare you a late breakfast."

So that explained it. Lady Atherly's interference in Stella's life was nothing new, but her intentions were well-meaning this time. Would Stella ever get used to it? She glanced around.

"I don't see Virginia?"

"She's not come down yet."

"I need to find her." She crouched beside her mother-in-law, who rolled her eyes at Stella's unladylike stance. "You didn't happen to notice which was her bedroom last night, did you?"

"Last one on the right." *The one Stella had found locked this morning.* Lady Atherly sat up a bit straighter and squinted at her. "Why?"

"I need to ask her something and I don't think it can wait."

"Then by all means." Lady Atherly shooed Stella away with the same wave she'd beaconed her with.

Stella straightened up from her squat and took a few steps

back toward the house. A loud *whack* like those she'd heard throughout the croquet game boomed close by, and a whistling sound like a fast-approaching flying arrow sent Stella, Lady Atherly, and Alice ducking for cover. But for Stella, there was none; no chair or table to hide behind. With a *whoosh*, something whizzed by, missing Stella as she dropped to the ground. The well-manicured turf cushioned her dive like a plush Persian rug.

"Good Lord!" Lady Atherly cowered in the lounge chair.

Alice gazed past Stella, her attention locked on the croquet ball landing with a thud in the grass several feet away. Their eyes met, and Alice covered her mouth with both hands. Stella had been in the ball's direct line of flight. If she hadn't ducked . . . Stella clambered to her feet.

"Bloody hell, that was close," Freddy swore.

"Who hit that?" Lady Atherly demanded. Heads shook, shoulders shrugged, and eyes sought out others for confirmation. No one would admit to it.

"Are ye all right, my lady?" Jeanie asked.

"I'm fine." Stella stood up, holding out her arms to show no damage done. Unless the knee-shaped grass stains on her skirt counted. She brushed grass clippings off her skirt and blouse. "Still in one piece."

But Stella wasn't fine. She was still trembling from the sudden shock but didn't want anyone to know. And she wasn't in one piece. Half of her was locked away in a dank jail cell while the real murderer was free to whack croquet balls at her. Of course it could've been an errant ball, an accident. But with no confession, it was more of a coincidence than she was willing to believe. Someone had deliberately tried to hit her. But why? Lyndy was in jail. For everyone but the actual killer, the murder was solved. Had that someone overheard her talking to Finn? Or seen them come out of Sir Edwin's room? Or knew Stella wouldn't give up?

With all eyes on her, she walked backward up the sloping lawn, unwilling to give the culprit another opportunity to strike, but nearly tripped on the hem of her skirt. Her exit and the lengthening silence were awkward as everyone watched her go. Jeanie tittered nervously. Once well out of range, Stella gave each croquet player a knowing glare, then pivoted and strode purposefully toward the house.

Stella spotted Virginia's linen dress like a white flag marching down the path away from the manor house.

"Virginia!" she called, but the mistress of Glenloch Hill continued walking and was soon swallowed up by the woodland that hid the laundry building. Stella gave pursuit.

"Bide a wee minute, lassie," Hamish called. When Stella didn't stop, he marched across the lawn after her. "Where ye off tae, Stella?"

Stella slowed, allowing him to catch up with her. "I was hoping to ask Virginia something."

"Ach, questions can wait. I havenae shown ye the rose garden yet, have I?" He eagerly gestured toward the walled garden. A little too eagerly.

Why was he trying to waylay her?

Stella studied him. His smile was plastered on his face as usual, but for once it didn't reach his eyes. A cryptic, almost desperate glint flashed there, convincing her to put off her errand and join him. Hamish held secrets. To free Lyndy, Stella might need to learn them too.

But the walled garden was already occupied.

"What an exquisite specimen of the Madame Isaac Pereire you have here, Mr. McEwen." Lady Atherly held a large shaggy bright pink bloom to her nose, closing her eyes as if doing so helped her smell better. Yet Stella could smell the rose's strong scent from feet away.

Stella sighed. Knowing her mother-in-law's love of gardening, she should've expected the intrusion. But why had her mother-in-law abandoned her chair on the lawn at this precise moment? And how could Stella question Hamish with her here?

"I'm delighted ye think so, Lady Atherly."

"Yes, and those cabbage roses." Lady Atherly pointed to a line of compact bushes with double flowers drooping under their own weight. "Is that Cristata, the Crested Moss rose?"

"Aye, it's a relic left by the previous owner."

"Your garden is quite splendid." A high compliment coming from Stella's mother-in-law. "But your groundskeeper has been derelict in his duties." Lady Atherly pointed to the many shriveled and brown rose heads scattered among the fresher blooms.

"Aye, that would be me. I enjoy maintaining this garden my-self—"

"A man after my own heart," Lady Atherly interrupted.

Stella fiddled with her wedding ring. Would Lady Atherly ever leave? Or should Stella excuse herself and continue her pursuit of Virginia? Stella wasn't going to learn anything useful standing around like this.

"But with the Open and all oor bonny guests," Hamish said, "I havnae had a moment tae spare."

Not to mention the two murders.

"Then you'll know these require frequent deadheading or you'll be done for the season." Without waiting for a word, she added, "I'll be needing a pair of shears."

Amused, Hamish opened the lid of a small wooden bench set on a built-in box. He procured a pair of heavy garden scissors and working gloves a size too large for Lady Atherly and offered them to her. "Be my guest, my lady."

Armed with her tools, Lady Atherly set to work.

"And what do you call this?" Stella moved to the other side of the garden. Hamish followed.

"This? It's—"

"I overheard your conversation with Sir Edwin the day he died," Stella said under her breath. "Or should I say your argument?" Hamish gasped sharply. "What did Sir Edwin demand to know?"

Hamish glanced over his shoulder at the preoccupied Countess of Atherly before leaning closer. "Based on some wee letters from Richard, Edwin suspected I could tell him something aboot his brother's death. That's why the fool invited himself here. But I didnae ken anything more than he did."

"But he had something you wanted, something he offered to bargain with. The nude photo of Virginia, maybe?"

Hamish blanched. Stella had guessed, but based on his reaction she'd been right. He shot a glance toward Lady Atherly again. Stella's mother-in-law was snipping off dead rose blooms with unfaltering gusto. Hamish's breath smelled of bacon and fear as he lowered his head to within inches of Stella's face.

"Please give it tae me, Stella."

"I don't have it."

"Then how . . . ?

"Lyndy's valet found it in Sir Edwin's suitcase when it was accidentally delivered to the wrong room. He returned it to Sir Edwin's room, but not until after seeing you leave. You were looking for the postcard, weren't you?"

"But it wasn't there." Hamish took a step back and Stella put another between them. "Now I ken why."

"Did you kill Sir Edwin because he wouldn't give it to you?"

"Wait! Whit did ye . . . Nay, absolutely not." He pointed back toward the croquet players away up the hill. Alice had taken Hamish's place. "I was in my study when Sir Edwin was killed."

"Alone?" Stella pressed.

"Aye. But I'd been holed up there every night. Ye can ask Freddy's caddie, Billy."

"What does Billy Birdwell have to do with it?"

"Today is Old Tom Morris's eighty-fifth birthday, and I've been planning a surprise party for the gaffer. Billy's been helping me."

"In what way? The two of you didn't even know each other until a few days ago."

"Aye, and that's whit made him perfect. He's an outsider, so Old Tom would never suspect."

It seemed a far-fetched excuse. Billy had been acting suspiciously, whispering with the other caddies and players, but was that why? He was helping Hamish plan a surprise party? Why not simply send invitations? She pressed Hamish on it.

"I did, tae those I ken," he explained. "I trusted Billy tae pass the word aboot tae those I didnae during the tournament." Although there was a ring of truth to what he said, Hamish still sounded like he was holding something back.

"Even if all that is true, you still could've found time to slip out and kill Sir Edwin."

"Ye have tae believe me, lassie. I had nothing tae dae with Sir Edwin's demise."

Did she believe him? She certainly wanted to.

"Would you mind if I took a cutting of this damask rose to take home with me, Mr. McEwen?" Lady Atherly called from among the rosebushes without looking up from her task.

"Not at all, Lady Atherly. Now, if ye'll excuse me, Stella."

"If you hope to find it in Sir Edwin's room now, I wouldn't bother. Finn and I searched it last night and it's gone—again." Hamish paled, his lip trembling as if he was about to be sick. "Who else would want that postcard, Hamish? Is someone else blackmailing Virginia over it? Or do you think Virginia . . ."

"I'll ask ye kindly to leave Virginia out of it."

Why hadn't Stella thought of it before? Virginia was the one in the photograph. If Hamish had been so determined to get it from Sir Edwin, how desperate might Virginia be? Could Sir

Edwin have approached her with the same blackmailing exchange and been killed for it? Did Hamish suspect the same thing? Was that why he tried to stall Stella, to stop her from talking to Virginia? How far would he go to protect her?

"You aimed that croquet ball at me," she said. It wasn't a question.

He tried to shrug it off. "Now, now, lassie. I admit tae hitting it yer way, but it was a mistake. If I'd aimed at ye, it would've hit ye."

"That was a dangerous *mistake*. You could've hurt me or worse. And for what? You just didn't want me speaking to Virginia?" She couldn't believe this affable man could be so callous. Maybe he did kill Sir Edwin.

"And I still dinnae, lass. Virginia's ill. Ye must see it too. She needs peace and quiet."

"Then why did I see her heading down the hill? Where was she going?"

A flicker of doubt crossed Hamish's face. He didn't know. Either why she was out or where she was going. Or both.

" 'Tis not for me tae say. But I can tell ye whit she doesnae need is for ye tae barrage her with questions, making her feel worse."

"Lady Lyndhurst rarely knows when to stop asking pesky irritating questions," Lady Atherly said, stripping the gloves from her hands as she joined them unexpectedly with the stealth of a hunting cat. Stella hadn't heard a whisper of her approach.

Stung by her mother-in-law's dredging up of that old complaint, Stella prepared to object. Lady Atherly, knowing Stella well, held up a finger forestalling her. "But I've come to learn, Mr. McEwen, that on occasion some questions need raising, and she's the only one willing to do so."

"Such as?"

"Why in heaven's name are you hosting a party when our

mutual dear friend Sir Edwin is dead and my son is in jail accused of his murder?"

Hamish, who'd drawn up taller, hoping to intimidate her to back down, saw his error. Lady Atherly held up her shears, using them to accentuate her point, backing Hamish into a thorny bush.

"Ow!"

As Lady Atherly continued to wave the scissors, Stella saw the opportunity to escape. She was beyond the walls of the garden and racing in the direction Virginia had taken when she heard Hamish say, "I mean no disrespect, Lady Atherly, but the party's been in the planning for weeks now. I couldnae call it off now if I wanted tae. Now, will ye please put down the shears?"

CHAPTER 28

Stella noticed Billy Birdwell alone on the putting green. She tried to ignore him, chasing Virginia before Hamish stopped her again, but something in Billy's stance, his motions caught her attention. He'd sunk a ball into the cup, squatted to retrieve a cloth from a leather case he'd left on the ground, and, pulling the putter into his lap, began wiping it clean with the fabric.

A pesky fly found him and he twisted and turned to avoid it, ducking and dodging the buzzing insect that hovered about his head. Never once did he swat at it. Never once did he raise his arms. Stella approached, waving and shooing at the creature until it whizzed away.

"Thank you, my lady," Billy said, "that was driving me crazy."

"Of course. Did you see Virginia pass by here?"

"Yeah. I did. Heading to the stables, maybe?"

Virginia would never wear a linen dress to go riding, but Stella didn't waste time illuminating the caddie. She felt drawn to follow Virginia, like the tug of an invisible halter's lead rope, but something caused her to ask, "Are you injured, Billy?" She pictured Hamish crumpling over the net on the tennis court. "I noticed you didn't raise your arms."

Had he ever, even when it was required of him on the golf course?

He shoved the putter into the bag beside him on the ground, gathered it under his arm, and pushed up to his feet. He regarded the croquet players far up the hill in silence for so long Stella wondered if he was going to answer.

"It was a long while back now, the injury. Carriage accident." He didn't elaborate and Stella didn't press. "Haven't been able to raise my arms higher than my waist since. I can still putt, but that was the end of my long game." The caddie forced a mirthless chuckle.

"Is that why Freddy always gets his own club from his bag?"

Billy demonstrated how raising the club from the bag required more height than his arms would go. "If he wants to play, he does." He chuckled again. "I can carry the bag, just can't get the clubs out of them. Freddy doesn't mind."

"It's unusual, though, isn't it?" Stella pictured what Lyndy called the caddie's *dodgy* behavior, whispering behind everyone's back. What had he been up to?

"Not for golfers like Freddy, who realize it takes a lot more than lifting a club to be a good caddie and who recognize a great one when they see one. I was a capable enough golfer before, but me, my lady, I'm a great caddie."

That was quite a boast. Stella couldn't suppress her skepticism. Billy straightened his shoulders in retort.

"Why'd you think Freddy insists on me being at every tournament? Any local chap could lug his clubs about, but I'm the one who can tell how the wind, the speed of the green, and the turf conditions will affect Freddy's game, aren't I? Those others don't know how Freddy hits his mashie when he'd not slept enough the night before, or how he gets impatient when too close to the rough. Freddy may fetch the club from the bag, but I'm the one who advises him which one to take. Despite my injury, Freddy knows he's a better player with me at his side."

"He trusts you."

With his injury, the caddie was the one person who couldn't have killed his father. But then why all the whispering, the need to change plans when Sir Edwin was found dead? And why was he holding a cloth similar to the one Aggie had been purposely scorching?

"What is that cloth, Billy?"

The caddie had finished with it and was putting it away. "Club heads get dirty. Grips get slick with sweat. Every golfer needs one to wipe down their equipment. Why?"

"I saw one before. It had a family crest embroidered where yours has tiny birds printed on it."

"Any clean rag will do, but most golfers, especially the serious ones, carry personalized cloths, often printed or embroidered with their family crest, as you say, or their initials, the name of a tournament they won, or a course they played. It varies."

"Kind of like a handkerchief for golf clubs."

"If you like."

"You said serious golfers, like Freddy, would have a cloth like that. But amateurs might use them, too, right? Men as well as women?"

"I don't see why not. This one here is mine. Keep it to remind me I'm still in the game, albeit in a different capacity. Why?"

"Just something I was thinking about."

Aggie was angry at the owner of the cloth she'd scorched. Could it be the key that unlocked what had happened to her? Stella didn't know how it fitted with Sir Edwin, who wasn't a golfer, and knowing anyone who played golf might have one didn't narrow it down much, but it was something.

But something *wasn't enough.* For Lyndy's sake, Stella needed more.

She assessed the caddie, who'd begun tapping the other balls scattered around the putting green toward the hole with the side of his foot.

"Where were you the night Sir Edwin died?" she blurted out.

It should've been enough, his injury and dissimilar drying cloth, for Stella to let him be. The caddie couldn't have bludgeoned Sir Edwin or even hanged Aggie, and Hamish had even given Billy an alibi, but he'd been acting strange since they arrived at Glenloch Hill and she had to know why.

"Me? I . . . I . . ." he sputtered, kicking one ball too hard, sending it careering across the green and into the lawn.

"We've all seen you whispering behind your hand, Billy. Slinking around like a snake-oil salesman well known to the local police. Does it have to do with the murders? Aggie's attack?"

"Oi! What're you going on about?" He backed away from her as if she'd spread a contagion. "I've got absolutely nothing to do with any of that."

"Then what? You were telling the other caddies about Old Tom's party on the q.t.?"

Hamish's excuse had sounded fishy. But now? If Billy confirmed it, neither he nor Hamish could've killed Sir Edwin.

"He told you about Old Tom's party?"

"He did."

Billy bent almost in half, snatched off his checkered cap, and wiped his forehead with it, the embossed bird on the brass button glinting in the sun.

"That's all right, then." He slapped his cap back on, stretching his shoulders as he straightened. "I've grown so used to trying to keep it under my hat." He chuckled at his unintended pun. "Keeping everything secret and all that."

"So, you were with Hamish?" Stella muttered her disbelief as a rhetorical affirmation to herself, but Billy squatted to collect the extra golf balls and responded anyway.

"I've been helping Mr. McEwen when I can, getting the word out, but I wasn't with Mr. McEwen that night. I went to see him in his study, but he wasn't there. And then later, me and a few other caddies convinced Old Tom to join us at the Cross Keys in St. Andrews. Mr. McEwen wanted to order Old

Tom's drink of choice for the party but didn't fancy it could be the ginger beer and lime the old golfer was known to enjoy on the links. So, we reckoned, what better place to wheedle it out of Old Tom than at the pub. I wasn't sure whether Mr. McEwen still wanted to know the next day, seeing what happened and all."

"So, Hamish wasn't with you the night Sir Edwin was murdered?"

Stella's stomach sank when the caddie shook his head.

Stella smelled it first before spotting the gray plumes of smoke rising above the tree line. Worried a building was on fire, Stella dashed toward the laundry house, which stood silent and empty. Fergus's cottage and the stables were intact too. Backtracking, Stella followed the scent into the woodland, up the path toward the hill's summit, where she'd first met the McEwens, picking up speed when she caught flashes of Virginia's white dress through the breaks in the trees.

"Why dinnae ye jist burn it?" Hamish was pleading when Stella burst into the clearing. "When sorrow sleeps, wake it not, I say."

Hamish stood with his foot resting on one of the granite stones encircling a large open fire, flickering and crackling and hot. He'd somehow escaped Lady Atherly and found Virginia before Stella did. Had he known all along where she was? Beside him, Virginia gripped the edge of one of a half dozen caned-back wooden folding chairs spread around the fire ring as if it was all that was holding her up. Clutched in her other hand, held out over the hungry flames, was the French postcard. When Stella approached, Virginia, startled, snatched the picture back from the fire.

Was that relief Stella saw flicker across Virginia's face?

"Stella, ye are nothing if not persistent, lass." Hamish McEwen wasn't the first to think so. "But it doesnae matter now. I failed. Virginia found out." He pointed to the offending picture.

"It's all right, Hamish," Virginia said. "Truly it is."

A breeze cut through the trees, fanning the flames but cooling the sweat beading on Stella's skin.

"You don't have to feign surprise, Stella. Hamish told me you were asking about it." Virginia waved the postcard as if fanning herself from the heat of the flames.

"But I am surprised," Stella said. "I knew a woman had been in Sir Edwin's room, but I'd assumed it was Jeanie from the lingering scent of her preferred perfume."

"It was Jeanie. She found it when she was searching his room. She'd thought she lost an earring when she'd had her little tryst with Sir Edwin. There's that look of surprise again."

How could Stella not have suspected? Jeanie and Sir Edwin lovers? Was that why the photograph of Sir Edwin and Lady Atherly was face down? A bit of competitive jealousy? Could Jeanie have killed Sir Edwin? Had a lovers' quarrel gone horribly wrong? Jeanie was as handy with a golf club as anyone. But how was the widow connected to Aggie?

"I thought Jeanie preferred Alasdair McCormack?"

Virginia swallowed hard, hesitating, her knuckles turning white as she gripped the top rail of the chair. "She did before Sir Edwin arrived."

"Jeanie prefers any man who's willing," Hamish muttered, poking the fire with a stick. A burst of embers sparkled up from the burning pile.

"That's not fair, Hamish," his wife scolded. "Jeanie is far more discerning than you give her credit for. She is a young widow after all. Would you have her live like a nun?"

Hamish sniffed his disapproval. "They're both married men, hen."

"Don't be so prudish, Hamish." Virginia held up the postcard for Hamish to see close up. "I mean, look at what your wife once got up to." Her laugh was listless and fleeting as she waved it at him.

"Jist burn the bloody thing, will ye?" Hamish muttered.

"Besides, even I knew Sir Edwin and Lady Isabella were no longer sharing the same bed," Virginia said.

"And Alasdair confided in me that his wife's left him," Hamish conceded. "Lass told him in a telegram."

"Really?" Virginia said, her face unnaturally flushed. Stella hadn't known that either.

Stella didn't care about what Virginia *once got up to* or the marital status of Jeanie Agnew's romantic interests. Unless it helped free Lyndy.

"Do you know when Jeanie and Sir Edwin were together?" she asked.

Virginia shrugged. "Jeanie didn't give me all the sordid details."

"Do the police know?"

Virginia waved away the accusation in Stella's tone. "As if Ian needed to hear about Jeanie and Edwin's tête-à-tête. Like Hamish, it's none of his business what Jeanie does with men."

Should Stella remind Virginia that it had nothing to do with impropriety but that in a murder investigation everything was the police's business? That no one could tell what bit of information would be the key to finding the murderer? Stella knew how true that was. But had the police ever asked Jeanie—or Virginia for that matter—anything that would help their investigation? Stella combed through her memory. She didn't think so.

Maybe I need to remind Inspector Docherty instead.

"Where were you that night, Virginia?"

If a possible lovers' tiff between Sir Edwin and Jeanie could cast enough doubt to free Lyndy, so, too, might Hamish's reaction to Sir Edwin withholding the nude photograph of Virginia from him. Hamish had been willing to scare Stella off with an errant croquet ball to stop her from questioning Virginia. What could he have stooped to if Sir Edwin had threatened his wife? And what about Virginia? She'd known Sir Edwin since their school days, and the day after he arrived unannounced he was found dead. Could she have done it?

"Yer starting tae sound like Ian, Stella," Hamish chuckled. When Stella waited expectantly for Virginia's reply, he added, "If ye must ken, Virginia and I were together after dinner and all night. She'd had another one of her spells. Does that ease yer mind?"

It didn't. Hamish could be covering for Virginia or vice versa. Just as Inspector Docherty suspected Stella was doing for Lyndy. And what was causing these *spells*? Guilt, maybe?

"And the postcard?" Stella pointed to it. "If Jeanie found it, how did you come to have it, Virginia?" After everything Hamish had done to procure it, it seemed odd that it would end up in Virginia's hands.

"Jeanie gave it to me this morning." Virginia looked at it, gazing at the woman she once was with a longing that hurt Stella's heart.

"She should've come tae me first," Hamish muttered.

"Why? Jeanie gave it to me to do with it as I wish. As Sir Edwin would've done if he'd been given the chance." What was she not saying? That Sir Edwin had offered it to her but died before he could track it down? Or had he refused her as he had Hamish?

"If we'd been able tae tell him what he wanted, perhaps," Hamish said, echoing Stella's thoughts. "Please, hen, jist burn it and let it go."

"You know I can't."

"Then let's go back tae the others. Alasdair may be a champion golfer, but ye could beat him at croquet with yer eyes closed."

Virginia took a step back and dropped into one of the folding chairs that looked more as if they belonged on the deck of a steamship than in the middle of a swath of dappled forest. She laid the postcard face down on her lap and cradled her face in her hands.

"I may as well throw myself into the fire."

What did that mean?

"Dinnae say such things, hen," Hamish pleaded. He shot Stella a look, urging her to leave, but Lyndy depended on her as much as Virginia did on Hamish, and Stella hadn't asked all her questions yet.

"What did you and Sir Edwin argue about, Hamish? What information did he want in exchange for the postcard?"

"I already told ye. Sir Edwin wanted tae ken more aboot Richard's death, but we didnae ken anymore."

"Don't we?" Virginia looked up, challenging Hamish. "Did you know, Stella, that Richard was why I sat for this photograph?"

"Ye dinnae need tae say more, Virginia. Yer not well."

His wife ignored him. "Richard's the reason, at least in part. My father's dying had something to do with it too." Tears welled in her eyes. "My father was a tutor at the school Richard and the others attended. I knew all three, but Richard and I courted. I thought we'd marry." She gave a weak smile to Hamish and reached for his hand. He quickly enveloped it in both of his. "But when my father died, my family couldn't afford the promised dowry. I was young and a bit daring in those days. Much like Jeanie, though we met much later. Maybe that's why we get on so well. Anyway, when the opportunity arose, I secretly posed for this photograph, hoping to earn enough money to marry Richard."

"But it wasn't enough?" Stella asked.

"I'll never know. After my father's death, Richard and Edwin's father withdrew his permission for us to marry. Richard was promised to someone else, and I didn't see him again until . . ." Virginia's voice faded as if it took too much effort to talk. Stella's heart went out to Virginia, having lost her father, her beau, and her innocence all at the same time.

"Virginia told me long ago," Hamish said, "but no one we ken ever learned aboot the postcard. Of course I wanted tae keep it that way. And then Sir Edwin arrived unexpectedly, brandishing the knowledge of it like a sword."

Was that why Sir Edwin was killed? Not for attacking Aggie but because he knew a secret Hamish and Virginia had hoped was long buried? One that could humiliate them in front of their children and friends, even threaten their position in society? If so, either Virginia or Hamish or both could've done it. Stella took an imperceptible step backward.

"He was blackmailing you, then," Stella said. "What did he want?"

Hamish snorted in surprise. "A tongue's a fearsome tool. And whit a tongue ye have on ye, Stella. Are all Americans so direct?"

"There are over seventy-five million of us, Cousin Hamish. *All* Americans aren't anything." Stella bristled at the worn-out accusation. "It's just that this one doesn't have the liberty of being subtle. Having my husband arrested for a murder he didn't commit saw to that."

"To be fair, it wasn't blackmail, Stella," Virginia offered. "Richard wrote something to Edwin referring to seeing Hamish, but it was vague and written the day he died. Edwin simply wanted to know what Richard was going on about."

"And what was he talking about?"

"How were we tae ken?" Hamish answered. "Besides, whit difference does it make? They're both dead now anyway."

Virginia slipped her hand from Hamish's grasp and hugged herself, staring vacantly into the fire. "Just tell her."

"Tell me what?"

What didn't Hamish want to say? Was there something more humiliating or damaging than the nude postcard of Virginia? Something else he might've killed to keep secret? Despite her suspicions and misgivings, Stella leaned forward in anticipation.

Hamish sighed. "If I tell her, will ye promise tae get some rest and try tae enjoy the party tonight?" Virginia nodded almost imperceptibly. Hamish sighed again before forcing out, "We were with Richard the day he died."

Stella struggled to keep the surprise from her face. Another Kentfield died around this couple? Stella took another almost imperceptible step back.

"We'd reconnected with him," Hamish explained, "because I wanted him, as a former champion cricketer, tae officiate at a cricket match I was sponsoring. We were passing through West Didsbury and paid him a call. He agreed. We arranged a date and time and left. It was nothing more than that."

But why would Sir Edwin blackmail them over that?

In answer to Stella's unspoken question, Virginia whispered. "And an hour later he was dead, drowned in the river, alone."

Virginia began sobbing, the steady unchecked streaks of tears on her cheeks glistening in the fire's glow. Hamish knelt beside her, a comforting arm around her shoulders while trying to propel her to her feet.

"If only we'd . . ." Virginia began, tears slipping between her lips.

If only they'd what? Was Virginia crying over Richard's loss? Or the regret over something she and Hamish had done?

"Live noo—no back," Hamish said, exasperated, as if repeating the same thing for the hundredth time. Stella had no idea what it meant. "We're not tae blame here."

"Then why not just tell Sir Edwin and get the postcard back?" Stella said.

Hamish could be rationalizing or he could be innocent, but Stella had to ask either way. She still didn't have anything that would see Lyndy's exonerated.

"I did! But would he believe me that I didnae ken more aboot how his brother died or why? No. He refused tae take my word for it. He refused tae give me that bloody postcard." Hamish grabbed it from his wife's lap and threw it onto the fire. The dry paper ignited immediately into yellow flame, burning its hungry way across Virginia's naked pose.

"No!" Virginia launched herself up and toward the flames, only Hamish's firm hold around her waist preventing Virginia from burning herself. She tried to snatch the stick from Hamish's hand in a vain attempt to salvage the burning postcard. "Why did you do that, Hamish? I wanted it. I needed it. To remind me of the time before . . ."

"Aye, I ken, hen," Hamish hushed gently, "but ye couldnae dae it, so I did it for ye. Now ye can leave Richard and all that sadness in the past where it belongs and get stronger. Ye can be happy again." Virginia buried her head in his shoulder and he stroked her hair, comforting her like a child. "I am sorry aboot ye photograph, but ye ken I'd dae anything tae see ye happy again."

Anything?

Virginia nodded weakly against his collarbone with a muffled, "I know, Hamish. I know."

Over her head, Hamish addressed Stella, too stunned at what she'd witnessed to move. "Now, Cousin, if ye've satiated yer curiosity, I'd appreciate it if ye'd leave us in peace."

Stella swiftly backed away from the fire ring, not needing to be asked twice.

CHAPTER 29

Stella ran her finger along the books as fast as her eyes could focus, searching for a particular volume. It didn't take long. Whether they spent their energies in sport or weren't a family of readers, the McEwens had acquired barely a quarter of the books found at Morrington Hall. Luckily, what she sought seemed to be required reading in every British manor house. She pulled a recent edition of *Burke's Peerage* from the shelf. Beside it sat *The Book of Family Crests*. Even better. She put back *Burke's*, grabbed the other book, and plopped into the nearest armchair.

After her conversation with Billy Birdwell, and then Hamish and Virginia, Stella didn't feel any closer to figuring out who'd killed Sir Edwin and Aggie. She'd been focusing too much on Sir Edwin because that's who the police accused Lyndy of killing. But when Hamish threw the postcard into the fire, it reminded Stella of Aggie angrily scorching the cloth and she realized her mistake. Poor Aggie's death had to be connected. Which meant a change in tactics.

Stella flipped open the book on her lap and looked up the family crest of every golfer at Glenloch Hill whose cleaning cloth might've made its way to Aggie: Agnew, Birdwell, Kentfield, McCormack, McEwen. None of them matched. She branched out to include the servants, golfers or not: Stevenson—though she could hardly imagine the stiff butler swinging a club—Mrs. Graham, Fergus Lorrie, and even Aggie Neely herself. When that didn't yield results, Stella scoured the book for other family crests—those of Docherty, Farley, Cuskar, and the other police, Morris, Braid, and every other golfer or caddie she could think of—and came up with nothing. She slammed the book closed in frustration.

Maybe she hadn't remembered the crest right. She'd have to see it again. Stella shoved the book into the empty spot on the shelf, her hand lingering on its spine. Could the scorched golf cloth still be in the laundry house? Or, like Hamish, had Aggie thrown it on the drying cupboard fire? There was one way to find out.

Stella cautiously pushed on the door when she reached the laundry building. She couldn't help but visualize the tragedy she'd encountered the last time she'd been there.

"Hello?" No answer.

The room was empty, but a fragrant dampness surged from within. Someone had taken over for Aggie and fired up the boiler.

"Hello?" she called louder.

Stella moved methodically about the room, peering under tables, opening drawers, and rummaging through basket after basket piled high with dirty clothes, bedsheets, and linen. Coming to the rinsing sinks, she pulled up her sleeve and plunged her hand into a vat of sudsy cold water, retrieving and inspecting each submerged washcloth and handkerchief. Not one displayed the singe marks or the family crest she remembered. Had Aggie thrown it in the waste basket? Stella searched there, too, but found nothing but a pencil nub, a torn soap wrapper, and a tangle of loose threads.

If it was still here, where could Aggie have put it?

She had looked everywhere but the drying cupboards. The last time she'd seen the massive built-in drying racks, they'd been slid open. Now their ends were flush against the wall. Stella studied the contraption, trying to figure out how they worked. There was no discernible handle or lever, so she pried along the edge of the nearest one with her fingertips, managing to crack it open. Stella gained a better purchase and shoved with all her strength. Heat blasted her as the cupboard's wheels rolled across the floor. Stella checked the dripping wet towels draped over the metal rods. The golfing cloth wasn't there. But then she spotted a patch of white fabric that had fallen to the floor in the back of the cupboard, out of easy reach. Kneeling, her shoulders resting on the cold cement floor, Stella stuck her arm through the gap in the wall, reaching as far as she could, stretching her fingers to their full length. It was no use. The fallen cloth was too far back. She'd need a stick or a pole to retrieve it.

Stella tried pulling back her arm, but her sleeve had caught on something. She wiggled and tugged, but she was stuck. With no other option, Stella yanked, ripping the fabric. But it was more tightly woven than she expected and the tear wasn't long enough. As she prepared to try again, she heard rustling outside, reminiscent of the suspicious sound she and Aggie had heard. Stella froze. Was it just the harmless rabbit she'd seen dash away that day or was someone lurking outside as she'd suspected at the time? Could it be Aggie's replacement returning from an errand or the killer returning, looking for evidence they left behind? Defenseless as she was, Stella assumed the worst. She jerked at her sleeve again and, with all the strength of her panic behind her, tore the fabric enough to free herself.

Stella lurched to her feet as the doorknob turned and scrambled to hide behind the door, grabbing a clothes iron as she passed the table. The door creaked open, the prowler pausing in the doorway. Not one of the maids or servants, then. With Stella poised to strike whoever it was, her arms shaking from the iron's weight, the person took a tentative step across the threshold. The shadow cast across the floor included that of a wide-brimmed hat.

Seeing Stella looming, the clothes iron held over her head, the woman cried out in surprise. "Stella!"

"Frances!"

Lady Atherly, her hand held to her heart, barked, "For goodness' sake, put that down." Stella immediately complied, gratefully dropping the heavy iron to the floor with a thud. "What were you going to do, thrash me with that thing? Of all the—"

"I thought you were going to attack me."

"Attack you? Why on earth would I? And what's happened to your sleeve?"

Stella glanced at the white eyelet fabric dangling in tatters along the entire length of her arm. "What are you doing here, Frances?"

Lyndy's mother notoriously made a point of never entering the servants' world at Morrington Hall or anywhere else. She closed the door behind her. "I saw you race out of the house and didn't like the look on your face."

"So you followed me here?"

"And what if I did? You appeared to be up to something and I wanted to know what."

"Did you just admit to indulging in curiosity, Frances?"

"Don't smirk. It's unbecoming. And yes, you seem to be corrupting us all. Besides, my son's life is at stake, not to mention that of his future heirs. So, are you going to oblige me or not?"

"You're right. I was looking for something."

Stella told her about the golf cloth, how she'd spotted it the day of Aggie's attack and again as Aggie was attacking it back.

"And you think there is some link between this cloth and Edwin's murder? A bit of a stretch, isn't it?"

Stella leaned against the wall, again beaded with water

vapor. She missed Lyndy. This was the longest they'd spent apart since their wedding. She yearned for his embrace, his level head, his faith in her. She missed hashing everything over with him.

Then why not do it now?

Invigorated by the idea, she thrust away from the wall with her elbows. "Everything seems a bit of a stretch until it points you in the right direction."

"Well, I can't possibly see how—" Lady Atherly was saying as Stella swung open the door. "Now where are you off to?"

"To see Lyndy." Stella strode past her mother-in-law and outside, the air almost chilly after the laundry house's humidity, and headed for the stables.

To her dismay, Lady Atherly matched her step for step. "You never answered me. What happened to your sleeve?"

"It's a long story."

"Then you can tell me on the way."

"On the way?" Was Stella hearing her right?

Lady Atherly strode into the stables as if she owned them and barked orders for a carriage to be prepared immediately. "You didn't think I'd allow you to see my son without me, did you?"

"Can we have a few minutes alone?" Lyndy heard Stella plead.

The receding boot heels clacking on the hall's wooden floor indicated she'd been granted her wish. Lyndy bolted from the bench and began to pace from wall to wall, all six feet of the cramped dank space, his chest tight in anticipation. But his lip curled as the surly ox of a man, Cuskar, stepped first into his line of sight. He wasn't who Lyndy had expected. Then Stella's head popped around the constable, and Lyndy forgot to breathe. Her alabaster cheeks were blushed with exertion, tendrils of her silky brown hair floated about her head like a halo, and her smile banished the dark, sending the vile creatures that lurked there scurrying. Lyndy had never seen anything so beautiful.

"My love!"

"Lyndy!"

Stella sidestepped the constable and ran forward, shoving her arms as far through the bars as she could, reaching out to him. Lyndy mirrored her response, pressing his body against the cold wrought-iron barrier between them, inhaling her scent and relishing the warmth of her embrace.

By God, how he'd missed her. *It couldn't possibly have been but one day, could it?*

"Back away, laddie," the constable instructed. "Or else this reunion is over."

Lyndy seethed at the belligerent tone, but he said nothing. But loathe to lose contact, he continued to cling to her in silent protest. When Stella complied with the constable's order and released him, lowering her arms and stepping back, it was as if he'd had a strip of porous plaster yanked off. Lyndy gripped the bars a moment before backing away.

"How are you holding up?" she was the first to ask.

What could he say? Admit that he'd slept but a few hours, his back aching from lying on the wooden bench that was his bed? That the food he'd been served wasn't fit for a sow or that in less than twenty-four hours he'd already begun to lose his bluster? That he'd never felt so pessimistic in his whole life? In the privacy of their bedchamber, he'd tell her, perhaps, but in front of that plonker Cuskar? Never.

Lyndy tugged at the sleeve of his shirt, flapping loose and open. They'd refused him cuff links. "As well as can be expected. How are you, love?"

Stella approached again and rested her forehead on the iron bars. Lyndy stepped closer, but not enough to invoke another rebuke from the constable.

"I miss you," she said.

"And I you."

"And I'm worried about you."

"I'm fine." She knew he was lying. Lyndy steeled himself as tears welled in her eyes. How desperately he wanted to cup her cheek and kiss her tears away. "Any developments?"

Stella wiped her eyes with a torn fragment of fabric that was once her sleeve and presumably had a story to tell before glancing back at the policeman, who'd retreated a few yards and was now preoccupied with picking his teeth.

"I have so much to tell you."

In a rush, Stella explained how she'd learned about Billy Birdwell's inability to raise a club above his head and his reason for all the whispering, about Fergus's alibi, about her failed attempt to link the golf cleaning cloth to anyone or to retrieve what she thought might be it from the drying cupboard, finishing with Jeanie Agnew's dalliance with Sir Edwin, the McEwens connection to Sir Edwin's brother, and the nude photograph of Virginia.

His wife had been busy.

"So, you believe one of the McEwens killed Sir Edwin?"

"I don't know what to think. No one seems to have an alibi except for Billy Birdwell and Fergus. It could've been anyone. If I didn't trust your sister to give him an alibi, I'd even suspect Freddy at this point. Hamish and Virginia certainly had reason to want to silence Sir Edwin. But I can't imagine why they'd kill Aggie too."

"I agree. The maid wanted to leave Glenloch. So why not just let her go?"

The sudden and loud intrusion of stomping feet compelled Lyndy to look beyond Stella toward the sound. The constable filled the door with his wide frame to prevent someone else from entering the cellblock.

"Get out of my way. I want to see my son!"

Lyndy retreated from the bars as his mother threatened to batter the constable's leg with her umbrella. Chuckling, the constable desisted, shrugging and stepping aside.

Emotions roiled through him—shock, shame, annoyance, and hope—but all he could sputter was, "Mother, what are you doing here?"

"I've come to see you get out of this . . ." she paused, taking in the dirty unadorned white walls, the flaking corroded iron bars, the dim inadequate supply of gas fixtures to seek an appropriate word, "establishment."

Lyndy shot a questioning glance at Stella, who mouthed wordlessly, *Alice wired her*, as she gave way to his mother at the bars.

As Mother approached, brushing her gloved hands against each other as if her presence here alone had soiled them, Lyndy crossed his arms, defiant, bracing for the requisite reprimand, the reiteration of her continued disappointment in him. He could hear it now. As if not producing an heir wasn't enough. What kind of son gets himself arrested and sullies the family name?

"Come closer, Lyndy. I want to see for myself that you haven't suffered under the hands of these brutes."

Mother's demands and outrage were as familiar to Lyndy as well-worn old boots, but there was something in her demeanor, a hint of something he'd never seen before. Was that a glint of genuine concern in her eyes?

Yet even with this hopeful possibility, Lyndy approached the bars tentatively, as if he'd already been convicted and Mother was the one to dole out his punishment. He wasn't prepared for the conspiratorial whisper.

"Did Stella tell you about the emblem on the golf rag?" When Lyndy nodded silently, she added, "Do you recall seeing such a crest before? Think hard."

But Stella had already asked, and he could hardly remember

the Atherly heraldry, let alone that of some other family. He said so.

Mother bristled, stepping back from the bars in a huff. "Are you purposely being obtuse or has one night in jail turned your head to mush?" There was the mother Lyndy knew. "You knew full well since you were in short pants you'd wax poetic about the horses courant on the Atherly coat of arms."

"Truly, Mother? You came all the way to Scotland to berate me about my memory of some archaic symbol created by the first Earl of Atherly several centuries ago? If you haven't noticed, there are far more important matters to attend to."

Stella suddenly grabbed the bars in both hands. "Lyndy, I've got to go." She reached between them briefly, grasping for his hand or shoulder, but her fingers barely brushed his sleeve when the policeman barked again.

"I said no touching!"

"Hamish is throwing a surprise party for Old Tom Morris tonight, and I have to prepare for it," Stella announced, her tone stilted, laden with meaning. But what was she trying to say?

He was poised to ask for more insight, but already she was drifting toward the door, her attention on sights unseen, as if she was playing chess and planning three moves ahead.

"What? That party? Is that all you can think of at a time like this?" his mother objected.

Standing in the doorway that led out of the cellblock, Stella glanced over her shoulder at him, meeting his gaze. *Bloody hell.* He knew that look. He was right. She was up to something.

"Stella, my love, don't . . ." he began, hoping to reason with her, but she'd already clutched her skirts and, a moment later, bolted down the hall.

Watching her go, Lyndy wanted to rattle the bars. What if her plan put her in danger? How could he live with himself if anything happened to her? "Stella!"

Her footfalls faded away until he couldn't hear them at all.

"Bloody hell! Mother, she thinks she's figured something out. Tell me you won't let Stella do anything foolish."

Mother sniffed. "I can assure you, that ship has sailed. Besides, we both know that wife of yours does as she pleases. Like ignoring the doctor's sage advice on how best to beget a child or abandoning her mother-in-law in a police station." It was meant to be Mother's attempt at humor, but when she glanced at the door Stella had disappeared through, she sniffed again. "I daresay, if I don't go this minute, your wife will most certainly leave without me." She turned away.

"Promise me, Mother," Lyndy begged through clenched teeth. He'd never begged his mother for anything, ever.

She regarded him, cocking her head as if looking at a specimen of a creature she had no name for. "I will do no such thing."

It was a slap in the face. But then, how could Lyndy have expected anything less from her?

"If Stella's antics can free you from your predicament and uncover Edwin's true killer, I wholeheartedly approve." And with that, Mother gestured for the constable to escort her out, the clang of the metal door reverberating as it slammed behind her.

CHAPTER 30

Finn blew out his cheeks, relieved to be back at the servants' entrance after his blood-pumping race to and from the stable yard. He had no time to lose. He hooked the crook of the umbrella over his arm and opened the door. Stepping across the threshold, Finn was immediately struck by the lingering delectable aromas of a day's worth of the kitchen staff baking, icing, and powdering numerous cakes and pastries for the party. He'd been promised a slice of Dundee cake, but that would have to wait.

He had to get to the library. Now!

With the hall empty and many of the servants preoccupied with the party upstairs, Finn broke into a sprint. He wasn't one to question his betters, but his promise would've been better kept if Lady Atherly hadn't insisted, at this most importune time, that he fetch the umbrella she'd left in the carriage. Or if Lady Lyndhurst hadn't insisted when she pulled him aside upon returning from seeing His Lordship, that Finn tell no one of her plan or his part in it. Finn had wanted to inquire after his master's welfare, but one didn't speak to the countess, and

Lady Lyndhurst was more agitated than Finn had ever seen her. Besides, from what Lady Lyndhurst had imparted, she seemed on the verge of a breakthrough that would bring His Lordship home.

All Finn had to do was man the library door.

"What do ye think yer doing?" Mr. Stevenson bellowed as he stepped from his study holding a serving decanter of red wine and a plain white tea towel draped over his arm.

Finn slowed to a more respectable hustle, believing his inappropriately speedy pace was his sole offense. But as he approached the butler, Mr. Stevenson blocked his progress instead of giving way.

"If you'll beg my pardon, Mr. Stevenson, but I'm in a bit of a hurry." That was putting it mildly. If he wasn't by the library door in ... Finn pulled the watch from his pocket, the one His Lordship had given him last Christmas ... in two minutes, Her Ladyship would be hard pressed. "Her Ladyship is expecting me."

The butler didn't budge or blink.

"If you please, Mr. Stevenson. Step aside."

"I will not. I have put up with the likes of ye for days now, and I say ye will not pass."

What nonsense was this? But Finn hadn't a moment to spare to appease or question his superior.

Finn made to pass by, sidestepping the butler, but Mr. Stevenson persistently matched his movements again and again.

"This is ridiculous." Finn tried elbowing the butler, shoving the man aside with his shoulder, but he was met with the strength of a tree rooted into the hall tiles.

Growing increasingly agitated, Finn swerved to the left and then dodged quickly back to the right, hoping to circumvent the man. Again Mr. Stevenson anticipated him and blocked his way. With no other recourse, the seconds ticking loudly in his brain, Finn knocked the decanter from the butler's grasp. The butler fumbled with the decanter, hoping to catch it in midair, spilling half the contents onto Finn's jacket as it bobbed about from the butler's fingertips. It eventually bounded out of Mr. Stevenson's grasp and shattered onto the floor, splashing the remaining wine across his and Mr. Stevenson's trouser legs. Finn didn't stop to gawk at the fragments of glass glistening or the bloodred wine seeping into the cracks between the tiles. He used Mr. Stevenson's outrage to skirt past and run toward the stairs, taking them two at a time.

"Blasted, man. I knew ye were no better than the killer ye serve!" the butler shouted from behind him.

Finn ignored him. He knew Lord Lyndhurst was innocent and he was going to help Lady Lyndhurst prove it. But not if he was too late!

Stella swallowed hard, her palms slick with perspiration, listening, waiting, resisting the urge to abandon her hastily laid plan and rejoin the partygoers, but she summoned the image of Lyndy in that dark jail cell over and over and stood her ground. Music and laughter slipped through as the library door opened behind her. Stella hugged the book to her chest and took a slow deep breath to steady herself, inhaling the comforting smell of leather and old paper. As the door closed, it muted the voices rising in song as string instruments picked up strands of "The Bonnie Banks of Loch Lomond." Stella suddenly felt very alone.

"I got yer wee note," he said, his voice husky and low.

He'd taken the bait. *Her.* Stella shivered in fear, clutching the book tighter, numbing her finger that marked a specific page.

Without the golf cloth Aggie scorched, without any witnesses or evidence, the only way she was going to free Lyndy was with a confession. And if this was the way to get it, so be it. She'd faced villains before.

Stella hefted the heavy leather-bound tome before her, cracking it open to the coat of arms she'd seen on the golf cloth, re-assuring herself this was all the proof she needed. She slowly turned to face Alasdair, leaning against the closed door. Blocking her way.

"Ye wanted to speak with me?" he said, a sly smile spreading across his face as he admired Stella, dressed in a forest-green silk gown and matching McEwen tartan sash the McEwens had given her the day she arrived. He, too, was dressed for the occasion. With his legs bare, he'd donned a kilt made from a tartan with a busy patchwork of color: bright yellow, deep blue, dark green, light green, orange, and, that which Stella's eyes kept darting to, stripes of bright red.

Before responding, gathering her courage, Stella glanced once more at the beautifully crafted illustration of the heraldry of the Earl of Camgossie before sliding out her finger and closing the book.

"I did." Stella's heart skipped a beat as he sidled slowly up to her.

"And what did ye want to see me about?"

Without any more encouragement beyond a request to speak with him and finding her alone, he presumed to brush an errant strand of hair along her forehead and behind her ear, his finger slowly tracing the contour of her face. Maybe she'd wanted to ask him something innocuous. Maybe she'd sought his advice on how best to begin learning the game of golf. But from the tension he exuded the second he closed the door, sealing out any interference from the world beyond, Stella knew exactly what he wanted. And it revolted her.

"I've always thought ye were the prettiest lass here."

Not to mention one of the youngest. Alasdair McCormack was old enough to be her father.

Stella resisted bracing herself, stiffening at his touch. It was too soon to reveal her true purpose. But flashes of someone else laying his hands on her, forcing a kiss on her, caused her ears and cheeks to redden as she struggled to control her anger. Alasdair got the wrong impression.

He placed his hands on either shoulder and leaned in close; his breath, already stinking of whiskey, was hot on her face. "Ye feel it too, don't ye? That something special between us. And now, with yer husband out of the way . . ."

"Is that why you falsely incriminated him? To get him out of the way? So, we could be together?"

Stella tried to use her most sultry voice, but the bile rose in her throat at his proximity and it came out more as a hoarse whisper. Her suggestion was ridiculous. It risked him seeing through her, but with her feet planted on the floor, her mind raced, and she couldn't think of any other way of bringing up Sir Edwin and Aggie's murders.

Alasdair chuckled indulgently, as if amused by the brutal honesty of a child. "It was a stroke of genius, I admit. Placing the bloody club in his trunk."

She'd done it. He'd confessed. But had anyone heard him say it?

He nibbled her earlobe lightly. "Now, how do ye plan to thank me for it?"

Stella pinched her lips into a tight grimace, trying not to let her disgust show and dissuade him from confessing more. Instead, Stella's stare bored holes into the closed door, willing it, commanding it to open.

Where was Finn?

"For killing Sir Edwin and Aggie and incriminating Lyndy for it?" she said as loud as she could muster, her voice shaking. "Like this." She raised the book and smashed him on the head.

Alasdair abruptly released her, his hands clasped against his head as he staggered back. "Ye dirty cow!"

Stella raced for the door and threw it open, expecting to see Finn waiting outside. At least that was the plan. Finn wasn't there. No one was there. Despite over a hundred guests attending Old Tom's party, the hall was empty, the music and the singing had stopped, and silence permeated the whole house. Where was everyone? She could hear the ticking of the grandfather clock, her ragged breath in her ears, Alasdair's heavy unsteady footfalls as he gained the door.

"Help!" she yelled.

"I'll teach ye to—"

Stella pivoted and slammed the door in Alasdair's face, twisted and crimson with rage. She slipped and scrambled across the recently waxed parquet floor, clinging to the book and nearly tripping on the train of her dress, hoping to reach the safety of the ballroom before her pursuer caught up with her. With a few seconds lead, she'd made it. The double doors were closed, but dozens and dozens of people were on the other side. Or at least there should be. Finn was supposed to be on the other side of the library door too.

Stella reached for the knob, but as she did, Alasdair snatched the fabric of her dress from behind, swirled her around and slammed her against the wall. She saw stars as her attacker's soft cold hands wrapped around her throat. Stella couldn't breathe. She couldn't scream. She struggled, clawing at his face, kicking his legs, each effort sapping her weakening strength as he grasped tighter. Ironic thoughts of dying the same way her father had, the way Aggie had, and the way Lyndy would now albeit at the end of a noose, drifted through her mind, crushing her spirit more effectively than any man's attempt to throttle her. Overcome with hopelessness, she began to lose consciousness, prevented from slipping down the wall to the floor by Alasdair's grip.

"Thought ye'd make a fool of me, did ye?" he whispered in her ear. "Like Sir Edwin. Like that stupid maid. Now I'll have to teach ye the same lesson." A suppressed cough and hushed whisper from the ballroom punctuated the end of his confession.

People. There were people a few steps away. They were unusually quiet and obviously unaware of her predicament, but they were, like hope for her and Lyndy, just on the other side of those doors.

As the edges of her vision closed in, Stella ineffectively slapped at the doors and unsuccessfully grappled with a doorknob. Alasdair snatched her hand away.

"Sorry, lassie. Can't have any witnesses," Alasdair taunted.

The doors suddenly flew open of their own accord. Flickering candlelight stung Stella's eyes and the heady fragrance of heavily applied cologne and perfume mingling with the sweet aroma of cake and other sweetmeats blasted her from within.

"Surprise!" a chorus of well-wishers cried joyously.

Then a woman screamed. Incoherent angry shouts and a stampede of footsteps closing in on her echoed painfully in Stella's ears. With the pressure on her neck abruptly gone, she doubled over, gasping. *Too fast, too much, too painful.* But she was safe now. Lyndy was safe. She'd exposed the actual killer. With nothing left to hold her up, Stella slumped forward and crumpled unconscious into a heap of green silk and wool tartan on the floor.

CHAPTER 31

Cold water from a dampened cloth pressed to her forehead dripped down the side of Stella's face. Murmurs and the rustle of silk prickled in her ears. Stella's eyes fluttered open to pale bare knees and dizzying tartan patterns filling her view. At first she couldn't piece together where she was or make sense of what she saw. Then Alasdair's attack flooded her memory. She rested her hand on her throat and risked glancing up. A cluster of concerned faces peered at her. Had they seen what he'd done? Heard what he said? She stirred, shifting her weight to ease the pain of sitting on the hard wooden floor.

"Don't get up," Alice said, holding the cloth and squatting beside her.

"Are ye okay, Stella, lass?" Hamish asked, worry lines etched on his brow.

"Alasdair—" Stella croaked, testing the use of her voice. It was raspy but didn't hurt as much as she expected.

"Almost killed you," Virginia said, hugging Hamish's arm as if it was all keeping her rooted to the ground. "We know. But you're safe now, Stella."

"He killed Sir Edwin and Aggie."

"After what he did to you," Alice said, her eyes skimming Stella's neck for marks to match those on Aggie's throat, "no one could doubt it was anyone else."

"And Lyndy?"

"Ian will have already telephoned the station," Hamish said.

"He'll sleep beside ye tonight, my lady," Jeanie Agnew, dressed in an eye-catching royal-blue, sea-green, and orange tartan silk-skirted dress, winked.

Freddy bent at Alice's shoulder, but when he caught Stella regarding him, he immediately shied away, looking vaguely toward the middle of the hall. "I'm ever so sorry I doubted him or you."

With her relief at being alive and knowing Lyndy would be released washing over her, Stella could forgive almost anything. Almost.

"It's okay, Freddy. Your father was murdered. You're grieving and need answers and justice. Believe me, I understand." And having gone through it herself, that was no idle claim. "Though you could tell Lyndy what you told me when he gets back."

Alice reached for Freddy's hand and he nodded at Stella in gratitude. "I will."

"Speaking of justice, did he get away?" Stella didn't have to say who.

As if in answer, Alasdair rounded the corner, struggling to free himself from the restraining grips of two male guests of the party. Inspector Docherty, resplendent in a black jacket and a red-and-black tartan kilt, followed behind.

"Unhand me! Get ye dirty hands off me! Do ye know who I am? Hamish, call off yer dogs!"

As they dragged her assailant back toward the ballroom, Stella used the wall to push and slide herself to her feet. Several hands reached out to steady her, but she waved them all off.

"Thank you, but I can manage."

Finn hovered on the opposite side of the open double doors, his shoulder against the wall, waiting for her to wave him over. He was swiftly beside her when she reached out as if in need of his assistance. He reeked as if he'd been stomping grapes in a wine vat.

"What happened to you?" she whispered, pausing, pretending to be more unstable than she felt. She'd needed the valet to get closer with impunity and remembered how effective Mrs. Graham's ploy had been. Her throat hurt, but there was nothing wrong with her balance.

"I can't apologize enough, my lady. There was . . . a bit of a delay." Finn glanced at the large dark blot on his jacket but didn't elaborate further. "By the time I reached the library, you were gone. I'm terribly sorry."

Stella laid a hand on the valet's shoulder. "I'm sorry too, Finn. I shouldn't have put you in that position." Lyndy would say she shouldn't have put herself in that position, but it had worked and she would never regret it. Ever.

With the others at her back, Stella stepped into the ballroom, smelling of sweat and sugar and champagne. The chandelier glittered high above the cake-laden tables. Most of the party guests, in all their Celtic finery, still mingled about the edges of the room, glasses in hand, their shocked, curious mutterings buzzing around the room like horseflies. A silent small-piece band, complete with accordion and bagpipes, crowded the far corner. Alasdair sat in the empty middle of the floor, like a pariah or an oddity in a zoo, restrained to a chair with a lady's green-and-black tartan scarf. Not familiar with the pattern or clan it belonged to, Stella glanced around, hoping to discern which generous lady she had to thank. Docherty and the two broad-shouldered guests he'd enlisted were keeping guard. Not willing to take any chances, Stella still didn't get too close.

"It's all her fault." Alasdair jutted his chin at her. "She hit me in the head with a book."

"Was it Sir Edwin and Aggie's fault too?" Stella demanded.

Alasdair struggled in vain against his restraints. "Aye, Sir Edwin most certainly earned his beating. Accused me of attacking that maid. As if I'd done something wrong in taking a few liberties. It wasn't as if she hadn't been offering up her delights to that groundskeeper moments before. I saw the pair when I returned from playing Hamish's course. Her bonny lips were still warm."

Stella shuddered. If she hadn't come along when she did, how many *liberties* would he have taken?

Alasdair's contemptuous laugh cut into her reverie. "Sir Edwin was one to talk. Did ye know he seduced my wife? And then, as soon as he arrives at Glenloch, he steals Jeanie's affections from me."

"How dare ye!" Jeanie snapped shut the peacock-feathered fan she'd been waving, stormed across the room, and aimed to smack Alasdair with it. Docherty stepped in and stopped her. "No one *steals* my affections, ye murdering scoundrel."

Alasdair continued as if he hadn't noticed, as if Jeanie's threats had no merit. He was warming to having an audience. "Sir Edwin had no problem with what I did. Not now, not back in school."

Someone gasped. It echoed in the vast almost silent room. As Stella sought the source, she caught Virginia beginning to sway even with her grip on Hamish's arm. Hamish patted her gloved hand and whispered something soothing. Had Virginia made the sound? Did she know something?

"You've done this before?" Stella's lip curled at the thought.

"Yes, he has." The small trembling voice came from Virginia.

Was that why Virginia was so often unsettled and shaky? It made sense. Stella had assumed her distress had grown out of her loss of Richard Kentfield, or guilt over causing his death, but looking back, Virginia was increasingly unsteady and skittish each time she'd encountered Alasdair or someone mentioned his name. They'd known each other at school. Had he assaulted her as he had the maid? Had Hamish, who'd been willing to do anything to protect Virginia's sensitivities, inadvertently invited his wife's former assailant to their home?

Stella could almost hear the irony land like a stone in the pit of Hamish's stomach, the ripples of mortification and disbelief spreading through his whole body, turning his face a hue brighter than Alasdair's hair.

"Aye," Alasdair said. "Boys will be boys with such depraved besom as yer maid and yer wife, eh, Hamish?" Alasdair smirked at Virginia.

Shying from the sudden scrutiny of everyone in the room, Virginia squirmed away from Hamish and ran with her hands covering her face, nearly knocking shoulders with Lady Atherly hesitating in the doorway. Stella's mother-in-law, dressed inappropriately in a mauve and lace tea gown, had refused to participate in a celebratory party while Lyndy was still in jail. Someone must've found her lounging elsewhere in the manor and told her what had happened.

"Ye bloody bastard," Hamish seethed, his fists curled.

The choice between punching Alasdair as Lyndy had Sir Edwin or comforting Virginia warred on Hamish's features. Hamish chose his wife, though not without casting a lingering hateful glance over his shoulder at the man in the chair before exiting the ballroom.

"And Edwin knew?" Lady Atherly stepped beside Stella, giving her a cursory glance from dancing slippers to tiara, lingering on her neck. She raised her impressive Roman nose at Alasdair. "I don't believe you."

"Believe it, Countess. It wasn't until after yer son gave him a good swipe that Sir Edwin threatened to expose me. Said he saw me leaving the laundry house."

"Maybe because that's when he realized you were still up to no good and decided it was finally time to expose you."

Stella hoped Lady Atherly's optimistic view was the right one.

"More like he couldn't abide being accused of something he didn't do," Alasdair said. "And I couldn't let him get away with it, could I? The philandering hypocrite."

"So you killed him?" Freddy asked. Luckily, he and Alice stood at a safe distance. After days of grief and sleepless nights, Stella couldn't imagine what Freddy might do.

"And look what it cost me!" Alasdair snapped. "If it weren't for yer father and all these distractions, I might've beaten Braid there."

"Holy Crivvens, McCormack!" James Braid, who'd been invited to the party, slugged back the entire glass of whiskey he held. The hand that was so sure and steady on the golf course was shaking.

Stella was stunned silent by Alasdair's arrogance and conceit. He'd murdered two people and had the gall to complain about losing a golf tournament? He made Lady Atherly look like Florence Nightingale.

"I promise you, Young Kentfield," he continued, tugging at his restraint again, "yer better off without him. Look how ye played those last three rounds. Ye could've given up, but ye refused, didn't ye? Ye have the making of a champion. And here ye father never once bothered to watch ye play."

"You killed my father with a golf club," Freddy said, as if he still couldn't come to terms with the truth.

"Ye can be reassured, it wasn't one of mine. Nay, a set had been left lying about in the grass near to where we argued. When Sir Edwin threatened to expose me, I grabbed one. And I hit him."

"At least three times," Inspector Docherty interjected.

"I wasn't using my usual swing. I had to make sure he'd stay down."

Freddy paled, and his posture stiffened like a windup toy about to spring to life. With one nod from Docherty, Freddy was willingly escorted from the room, his eyes pinned to Alasdair's face until he was out the door. Alice would've followed, but Lady Atherly grabbed her hand as she passed and shook her head, forcing Alice to stay.

"And that poor laundry maid?" Jeanie asked. "Why kill her, ye brute?"

"Now she was an ungrateful cow. If she'd only just kept her mouth shut. I'd impressed upon her the importance of it." Stella envisioned the finger-shaped bruises on Aggie's cheeks. Her ears burned at his cavalier attitude. How could she have not seen it before? "And when she blamed Sir Edwin, I thought we had an understanding. Even stopped by that stinking hot laundry building a few times to make sure."

Had he been the one creeping around outside, eavesdropping on poor Aggie to make sure she didn't say the wrong thing? Stella didn't doubt it.

"But then you found out from Virginia that Aggie was trying to leave Glenloch Hill," Stella said. "You knew you couldn't stop her from talking if she left. So you stopped her from leaving." It was a guess, but it sounded right after what he'd confessed to.

"Aye. Like most lassies, she couldn't be trusted." He glared at Stella, who returned his unblinking stare. He looked away and shrugged, chuckling. "Which, of course, made it easier to make everyone think she'd lied and killed Sir Edwin herself. She was just a wee spiteful maid. Who'd question it?"

"Lady Lyndhurst did." Inspector Docherty said, nodding for the constable who'd arrived to join them, his simple dark uniform in stark contrast to the riot of color worn by the guests. "I should've listened to her instincts."

"But if she'd just kept her bonny mouth shut, perhaps Lord Lyndhurst wouldn't be in jail now, would he?" Again, he stared at Stella, leering and admiring her facial features as if he were kissing her with his eyes. It made her skin crawl.

"So, ye admit to purposefully incriminating Lord Lyndhurst

for the crimes you committed?" Docherty said as the constable handcuffed Alasdair, untied the scarf, and hoisted him roughly from the chair.

Alasdair shrugged as the constable led him toward the door. Stella couldn't wait to see the back of him.

"Ye give me more credit than I deserve, Inspector," he said over his shoulder. "Aye, I tossed the bag somewhere the butler would find it, though not straightaway, and kept the bloodied club. I hid it in a trunk in the storage room, assuming it was Sir Edwin's. Wasn't he always going on about missing his luggage? I enjoyed the irony of it. But when I learned it was Lord Lyndhurst's, I wasn't going to correct yer mistake, was I? I regretted it, though. I respect Lord Lyndhurst. The viscount's a proper gentleman. I did try to cast suspicions on that wee caddie I'd caught sneaking around Hamish's office. And left the clubs near the wine cellar to muddy the waters."

"You were going to let Lyndy hang!" Stella said, outraged by his attempt to mitigate his evil intentions.

Alasdair shrugged. "Couldn't be helped, I'm afraid. It was either him or me."

"Besides, Billy was helping Hamish with this." Jeanie spread out her hand to encompass the gathering. "Which reminds me . . ." Jeanie's hand flew to her mouth. "Ach, Tom!"

Old Tom Morris, dressed in his Sunday best, a well-tailored tan suit, appeared in the open doorway. He ran his hand down the length of his long white beard. "Whit's this all aboot, then, eh? I was told we were having a wee bit of supper."

"Surprise!" Alasdair mockingly cried as Docherty shoved him past.

CHAPTER 32

Lyndy threw open the carriage door and leaped down, his hat blowing off in a strong gust of wind. He waved off the footman poised to chase after it, sending the man back toward shelter, and lifted his face to the sky, inhaling the fresh air, relishing the cold rain splattering his skin.

By God, it was good to be free.

Crunching the wet gravel as she ran, Stella, who must've been watching from the door, launched herself into his arms. As large raindrops pelted them, Lyndy buried himself in her hair, her scent as intoxicating, warm, and welcoming as a glass of that Royal Brackla whiskey Hamish introduced him to.

"Oh, Lyndy!" His chest tightened. Her whisper in his ear was warm but raspy and quivering. It was unlike her. But they'd never faced such a precarious situation before, had they? Weren't they both a bit shaky with relief?

"I do believe you missed me." He pulled her tighter.

"I worried you'd hang."

He didn't want to admit, even to himself, how many bleak dark moments he'd allowed that fear to overwhelm him. He'd never been so cheered to see that boorish Cuskar as when the constable fitted his key into the lock announcing McCormack had confessed to the crimes.

"Can't get rid of me that easily." Lyndy forced a chuckle and was rewarded with Stella's smile. "Now, shall we get out of this bloody rain?" He slipped his fingers between hers, and they dashed toward the glow emanating from the McEwens' hall like a welcoming beacon.

Lyndy gratefully stepped into the warmth, turning to admire Stella's features in the full brightness of the hall. But what were those? Red marks and dark bruises marred her porcelain skin. She'd been hurt like Aggie, the laundry maid. Lyndy's temper flared, not at his beloved wife, but at his failure to protect her. He curled his fist, but who had he but himself to punch? And wasn't it his temper that had gotten them into this fix in the first place?

As calls for hot baths to be drawn were made, Lyndy relaxed his hand, gently brushing Stella's cheek instead. "My love, what happened?"

Stella self-consciously put her hand to her neck. "Before you ask, I'm fine but have so much to tell you."

"A sight of ye is guid for sair een!" Hamish McEwen said, popping into the hall and welcoming Lyndy back as Stevenson provided him and Stella with thick dry towels. "Old Tom's party was ruined of course, but one's got tae make the best of a bad bargain, eh? Now at least there's plenty of extra whiskey tae go around. We can toast yer safe return, Lyndy." Hamish motioned for the pair to join him in the drawing room. Drying off his neck, Lyndy tried to follow Stella, but his mother blocked his way, forcing him to step back into the hall. She hesitated before him, not able to meet his eyes.

"Mother?"

She haltingly approached and wrapped her arms tentatively around him as Lyndy stood stunned into stillness before quickly backing away. She tightened the embroidered silk shawl around her shoulders. "I'm relieved to see you free from that wretched jail. I expect there will be no other such occurrence?"

"If you're asking if I plan to get arrested for murder again, Mother, I can assure you, I do not."

"Very well, then." She tilted up her nose and returned to the company of the others, leaving Lyndy, touched and surprisingly bereft, to follow. He'd missed his opportunity to return her embrace.

A fire flickered in the fireplace, its warmth not quite reaching Lyndy as he stepped into the drawing room. Alice jumped from her seat beside Freddy and without reservation embraced him wholeheartedly. Lyndy welcomed it, enfolding his sister as he'd never done before. "We're all so happy to have you back."

Freddy stood and offered Lyndy his hand. "No hard feelings, I hope."

"None." Lyndy couldn't blame the grieving son for his misgivings. Besides, Freddy was soon to be family. For Alice's sake, Lyndy wouldn't hold a grudge. As Stella patted the seat beside her, he added, "But I would like a bit of an explanation."

That was an understatement. Once so apathetic to anyone else's affairs, Lyndy was bursting with curiosity. *How much he'd changed!* Lyndy chuckled to himself.

"I agree." Jeanie Agnew lounged on the arm of the velvet sofa, draping her arm across the back where Virginia sat. "I still don't know how ye figured out Alasdair killed Edwin, Stella."

Lyndy would've asked first about those bruises on Stella's neck, but any information was better than remaining ignorant of everything.

"It wasn't easy. With few of you having alibis, it took me a while to realize it," Stella said, her hand still resting self-consciously on her neck, "but Aggie was always the key. I believed her when she was first attacked and blamed Sir Edwin for it. But then came the incident with the golf towel. Aggie was purposefully scorching it. There had to be a reason. After Sir Edwin was killed, I started to suspect she wasn't telling me the truth, or not the whole truth anyway. As others pointed out, why would she insist on leaving Glenloch Hill immediately, even after Sir Edwin died? What was the rush? She and Fergus planned to elope, but they weren't financially ready yet, and she knew she'd never get another laundry maid's position."

"Why wouldn't she?" Virginia said. "She was such an excellent loyal worker, and I would've seen that she got a good reference."

"Because Aggie couldn't read or write and could only do her job because Mrs. Graham helped her."

"I had no idea," Virginia said. "About so many things."

"Yer not to blame, Ginny," Jeanie said. "Sounds like Aggie was good at keeping secrets."

"Which I didn't know at first either," Stella said. "But I kept wondering why she would endanger her future." Stella hesitated, allowing the question to settle. When no one offered an answer, Stella provided it. "Precisely because she was keeping secrets and felt more in danger staying here."

"And she was right," Lyndy said. "Her attacker came back and killed her."

"Exactly," Stella agreed.

Virginia gasped. "That poor girl. I should've spoken to her woman to woman instead of mistress to maid. Perhaps I could've prevented all of this. If only I hadn't been so ashamed of my own . . ." she paused to chew on a thumbnail, "encounter with . . . Alasdair all those years ago. How, I don't know, but he found out about the French postcard of me and thought that meant . . ."

McCormack had once attacked Virginia as well? Lyndy shot a questioning glance at Stella, who confirmed with a slight nod what Lyndy had concluded. No wonder Virginia often appeared like a nervous wreck. It had nothing to do with Richard

Kentfield but with the predator prowling the halls of her house. And no wonder Hamish was so protective. He loved his wife.

But why, then, invite McCormack to Glenloch Hill in the first place? The blackguard could've stayed in St. Andrews with most of the other participants of the Open. Stella voiced what he'd been thinking. *Per usual.*

"I didnae ken," Hamish said, anguish coloring his voice. "I thought Virginia was ill, in need of quiet and rest. I thought she still grieved Richard's death. As I already said, that's where she and I were when Sir Edwin was killed. Virginia had another one of her turns. So I stayed by her side until she rested and recovered. Why didnae ye tell me, Virginia?"

Lyndy could imagine what he was feeling. Thank heaven there were no secrets between him and Stella.

Virginia gazed at Hamish. "It's not something I'm proud of and I just couldn't face telling you."

"Even after I invited him for the tournament, thinking I was doing ye a favor, inviting yer old school chum? He a champion and all?"

"Especially after that."

Mother lowered her gaze and plucked at the folds in her skirt. Alice and Freddy shot questioning glances at each other, hoping the other knew what Virginia was talking about. Lyndy sought Stella's hand and laced his fingers with hers.

"I'm so, so sorry, hen," Hamish said, cupping his wife's cheek.

"Ye have nothing to be ashamed of," Jeanie said, resting a hand on Virginia's shoulder but including Hamish in her gaze. "Neither of ye. Alasdair is Auld Clootie if I've ever met him."

"Yet we shan't talk about it again," Virginia said. "The children need never know," she pleaded, eliciting an unspoken promise from all.

"I find the less the children know, the better," Mother said. It was last Christmas that Lyndy had learned that his mother had had an affair with Sir Edwin. Was there more she wasn't telling him? She must've caught his expression. "Must you look at me like that? Can I help it that the man still carried a torch for me all these years later? Keeping that photograph of us and carting it around." She scoffed. "What utter nonsense. He should've moved on."

"Look afront tae where ye'll live, eh?" Hamish said, a hopeful brightness in his tone.

"That's it exactly," Mother agreed.

"Aye. *Live noo—no back*," Virginia said, mimicking Hamish's accent with a lightness Lyndy had never seen in her before.

"But you still haven't explained how you figured it was McCormack and not someone else, Stella," Lyndy said, burning to know. She smiled at his persistence.

"I kept coming back to why Aggie would be scorching the golf cloth. Was she taking her anger out on it because it was handy or because it represented something? Or someone? When I realized the significance of the emblem stitched into it, I searched *The Book of Family Crests* but didn't find a match for anyone who could have attacked Aggie or killed Sir Edwin. I admit I was stumped. Then something you said, Lyndy, about your family heraldry made me realize my mistake."

"I aided you after all?"

"We make a pretty good team, don't you think?" Stella inched closer until their thighs touched and she hugged his arm, momentarily resting her head on his shoulder. How long had it been since they were this close? Yet the disconcerting bruises on her neck cooled his sudden ardor.

"Aye," Jeanie said, "but what was yer mistake?"

"When I consulted *The Book of Family Crests*, I searched for the surname of McCormack when it was the Earl of Camgossie's, Alasdair's noble crest, I should've been looking up. When I checked *Burke's Peerage*, it was there, and it was a match. But I was still guessing, so I lured Alasdair to the library to see if I could get him to confess."

"You did what?"

"Believe me, Lyndy, I didn't plan for him to strangle me." Her hand went to her neck again.

Here he was, locked behind bars, helpless, while Stella was out risking her life. Rage and relief warred within him. How dare that scoundrel hurt his Stella. He'd punched Sir Edwin for less. Lyndy was grateful the scoundrel was locked up, taking Lyndy's place in that dank cell. Lyndy didn't know what he'd do if he faced McCormack again, but whatever it was, it would assuredly make things worse. Wasn't it enough that Stella was alive and would heal? That they were together?

Besides, he had no desire to see the inside of a jail cell again.

Lyndy drew in a long slow breath. Trying to ease his anger by satisfying his curiosity, he asked, "What was the plan, love?"

"Finn was supposed to help me by waiting outside to hear the confession and barge in if anything went wrong."

"Obviously it all went terribly wrong." Lyndy brushed the angry red marks on her throat gently with the pad of his thumb. "What happened?" Lyndy was more than comfortable with his valet, if not fond of the man, but if he'd neglected to come to Stella's aid when she needed him most, Lyndy wouldn't hesitate to sack him immediately.

"I believe, my lord, that I'm to blame," Stevenson, the butler who'd posted himself beside the whiskey tray, said. Like all good butlers, his expression revealed nothing of the man's thoughts.

"Yes?" Lyndy's tone demanded further explanation.

"When Mr. Finn returned to the house after leaving on an errand, I sought to prevent him from entering."

"And why would ye dae that?" Hamish asked before Lyndy could.

Lyndy didn't think it possible, but the butler stiffened even more. He stole a quick glimpse of Lyndy from his hooded eyelids. "I mistakenly believed Mr. Finn was the valet of a murderer, sir. I believed it best served ye and Mrs. McEwen to keep such riffraff out."

"Ye meant well but were way out of line, Stevenson."

"Sir."

"Be that as it may," Lyndy, unwilling to let his wife off as easily as Hamish had the butler, returned to the previous topic. "You put yourself unduly at risk, Stella. I wouldn't have been able to live with myself if something had happened to you."

"It's not always about you, Lyndy," Mother scolded him as if he were still a child. He bristled at her tone.

"But by God it's true—for me, for you, for all of us, and you know it, Mother."

"Then stop chastising her and be thankful! Your wife's risky behavior uncovered Sir Edwin's killer and saved your life. Not to mention ensuring Morrington's future. Must I remind you that you can't pass anything on to your son if you die before you have one? No, you should be expressing your gratitude and not griping, don't you think?"

It was one of those rare moments when his mother was undeniably correct.

Lyndy raised Stella's soft warm hand to his lips. "Thank you, my love, for everything." He wanted to keep going, up her arm, to her collarbone, to the marks on her neck, kissing the pain and the memory away.

"I don't need thanks, Lyndy. I'm just glad you're free and cleared of any wrongdoing."

"As we all are, laddie," Hamish said.

"I am sorry about Sir Edwin, Mother."

"I am too. Edwin was a rogue, but he was never evil. He loved me. He loved you, Freddy. Very much. And once he learned of Mr. McCormack's unspeakable acts, he planned to expose him and died for it. His teasing you about your parentage, Lyndy . . . well, that was just his wishful thinking. The man did make me regret naming you for him, but all the gladder that I married your father instead. And for that I'll be forever in his debt."

"Oh, aye? Is Lord Atherly quite the catch, then?" Jeanie Agnew asked, a playful smile on her lips.

"Well, I don't know about that."

"Well, aren't I a wee bit jealous," Jeanie said. "Just look at ye all. What lovely couples. Even Lady Atherly admitted to being happily married."

"Did I?"

"I can only wish for such luck. I guess I'll have to stick to golf and, uh, other sports where I can make my own." Jeanie winked at Stevenson, the sole unspoken for man in the room. The butler's eyebrows raised in alarm.

"On that note, anyone up for a distracting game of snooker?" Hamish suggested.

"Not for me," Lyndy said. He just wanted to be alone with his wife.

"Or me," Stella said. "I don't have to say how difficult a day it's been." Her hand went to her throat. "I think we'll call it a night."

After enduring a round of well-meaning "Pleasant dreams," "Guid nicht," "Coorie doon under the bedcovers," and "Go make me a grandson" from his mother, Lyndy and Stella mounted the stairs, finally alone.

"Does it hurt?" he asked.

"Not too bad." She knew what he meant. Stella slipped her hand into his. "I won't be singing solo anytime soon, but I'll be fine. How are you?"

When they reached the top of the stairs, the grandfather clock in the hall below chimed the hour. Waiting for the resonating bell to fade into silence, Lyndy paused to brush a loose strand of her hair behind Stella's ear. "More shaken than I'd care to admit."

"Me too, to be honest. But what was it Hamish said, look afront to where you'll live?

"Excellent advice. As long as that future holds you, my love."

Stella beamed, joy mingled with relief shining from her eyes. He didn't know precisely what he'd said that pleased her, but it made him weak to see her happy again.

"Which comes back to what you said earlier." Like a playful pixie sprite, Stella mischievously tapped the tip of his nose. "Can't get rid of me that easily."

"Now, aren't ye a cheeky wee lass?" Lyndy teased in his best imitation of Hamish, cringing as he spoke. It was no good. His accent was terrible. But it made her laugh. Pleased with himself, he swept Stella off her feet and into his arms, and together they giggled all the way to bed.

ACKNOWLEDGMENTS

Writing a story with golf as the backdrop was a lifetime in the making. I've only played a few rounds myself, but I have learned a deep appreciation for the sport through my family. One of my earliest memories is of my grandparents' home filled with the whispered commentary of a televised golf tournament. My grandfather, Thomas Lynch, made me my first (and only) set of golf clubs. My grandmother, Maryon Lynch, showed me during an age when I didn't know women played sports, that she not only played but could beat the men. And then there's my father-in-law, Harold "Hal" Wilsey, who treated the game as a way to extend quality family time (graciously letting me ride in the golf cart), my brother-in-law, Michael Wilsey, who never needs an excuse to be on the course (even in the worst of weather) and my husband, Brian, an avid player who over many years patiently taught me the nuances of the game. I'm grateful to them all.

I'd also like to thank Jacqueline, who read every line of dialog and helped me translate the necessary bits into Scottish (and for laughing with me at my feeble attempts at a Scottish accent). If something was lost in translation, that's on me. Thanks to my mom, my biggest cheerleader and harshest beta reader, who undeniably made the book better, and to my teenage daughter, for hanging out with me during the Open Championship when she'd have rather been doing absolutely anything else.

Finally, I want to express my appreciation to the many Scots I met during my travels while researching this book.

From the cab drivers, Airbnb hosts, and museum guides to those three police officers (long story) and the gentleman at The Old Course who helped me when I lost cell service and couldn't get my e-tickets, I've never met such a nation of kind, friendly people. Slàinte Mhath!

AUTHOR'S NOTE

Writing historical fiction allows me to blend inspiration with imagination. Through research, I discover people, places, and historical facts that I can use to weave into my fictitious world to create authentic-feeling stories set back in time.

"Old Tom Morris" is one such person I discovered. Rightly called the "Grand Old Man of Golf," he, more than almost anyone, put his stamp on the modern game. Born in St. Andrews in 1821, he was not only a championship golfer (winning the Open Championship multiple times), but an innovative greenskeeper, successful club and ball maker, business owner, and renowned course designer who, among other accolades, created the first 18-hole golf course. His son, "Young Tom Morris," is considered one of the greatest golfers ever to play the game. As in the book, Tom Morris' eighty-fifth birthday fell on June 16, 1906, and his comment about children from St. Andrews being born with webbed feet and a golf club in their hands is a direct quote. The other historical figures I mention in the book include Richard Kentfield, Willie Park, Harry Vardon, and James Braid, the golfer who won the 1905 and 1906 Open Championship.

Two prominent places inspired this story: the Old Course and the Hill of Travit. I visited the Old Course, the oldest and most iconic golf course in the world, during the 150th anniversary of the Open Championship. Although the course has changed little in the past hundred years, allowing me to describe what I experienced, I did consult authoritative sources of its history when necessary to reflect the course as it was in

1906. The Hill of Travit, the Edwardian country estate that became the fictitious Glenloch Hill, is run by the National Trust of Scotland. It is open to the public for tours and overnight stays. I was lucky enough to have the servants' quarters as my home while I attended The Open. Although I may have changed or embellished aspects of the estate to fit the mystery, I portrayed the summerhouse, the laundry house, and the gardens as they were and still are today.

As with all my books, I try very hard to get my historical details right. However, this being a work of fiction, I allow myself a bit of leeway if necessary. I confess I made one major change. Since The Old Course is iconic, I wanted to set my story there. However, the historical timeline didn't align with Stella and Lyndy's. The Open Championship was played on June 13-15, 1906, as in the book. However, it was played at Muirfield in Gullane, East Lothian, Scotland, having been played at The Old Course in St. Andrews the year before.